Terrinoth: an ancient realm of forgotten greatness and faded legacies, of magic and monsters, heroes, and tyrants. Its cities were ruined and their secrets lost as terrifying dragons, undead armies, and demon-possessed hordes ravaged the land. Over centuries, the realm slipped into gloom...

Now, the world is reawakening – the Baronies of Daqan rebuild their domains, wizards master lapsed arts, and champions test their mettle. Banding together to explore the dangerous caves, ancient ruins, dark dungeons, and cursed forests of Terrinoth, they unearth priceless treasures and terrible foes.

Yet time is running out, for in the shadows a malevolent force has grown, preparing to spread evil across the world. Now, when the land needs them most, is the moment for its heroes to rise.

ALSO AVAILABLE IN DESCENT: LEGENDS OF THE DARK

WAIQAR

ROBBIE MACNIVEN

First published by Aconyte Books in 2023

ISBN 978 1 83908 210 8

Ebook ISBN 978 1 83908 211 5

Cover art by Joshua Cairós.

Map by Francesca Baerald.

Distributed in North America by Simon & Schuster Inc, New York, USA

Printed in the United States of America

9 8 7 6 5 4 3 2 1

ACONYTE BOOKS

An imprint of Asmodee Entertainment Ltd

Mercury House, Shipstones Business Centre

North Gate, Nottingham NG7 7FN, UK

aconytebooks.com // twitter.com/aconytebooks

*Dedicated to this book's wonderful
editor, Lottie, a masterful wrangler
of novels about baddies.*

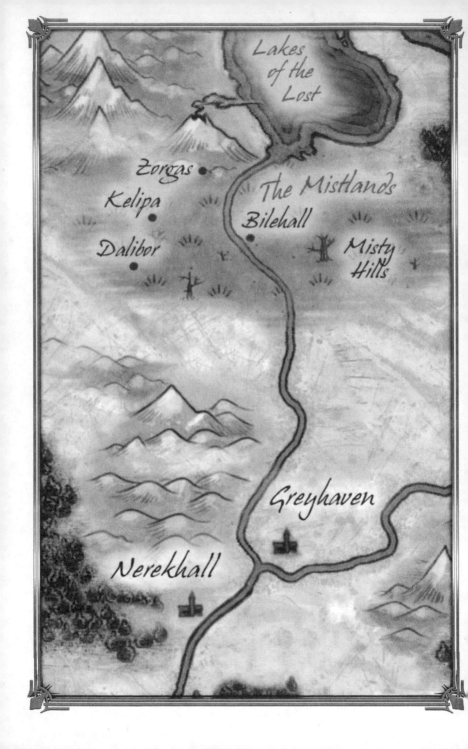

PART ONE

ZORGAS

CHAPTER ONE

Tomaz's friends took him on the thirteenth day of Chillwind.

It was during the night. The first he knew of it was a hand clamping over his mouth, stifling him. He tried to fight back, but others gripped him, unseen in the dark, three or four assailants who hauled him up from his bed and half-carried, half-dragged him out of the university dorm hall.

Tomaz tried to scream, but could not. He tried to struggle, but failed to break free. It seemed incredible that none of the other Greyhaven students in the long, vaulted room would be awoken by the commotion, and yet none came to his aid.

He was taken outside, feeling the cold bite of the new winter wind that knifed through the alleys and around the slope of Winding Hill. A gibbous moon leered down at the city, offering him the faintest half glimpse of his attackers. They were robed, with raised hoods and black rags bound around their lower faces.

"Put the robes on him," one snarled. Tomaz realized they

had taken his long, gray student's robes with them from the dorm, and now one stuffed them over his head.

Tomaz was terrified. Was it the runemasters? Was it witch hunters, come from Nerekhall? Was the Death Cult of Greyhaven about to be purged by the authorities?

He should never have joined in the first place. He knew necromantic magics were forbidden, that those at the university who practiced such dark arts did so in secret with good reason. He should have stayed his curiosity and never gotten involved.

"Not here," said one of his assailants as they held him for a moment longer, seemingly uncertain about what to do next. "Up the slope, to the alley."

Tomaz was marched into the fetid darkness between the buildings just uphill from the Hall of a Thousand Scribes. He heard the bell on the Celestial Observance begin to toll the hour, the dolorous chimes a fitting backdrop as he was shoved down onto his knees in the dirt.

Oh gods, they were going to slit his throat. The hand across his mouth came away, and he began to babble, fear rendering him incoherent.

"Please," he managed, looking up at the dark figure standing over him. As he did so, something pierced the panic, a moment of realization that made him pause.

He knew the robes.

"Wilem?" he asked disbelievingly.

"I told you he'd recognize us," hissed another of his assailants. Tomaz knew that voice.

"Viktor?" he said. He began to laugh, his fear replaced by a surge of relief. "Oh, praise the Great Necromancer!

I thought you were witch hunters! I thought we'd been discovered!"

They were his friends. Or, more accurately, his fellow cultists, members of the society that concealed itself in the midst of Greyhaven's student population. Death Cults, dedicated to the study of necromancy, were said to proliferate all over Terrinoth, and the arcane university was no different. Tomaz had found the members insular for the most part – and understandably so, given that practicing dark magics was a capital offence in the Free City – but since his first day with them he had found it all wonderfully exciting, a thrill compared to the drudgery of most of the first-year lectures. A few of the cult's members had even seemingly grown accepting of him.

Now, apparently, they'd decided to play a joke on him. Or perhaps they had more practical intentions – they were always talking about kidnapping one of the university's runemasters. Clearly, they were just practicing.

"You could have warned me a bit sooner," he said. The figure in front of him dropped his hood and pulled down his rags. It was indeed Wilem.

He said nothing. Instead, he punched Tomaz in the face.

The younger student reeled, tasting bitter blood on his lips. Before he could recover, they were on him again, pinning his hands behind his back and binding his face. He was gagged and blindfolded, his wrists lashed together behind him. Helpless, he was heaved back onto his feet and marched from the alleyway.

Confusion and terror, even more acute than before, threatened to overwhelm him. This couldn't be happening.

These were his friends. Why were they doing this? Where were they taking him?

"Lift him," he heard Wilem order. He was shoved up and forward, landing on what felt like wooden runners. He could smell old straw and dung. A cart, he realized.

He tried to speak, but the gag made him choke. He rolled over, but felt a foot plant itself on his chest, keeping him down. Moments later it was replaced by something heavy and yielding. More was added, pressing onto him, heaped one atop the other. Sacking? He was being concealed.

The cart lurched into motion. He gave up struggling momentarily, panting through his nose, his thoughts in turmoil. A part of him still wanted to believe this was all some elaborate joke, or training, or preparation for some greater scheme. He was a junior inductee, a Mortificer, whereas Wilem was a High Mortificer, the cult's chief lieutenant and second only to Tarmond, the Arch Mortificer and most senior student. Perhaps he'd just been chosen because he was new? Or maybe this was some sort of test, or a rite of promotion?

He tried to stay with that theory as he endured the juddering motion of the cart over Greyhaven's worn cobbles. He expected it to stop at any moment and for him to be bundled out at their destination, but it didn't. It kept going. Eventually the uneven movements became less intense, and he realized that they were no longer traversing the city's streets. They were out on a country road.

He didn't know how long the journey lasted, but it was not short. The first time he stopped and the sacking was hauled off, he hoped that he would be untied, but all that was removed was the gag. He hoped desperately that his absence in the dorm back in Greyhaven would be noticed, that someone would come looking for him, even the authorities he had once dreaded. But there was no sign of pursuit.

"Please, where are you taking me?" he pleaded, panting fearfully.

"Drink," snapped Wilem's voice. A flask was pressed to his lips. He gulped down the tepid water, almost choking.

The gag was immediately reapplied, and he was thrown down again. The cart set off. So it continued.

Blindfolded the whole time, it was impossible to tell day from night. Sometimes, when they had stopped, Tomaz would try to arise from the cart, but a hand would always shove him back down and a voice – Wilem, Viktor, Lillian the final year head-of-class or Fergas, the highest-graded student in Tomaz's cohort – would snarl at him to lie still. He slept intermittently, too afraid he'd wake up to the stabbing pain of a dagger in the ribs or at his throat. They fed him, bread and cheese mostly, and untied his wrists when his moaning indicated he had to relieve himself, but beyond that there was no reprieve.

It was like a nightmare, and it was going to become so much worse.

Eventually, the blindfold was snatched away. Tomaz grunted, squinting in the pallid daylight. Viktor and Lillian were standing over him, their robes and rags discarded, their clothing muddy from days on the road.

They manhandled him down off the cart. He looked around, groggy, trying to get his bearings.

He certainly wasn't in Greyhaven anymore, nor anywhere near it. The cart seemed to have stopped in the midst of a bog. The ground around them was a festering morass of black mire and springy tussocks, all shrouded in a gray mist that coiled languidly around them like a predator, hemming them in. The whole place stank of decay.

Tomaz wanted to ask where they were, but the gag was still constraining him. The others stood around him, gazing not at him, but off into the mist. It looked as though they were waiting for something. Judging by their expressions, it wasn't something good.

He was regretting ever meeting any of them. He had only been at Greyhaven for a few months when he had first befriended Wilem during his early elementalism lessons. It was through him that he had met the others. His own father had been a minor dabbler in the art of necromancy – nothing major, of course, but he had once managed to briefly reanimate the family cat. After that he had seemed like a changed man, living in constant fear. He had left home, claiming the priests of the Church of Kellos were hunting for him, and had never returned. It had all left a powerful impression on Tomaz, who had been fascinated by the concept of the Sphere of Death, and had worried that during his arcane studies at the university he wouldn't have an opportunity to pursue his real interests.

What they called "fell" magic was strictly forbidden at Greyhaven, but the university was renowned as the seat of Terrinoth's learning and his parents insisted he attend. It turned out that Tomaz had not been alone in harboring a secret interest in the magics of the afterlife.

He was now very much regretting that fact.

He whimpered. In vain, he tested the bonds at his wrists, and immediately wished he hadn't. The cords had chafed his skin raw. His whole body ached, and he was desperately hungry. He briefly contemplated trying to run out into the bog, but knew he wouldn't get far. He wasn't exactly the fittest of Greyhaven's student cohort, and both Wilem and Viktor were older and taller than him.

Besides, as bad as being kidnapped by his erstwhile friends was, he'd still rather be with them than find himself alone in the sinister marshland.

A noise disturbed his reckoning, making everyone start. It sounded like the call of a hunting horn. It came a second time, echoing in the mist surrounding them.

"They're coming," Lillian said, fear in her voice.

"We should just abandon him," Fergas added urgently. "They'll find him easily enough!"

"The Arch Mortificer was clear, we make the handover in person," Wilem said, apparently struggling to hide his own apprehension. "You should be glad, Fergas. This is a great honor."

"If it's such an honor, why isn't Tarmond here himself?" Fergas pointed out.

Wilem didn't answer. There was another noise now, more regular than the sound of the horn – the splashing of something in the mire. It grew steadily louder.

Tomaz's heart was racing. Despite the pain in his wrists, he squirmed against his bonds. Lillian noticed and snatched him under the arm to hold him firm.

What did Wilem mean by a "handover"? Why had he

been dragged here, to the middle of some cold, foul bog? Had he displeased the cult in some way? Perhaps they thought he was an informer? Or not dedicated enough to the cause?

The splashing grew louder. The mud-spattered pony that had been hauling the cart snorted and strained against its bridle, seemingly aware of what was coming.

Shapes swept toward them from out of the fog, a trio of towering figures, mounted on great steeds. Tomaz only understood the true horror of them as they reined in before him.

They were, or had once been, knights. They wore plate armor, black lacquer that had been slashed and scarred and scraped in a thousand places. Their pauldrons and gauntlets were studded, as was the barding on their steeds. At their waists they bore great weapons, a massive broadsword for one, a jagged mace for another and a wicked looking war hammer for the third. Shields were slung against their saddles, as battered as their armor, all three bearing the same device – a white skull with the antlers of a stag, set against a field of black and purple.

All three of the riders were long dead. Their great helms, crested with antlers like their sigil, hung about their saddle pommels, leaving their heads exposed. All were completely skeletal, nothing but bare bone, a trio of skulls that grinned broadly down at Tomaz as he stared up at them in abject horror. Only their eye sockets indicated the source of their sentience. Deep purple witch-light glowed there, and it flared in the fog as they sat astride their equally skeletal steeds.

Three riders, risen from the dead and come for him. Tomaz felt close to fainting. He knew the stories, and knew the device on the shields, the horned skull. Even those who didn't hold secret allegiance to a Death Cult recognized that mark. It was engrained into a thousand cautionary tales and dark fables, woven into tapestries and inked onto the pages of histories and fantasies alike. It was seared into the folklore of Terrinoth, into the legends from Forthyn to Trast, from the shores of the Sea of Redtyde to the barren borders of the Ru Steppes.

It was the sigil of the Great Necromancer, the Undying One, the Betrayer. It was the mark of Waiqar.

Viktor pulled away Tomaz's gag. He tried to speak, to beg, but cold dread killed the words before they could be uttered.

"Take him," Wilem said hoarsely, addressing the riders. The others had all backed off. Tomaz remained frozen, unable to move as, wordlessly, the lead knight dismounted. It waded through the cloying bog until it was towering over him, the foul light festering in its eye sockets pulsating.

Tomaz burst into tears. The horror snatched him and, with no apparent difficulty, lifted him up and carried him by the scruff of his robes. He couldn't find the courage to fight back as he was slung like a sack of vegetables across a moldering blanket rolled up on the rear of the knight's saddle, before being lashed there. The undead warrior mounted his steed once again and, without even glancing at the rest of Tomaz's former friends, turned and galloped into the mist, followed by its companions.

Over the splashing of hooves and his own sobbing,

Tomaz heard Wilem calling out after him, voice echoing through the mist.

"You were always talking about serving the Great Necromancer, Tomaz! Well, now you can!"

Waiqar took to his throne just before the start of the banquet.

The grand hall of Zorgas was bedecked in its finery. It was the Night of the Red Feast, the time when the lords of Bilehall, Dalibor and their lesser coven-kin renewed their oaths of subservience to the Undying One. Waiqar found little pleasure in their company, but a part of him still enjoyed the act of hosting the occasion. What was the point in ruling if he could not, at times, display the more lavish trappings of his power?

Tonight the hall reflected that. The lost spirits that wandered Zorgas had been momentarily banished and the braziers had been lit, partially illuminating a cavernous, vaulted space constructed from dark mirestone, its ceiling arching away into shadow. The walls were hung with tapestries portraying Waiqar's life and un-life, while two dozen armored figures were arrayed around the hall's edges, each carrying a banner displaying the heraldic crests of one of the Bilehall families – the black serpent of the DeVays, the skeletal scorpion of the Balthazars, the horned drake of the Torvics, and more besides.

Those same families were now gathered like a pack of savage beasts around the feasting pit in the center of the hall, bedecked in their finery, trying to show restraint as they waited on Waiqar's permission to begin.

They were no better than dogs, Waiqar mused. He had vague recollections of a canine he had known in life. He had trained it to overcome its excitable nature, until he could hold food before it and know that, even when it hungered desperately, it would not dare to eat before he gave it permission.

It was the same with these pets, he decided as he watched them struggling to control their bestial nature. Describing them as dogs was not wholly accurate though. They were more like parasites, leeches or fleas dressed up in red silk and gold and black velvet. They could only be strong if others were weak. Without the existence of hopeless, vulnerable prey, they would not be able to survive. That in turn made them contemptuous to Waiqar. They were nothing like him and his Deathborn. He did not even consider them immortal.

But they had their uses, and so Waiqar was hosting the vampire families of the Mistlands. He had even dressed for the occasion, garbing himself as befitted a warrior-king. His ashen gray hair was slicked back from his pale, hard-boned face. He wore his armor, plate and scale mail, intricately etched with a thousand grimacing rune-skulls and edged with brass. At his shoulders were the antlers of the Great Stag, Morkai, which he had slain in life, and a cloak of deepest, imperial purple. At his waist was the ensorcelled horn of the Death Hunt, and resting to his right was his broadsword, Bitterbite, and the great war axe, Doom's Edge.

The throne completed the image, a construction of black stone with a high, arching back carved to resemble the mythical hooded reaper of death. Behind it was Waiqar's standard, a black and purple banner bearing on it the white stag's head that was his ancient crest.

Only one other figure was permitted to occupy the dais, sat on a lesser throne to Waiqar's right. His name was Tristayne Olliven, and like Waiqar he was no vampire. Like all of the other undead nobility in the chamber, he had cast a glamor about himself to hide the rotting effects of time, assuming his former, mortal appearance to those he valued – a nicety not followed when it came to the lesser dregs and thralls, who saw them all for what they really were. To Waiqar, Tristayne resembled a man reaching the end of his youth, pallid, with languid, jet-black hair and equally dark eyes. He was clad in his robes and bore a long-handled scythe that was currently resting against the side of his throne. He was Waiqar's apprentice in the arts of necromancy.

Normally Waiqar kept him separate from matters of state, desiring that he focus only on his arcane studies, but he had chosen to permit his presence tonight, hoping that he would learn something of the primitive mindset of the so-called lords of Bilehall and Dalibor. Such an experience might be useful in the future, and besides, Waiqar wished to test him.

"What do you think of our guests?" he asked, leaning toward Tristayne. The younger necromancer gave a small, non-committal shrug.

"They look hungry," he said. Waiqar laughed, causing some of the vampires to tear their eyes away from the feast arrayed in the pit beneath them.

"Note that," Waiqar told Tristayne. "These creatures are

always best to deal with when their thoughts are on their food."

"Lord Waiqar," called out one of the Bilehall lords, Naythen Torvic. Waiqar found him a particularly detestable creature, though unfortunately he and his sister Lucrezia were also the most powerful of the Bilehall nobles. He was a pallid, bald-headed figure with flabby, waxen-looking skin, dressed in oversized finery, and now he dared address Waiqar from the far side of the pit.

"Do we await only your pleasure, lord, or might we begin?" he demanded. "Given that our latest oaths of allegiance have required that we increase our tithes, I would have at least expected the Red Feast to start on cue this year."

The other lords of Bilehall ceased their hissing, and a deadly quiet settled over the hall. Waiqar held Torvic's gaze, until his sister tugged urgently on the sagging creature's arm, hissing words in his ear.

"Not, of course, that we are anything other than grateful for your hospitality," Torvic added with obvious difficulty, no doubt on Lucrezia's advice. Waiqar let the tension run a little longer before replying, his voice cold.

"I wish to make a public gift to my apprentice," he said. "I assure you that is all we wait for, Lord Torvic. It shall not be long."

In truth Waiqar had been waiting to see how long it took one of them to complain, wondering which would have the courage or the arrogance to speak first. Of course it had been Torvic. It only further confirmed his suspicions. His instincts craved to punish the vile creature before his simpering underlings, but he restrained himself. There would be time for that. Time was always on his side.

He reached out with his mind, brushing aside the anguished souls that sought to latch onto his spirit-thoughts as they located the brooding, brutal presence of Ardus Ix'Erebus. The champion of Waiqar's guard was standing just beyond the hall's great doors, bearing the gift. Wordlessly, Waiqar instructed him to enter.

The doors swung open and Ardus strode inside, the light of the braziers glinting from his heavy armor. One great gauntlet was planted on the shoulder of a short, rotund figure, who visibly quaked with terror as he was led up onto the dais. It was a human, hideously mortal and far too alive. Waiqar glanced only briefly at the shaking, fleshy thing, focusing his attention instead on Tristayne.

The necromancer was frowning, clearly confused.

"What is it?" he asked.

"A gift," Waiqar said, almost teasingly.

"Yes, but why? What does it do?"

Waiqar briefly considered ordering the mortal to say who he was, but he looked to be on the cusp of passing out and was certainly in no fit state to explain where he'd come from. Waiqar did it for him.

"He is from Greyhaven. A student of the runemasters who have been dabbling in our beloved arts. I thought it was about time you had a servant of your own, and since you, too, were once a student of Greyhaven, I believed it might amuse you to have someone you could reminisce with."

Tristayne looked less than thrilled. Waiqar had always

found his apprentice's moods easy to read, even without driving his own thoughts into the younger necromancer's mind and ransacking them for the truth. It was easier this way.

"Must I feed it? Find it somewhere to sleep?" Tristayne asked.

"Do not be petulant," Waiqar said. "It is important you have something else to focus on besides your studies. I expressly forbid you from reaping its soul with your scythe. It has claimed enough already."

"If you're quite done, my lord?" Torvic interrupted again. Waiqar glared down at the vampire for a moment, noting how he was practically shaking with hunger. He resisted the impulse to chastise Torvic. He had pushed them all just far enough tonight. That was a start.

Instead, he smiled, and spread his arms wide, his deep voice ringing through the hall.

"Of course, noble Lord Torvic. Let the feast begin!"

Tomaz felt close to collapse, but the skeletal monstrosity gripping him held him up without tiring.

The kidnapping had been bad, and even worse the journey to a vast, terrible citadel that he had caught only glimpses of as he endured the brutal ride, but none of it compared to this. He had been dragged up a barren slope and in through a cyclopean portcullis, his ears filled with wailing and terrible, disembodied whispers. From there it had been up flights of spiral stairs and along black, ruinous corridors where shambling half-dead things and spectral apparitions had fled before the implacable advance of his captor.

One thought kept returning over and over, the only coherent one he seemed capable of anymore. He hadn't really believed the stories. He hadn't really believed that the Great Necromancer had returned, that he now ruled from a stronghold deep in the blighted northern marshes.

But it was all true.

He had been a fool, and now he was terrified not by the prospect of death, but the realization that something even worse surely awaited him.

He envisioned being flung in some dungeon or charnel pit, his soul wrenched from his body by hungry fiends and accursed spirits, yet when the last set of doors before him swung open he found himself being brought into what could only be the hall of some great lord or king. And that seemed worst of all.

Tomaz had never been within the chambers of a noble, but this one seemed like a nightmarish parody of the ones he had imagined. It was crumbling and dank, and echoed with low hissing and snarling, as though it was playing host to a pack of beasts. Rusting, seemingly empty suits of armor stood arrayed around the walls, holding great red and black banners displaying horrific devices.

In the hall's center was a pit around which a mass of figures crowded. For only the briefest second, Tomaz felt something approaching hope. It seemed as though the assembly were humans, all of them noblemen and women dressed in their finery. But as he was dragged forward, he discovered his mistake. None of them were any more alive than the skeletal brute gripping him.

Their seemingly fine clothing was raggedy and

bloodstained, their flesh pale as marble, and their faces were contorted with ugly, inhuman expressions that bared their unnaturally wicked canines. They looked at him with a naked hunger as he passed, eyes gleaming like predators in the flame-shot darkness. He was convinced the nearest were about to lunge for him, but none dared.

He was marched on, to a dais at the far end of the hall. Despite his exhaustion, despite his fear, his body still responded instinctively, trying to break free from the iron grip as he saw what was waiting for him.

Two figures sat on thrones atop the raised platform. The smaller was occupied by one particularly gaunt skeleton, clad in what looked like the ragged remains of the dark robes worn by senior students of the Academy at Nerekhall. In one hand it clutched a long scythe, the blade gleaming in the firelight. Sickly yellow luminescence pulsed from within its skull.

The other figure was even more terrible. It, too, was completely skeletal, but far larger. It was clad in heavy armor, and bore at its side great weapons. Gnarled antlers framed a grinning skull that turned slowly to regard Tomaz as he was brought before it. Purple witch-fire, like that of the knights who had brought him to Zorgas, flared powerfully in the hollows of its eye sockets. It radiated controlled power, and a palpable malice that made Tomaz feel sick.

If there was any doubt about its identity, the raggedy banner behind the throne dispelled it. The emblem was of a white, human skull with the antlers of a stag, the sigil of Waiqar.

Tomaz had been brought before the Undying One, the Great Necromancer.

He fell, and had to be physically hauled up onto the dais. He kept his eyes on the stone beneath him, quivering, ill. He was vaguely aware of words being spoken, though his mind failed to register what they were. Not daring to raise his gaze toward the seated figures, he turned instead to the rest of the hall, seeking any sort of reprieve.

It was then that he realized he was not the only living being in the chamber.

The pit in the hall's center, the one surrounded by the vampiric nobility, was filled not with a feasting table, but with people. They looked as ragged, desperate and afraid as he was.

The monstrous skeleton on his black throne, Waiqar, said something that Tomaz's fear-addled mind could only partially understand. The coven of vampires below let loose a dreadful howl and threw themselves down into the pit with the corralled humans.

That was when the real screaming began. It lasted for a long time.

CHAPTER TWO

For once, the mist had rolled back from the walls of Zorgas, exposing the leagues upon leagues of flat, fetid marshland that lay beyond the citadel's craggy mount.

One man was dying in that bog. Tristayne watched him dispassionately as he gargled his last, his throat cut by the necromancer's bone-handled knife. Waiqar had forbidden him from using his scythe, saying that it would defeat the purpose of the exercise – as a conduit to the Black Realm, it enhanced his abilities, and Waiqar wanted his apprentice to rely on nothing but his own raw power that morning. It frustrated Tristayne, but then there were many things about his apprenticeship to the Great Necromancer that frustrated him.

The man's thrashing stilled, and he began to sink into the mire. He was one of the living cattle kept at Zorgas, fodder for experiments such as these or for visitors from Bilehall or Dalibor. Perhaps in his last living moments he had assumed that, with the ending of his life, his suffering was finally over, but that was not the case. He would not be free yet.

"*Ki-búr gidem,*" Waiqar said, one hand extended over the body. "*Gaba zidug.*"

Tristayne felt the terrible powers that flowed around the Great Necromancer stir. To someone attuned to the essence of death, it was possible to always feel the foul magics that seemed drawn to Waiqar, but when he turned words and thoughts to harnessing that energy, it responded with a speed and force Tristayne himself had never known.

A choking scream filled the air. Tristayne continued to watch, unmoved, as pallid smoke rose from the dead man. It twisted and coiled around Waiqar's outstretched hand, slowly materializing into something vaguely resembling the unfortunate victim. The screaming continued, broken and gargling.

"Silence him for me," Waiqar instructed.

Tristayne raised his own hand and, with a word, drove a flurry of arcane pins through the insubstantial gap that formed the spirit's maw. The screaming was immediately reduced to a low, disembodied moan.

"Good," Waiqar said, and clenched his fist. The phantom, which had been coiling and twisting around his arm like marsh mist, suddenly ceased its motion, remaining firm, almost tangible.

"Now, what can this one tell us?" Waiqar asked rhetorically. He spoke another incantation. The spirit shuddered, but remained firmly in his grasp, its moaning rising.

"He is from Trast," Waiqar continued, talking through

what he was discovering. "A trader by profession. Tell me where my servants captured him."

The Undying One turned his gaze on Tristayne. For all that he had grown accustomed to being in his master's presence, a part of him still baulked. There was no being as powerful as Waiqar – yet. When he had been freed and taken on as an apprentice by the Great Necromancer, Tristayne had initially rejoiced. With his own formidable abilities married to the higher knowledge Waiqar could teach him, he would become second to none in the dark arts. Secretly, he intended to become even more. There were times though when he still found himself in awe of his master.

Angry at his own weakness, he repeated the short chant that Waiqar had spoken, reaching into the elemental Mortos surrounding them both. Drawing upon that magical essence of the Sphere of Death allowed them to fashion the designs of those who practiced the so-called dark arts. The energy itself was usually only visible to those with the witch-sight, and often looked like coiling strands of pale luminescence or ectoplasm. Today, the energies of death responded sluggishly, as though reluctant to cease being attentive to Waiqar and bend to Tristayne's will instead.

He reached his own hand out, holding it over Waiqar's as he sought to drive his mind into that of the captured spirit. He remembered making similar endeavors when he had still been a mortal, dabbling in foul magics while enrolled at Nerekhall.

Then, seeking to commune with the departed had

felt physically abhorrent. It had been like he had been submerged in icy waters, shocking at first and then, after a while, numbing. Now though, he felt nothing as he pierced the spirit's essence. He had been cold for a very long time.

His mind met that of the murdered man's. Horror immediately sought to overwhelm him as he experienced exactly what the victim was feeling.

"Please," Tristayne said. "Oh gods, please, what is happening?"

"Control it," Waiqar snapped. Tristayne glared, his own embarrassment briefly flaring through the fug of the spirit's emotions. With their minds connected, he had accidentally channeled the soul's thoughts, giving vent to the words its own bound lips could not.

He snarled, twisting the mental probe by clenching his fist. The spirit twitched and writhed in pain, and he drove deeper into its consciousness, doing his best to ignore the fear, confusion and agony that was momentarily becoming his own.

He was seeking the soul's memories, rather than merely its thoughts. It was like trying to work his way through a maze – every turn seemed to lead only to dead ends filled with anguish and horror. He felt the pain of the knife at his throat, which in turn triggered his own memories of the noose that had once choked his own life from him.

He almost lost control. Rigid with effort, he anchored his thoughts with a focus word and pressed on. There, finally, was a vision, a true and tangible memory.

"He had a wife, and a son," he said through his clenched jaw.

"That isn't what I asked," Waiqar said sternly. "Where was he taken?"

Tristayne forced his mind on, seeking furiously, letting his own desire to not fail, to not embarrass himself before his master, burn away the miseries threatening to overcome him. At last, for the briefest second, he saw another of the sights that the man had once seen, a brief glimpse of yurts and tents and, beyond them, the rising sprawl of an ungainly town of timber and thatch, chimney smoke and campfires dirtying a slate-gray sky.

"Frostgate," Tristayne managed to say. "He was taken in Frostgate."

"Good," Waiqar said. "Now, keep hold of it yourself."

Without warning Waiqar removed his arm from the spirit's semi-corporeal form. Tristayne immediately felt it drag at him. It was trying to escape, to dissipate and finally leave the horror of its existence behind.

"You are losing control," Waiqar said.

Tristayne knew as much. He spoke another binding incantation, but he couldn't stop it. He couldn't pin the soul in place for any length of time, the way Waiqar did seemingly without effort. It was like trying to snatch water. It squirmed its way from Tristayne's grasp, breaking the bindings on its mouth as it went. With one last terrible shriek it dissolved, taking its pall of fear and pain with it.

Tristayne cried out in frustration, letting go of the energies he had been harnessing. They fled back to Waiqar, who stood impassively, waiting for Tristayne's anger to spend itself.

"You are not progressing," Waiqar said.

"Because this is pointless," Tristayne said. "Mere parlor tricks. Any necromancer can commune with the dead! Why are you continually testing me on this when we could be binding powerful constructs or summoning armies?"

"Interrogating departing souls is no mere trick," Waiqar said. "And you are not communing with it. A hedge wizard can converse with the dead. Souls bound for the afterlife or dragged back from it cannot be trusted to speak honestly or coherently. This method delves into their very memories. Those are far more valuable. You will be able to see the realities of places and peoples far from here. It is essential if you are to exert influence beyond this benighted swamp. That is something no mere army or barrow wyrm can do."

"I would exert even greater influence with undying hosts at my command," Tristayne said, letting his bitterness show. More and more, it was beginning to feel as though Waiqar's tutelage was restraining him, rather than increasing his abilities. "We torture lost souls when instead you could be teaching me the incantations to raise razorghasts or barrow wyrms. Terrinoth would tremble before such power!"

"I have told you before, the wyrms are beyond your abilities. You would not survive the clash of wills necessary to tame the lingering spirit of one," Waiqar snapped, and Tristayne couldn't avoid a rattling shudder as the energies that surrounded the Unliving turned acerbic, making his bones ache and causing the sunlight to momentarily flee from around them.

"You will only learn such spells with time, if I choose to teach you them at all," he continued. "Do not ask me again."

Tristayne had long learned when not to push Waiqar any further. He managed to make himself incline his head, forcing forth words of submission.

"My apologies, master."

Waiqar grunted, seeming to glare at Tristayne for what felt like an uncomfortable length of time.

"I will have Ardus bring more chattels, and we will continue until you are capable of holding and extracting something of note from one of them."

A day and a night passed before Waiqar relented and allowed Tristayne to pass back into Zorgas. He still hadn't made any headway. Frustration radiated from the apprentice as he stalked the crumbling halls and corridors, lashing out at any spirit unfortunate enough to pass him and holding them in his grasp.

At first, he spoke to them of his frustrations, ignoring their wailing and screeching, but eventually, growing bored of their inability to comprehend corporeal struggles, he went in search of his servant.

Tomaz was his name, or at least that was what Tristayne thought. He struggled to remember such insignificant things. In fact, he would have forgotten all about the foolish thing's existence had Waiqar not insisted he assign one of his reanimates to care for the mortal. A week had passed since the Night of the Red Feast, and it seemed the undead construct that had been bound to feed and water the human had succeeded in keeping him alive, if apparently not wholly sane.

Tristayne swept into the cell where Tomaz was being

kept, wondering if he knew what a privilege it was to get his own space away from the rest of the cattle. The human whimpered and cowered atop rotting old straw, shying away from Tristayne as he always did whenever the necromancer looked in on him. He was filthy, his Greyhaven robes barely recognizable.

"On your knees before me," Tristayne commanded, speaking loud and slow in the hope that the stinking, mangy creature might understand him. It seemed he did. Tomaz crawled from his corner to kneel in front of him, eyes averted.

"Can you speak?" Tristayne demanded. Tomaz managed to nod and croak.

"Yes."

"You will address me as master."

"Y-Yes, master."

"Do not say anything more unless I question you directly," Tristayne said. "Remain at my side at all times, and do what I say immediately and without question. Do you understand?"

"Yes, master."

"Good. Follow."

Tristayne turned and paced away down the corridor. He heard the shuffle of feet as Tomaz scrambled after him. He hadn't wanted a servant, much less a mortal one. Sometimes he worried that in ways he, too, was no more than a servant to Waiqar. He owed his freedom from the Black Scythe to him, after all. That was a debt Waiqar rarely made mention of, but it loomed over him all the same. He sometimes felt he had to prove himself, prove that he was worthy of Waiqar's favor, but that was a foolish notion. Tristayne needed to prove himself to no one. Still, it was surely a good sign that the Great Necromancer had gone to the trouble of finding and gifting him a mortal.

He led Tomaz through Zorgas and out of one of the sally ports, reaching ahead with his magics to cause the reanimates guarding it to swing it open for him. All of the garrison were nominally under Waiqar's control, but it amused Tristayne to sometimes wrest that power for himself, if only briefly. He wondered if Waiqar knew he sometimes took ownership of his warriors. He doubted it. The old fool was too busy prowling the battlements and talking to himself, or locking himself away in the great hall with only the spirits for company.

He took the winding path down the eastern face of Zorgas' crag, then out into the marsh beyond. To his credit, Tomaz said nothing, merely wrapping his Greyhaven robes tight and struggling after Tristayne through the muck. The necromancer found himself again considering the mortal's presence. Fear and desperation radiated palpably from the pathetic creature.

"You were a student at Greyhaven?" he asked. Tomaz seemed uncertain as to whether the words were a question or a statement – he said nothing.

"Answer me," Tristayne snapped.

"Yes, master, a student of the runemasters," Tomaz stuttered.

"Did you enjoy it?"

"I… I do not know, master. I was not there long."

"I studied at Nerekhall once," Tristayne mused, hitching

his own ragged robes up, though he needn't have bothered – they were already befouled with bog muck.

"At the Academy," Tristayne repeated. "Until they put a rope around my neck and left me to dangle."

He raised a hand to his throat, running his fingers along where the scar had once been. He could still remember it. The choking, twitching horror of it. The searing panic of being unable to draw breath, the ache in his lungs only making it worse. Finally, gray walls closing in, a numbing oblivion that he had almost welcomed.

He had died many times since that day, but none had stayed with him like the first. The memories endured, long after he had forgotten what it truly felt like to experience air in his lungs or the warm vitality of his own heartbeat. They haunted him like a phantom that he could neither bind nor banish.

He realized that Tomaz was falling behind. He paused to allow him to catch up, leaning on the haft of his scythe as he did so. It was an affectation that he had a habit of adopting without realizing – after all, since he had passed from life to undeath, he had no need of rest, sleep or any other worldly sustenance. He did not tire dragging his body through the marshland's cloying ooze, and failed to understand Tomaz's difficulties as he watched him flounder.

"How did you come to be here, you miserable little thing?" he asked as the mortal finally caught up, struggling for breath.

"I was betrayed, master," he whined. Tristayne laughed, a low chuckle as thick and foul as the bog.

"Weren't we all. You belonged to the cult?"

"Yes, master."

The Death Cults were Waiqar's eyes and ears throughout the baronies of Terrinoth. They had roots in every city, and counted among their ranks everyone from criminals and killers to knights and professors. Tristayne himself had been a member of Nerekhall's students' cult, though his interest in necromancy had swiftly outgrown them, even more so when he had taken the Black Scythe from the city's Shrine of Nordros and corrupted it.

"You were a fool to trust them," Tristayne told Tomaz.

"Yes, master," the wretch replied. Tristayne set off once again.

The mist had withdrawn from the castle crag that morning, but they were now deep amongst it, wading through an ethereal world of muck and tall bog grasses, all shrouded in the slowly shifting miasma. The only landmarks were the occasional tree, short, twisted and leafless, and the barest hint of old walls and ruins that protruded from the tussocks. Tristayne was unconcerned. He would find his way back to Zorgas easily enough. To one such as him, its accumulation of dark energies was like a beacon on the horizon.

"You must consider yourself very blessed, I suppose," he said to Tomaz as they went. "A mortal who has set eyes upon the Undying One and still lives. Few can claim such a thing."

"Yes, master," Tomaz said, though he sounded anything but thankful.

"Sometimes I wish I had not encountered him," Tristayne admitted, realizing he was partially enjoying unburdening himself to a being he knew was powerless to do anything with the information he gave him. A mortal servant in a place like Zorgas was less than nothing. That in itself made Tomaz somewhat valuable to him. "I know it sounds like foolishness, but he freed me from my imprisonment. To be chosen by him, to receive his tutelage, there could be no greater honor. But his arrogance is unbearable. He thinks himself a god. He believes he is the master of life and death, yet he cannot even raise up the bodies of the slain, not without his dust. He is no more powerful in that regard than I am."

Wisely, Tomaz said nothing. Tristayne supposed it made little sense to the worm, even if he had been in a Death Cult. Necromancy was an imprecise and complex art, and never more so than when it came to the specific act of raising the dead. Ynfernael energies or the unknowable workings of the Everliving Engine could imbue unlife into a corpse, but the only sure way to create undead capable of acting independently was to use the infamous bone dust of Waiqar's Deathborn Legion, coupled with the Black Invocation.

The tale of how the dust came into being was legendary, and well known even beyond occult circles. When Waiqar had ascended amidst the horror of the Black Rain, his army had suffered and been reborn with him in undeath. The skeletal warriors of his personal guard, now the Deathborn Legion, were so redolent with necromantic energies that it had sunken itself into their very bones. Grinding those same bones down produced powder which could be combined with certain delicate rituals to reanimate the dead. This was the only certain way of producing a host of unliving minions.

It was a curse that all necromancers had railed against at some point but, thus far, even the mighty Waiqar had yet to find a way to bring back bodies without the use of the dust, finite though it was. Spirits could be harnessed by the Everliving Engine and brought forth from the afterlife, but they were not enough to build an army. And that was what made Tristayne doubt his erstwhile master.

Really, the Great Necromancer was no greater than any of them. Without the essence of his warriors and their remains, he was nothing.

"He would do well to remember that," Tristayne said out loud. Tomaz, stumbling behind, clearly thought better than to ask what he was talking about.

"Were your masters in Greyhaven fools as well?" Tristayne demanded.

"Yes, master," Tomaz said.

"Elaborate."

"They… did not appreciate the power of the necromantic arts, master," Tomaz said after a pause, erring on the side of caution.

"We will show them the error of their ways then," Tristayne said. "Sooner, if I had my way."

He had been right to drag along his pet – it was good to speak his thoughts to something other than the mist or the bog. He forged out into the marshland whenever Waiqar's tutelage frustrated him, allowing his thoughts to fester quietly, away from Zorgas and its desperate wails and echoing halls. Out here there was rarely anything but the dull popping of the sump and the occasional, far-off screech of something unearthly. Nothing dared disturb him.

He liked to be out in the open, too. His imprisonment was the only thing that haunted him more relentlessly than his hanging. To be bound, sealed in, unable to move so much as a finger, his magics useless, his very thoughts held captive...

He shook off the memories, aided by the fact that Tomaz had started to whine. He again stopped and looked back dispassionately at the human. He was muddied from head to foot and looked close to collapse. Tristayne had forgotten how easily exhausted mortals were.

"I will see you well-fed when we get back to Zorgas," he told him. "Or you can stay here and become food yourself."

"Master, it grows late," the fool dared complain. Tristayne was about to punish his presumptiveness when he realized that, actually, Tomaz was right. Days in the Mistlands were always short, and the weak light fighting its way through the fog was fading fast. They had been wandering for longer than he realized. He had never had someone to converse with on one of his marshland journeys, and time had slipped away from him as thoroughly as one of the souls Waiqar had demanded he interrogate.

"We turn back," he said brusquely, coming about and passing Tomaz in the other direction. The servant dragged himself after him once more.

Perhaps he had been unwise to come this far. One such as he could pass without concern through the Mistlands during the hours of daylight, but when darkness descended, none but Waiqar could walk abroad in total confidence.

There were things out in the marshes that defied any but the mightiest necromancer, ancient evils that had writhed and squirmed, haunted and hungered since the rot had first taken root in the thirteenth barony, millennia before.

Tristayne believed absolutely in his own abilities, but he had no wish to test himself against the creatures of the marsh. Not yet, anyway.

"Quicker," he snapped back at Tomaz, considering leaving the servant. He was surprised something hadn't snatched him from the mire already. They did not dare while he was here, he thought. But that would change in the dark.

Night came on quickly. Zorgas was still far off as the marsh faded into the gray twilight, the grass and broken trees growing indistinct, the mist seeming to thicken. Amidst the day's last dying, Tristayne made out a few pieces of broken stone jutting up like great old bones from the marsh. He altered course for them, discovering a long-abandoned, partially submerged ruin, all crumbling walls and thick lichens. The marshes were littered with such places, most now barely distinguishable from their surroundings, relics of a time before the Second Darkness when the Mistlands had been a prosperous and peaceful barony in its own right. Such a place hardly constituted as shelter – indeed, many harbored cursed spirits and foul monsters in their own right – but it was preferable to being caught out in the open after dark.

Silently, he cursed gods he had long ago stopped believing in. He had let his bitterness get the better of him. He had been gone for too long. Tomaz managed to join him between the remains of the broken walls, collapsing on a patch of semi-solid ground.

"If you wish to keep hold of your body and soul this night, you will not interrupt me," Tristayne told him. The servant didn't reply, but blanched with fear.

Tristayne had heard something as they reached the walls, a distant, ghastly shriek. He began to chant under his breath, using words as tools, to shape the energies around him. As he did so, more howls became audible, and soon the whole twilight was resounding with an unearthly cacophony, surrounding the ruin.

There were many strange and unknowable things in the Mistlands, but Tristayne knew exactly what was making this particular din. Ferrox. The ghoulish beasts infested the marshes, neither truly living nor dead, cannibalistic humanoids with a disputed origin.

Some claimed they were the descendants of the peoples who had once inhabited the thirteenth barony, others that they were the result of a diabolic sorcerer's melding of humans with great razorwing bats. Regardless of how they had come about, they inhabited vast tracts of the Mistlands. A powerful necromancer was able to bind them to their will, for a time, but for the most part they knew no master other than their own hunger. A hunger that now seemed to be directed at Tristayne and Tomaz.

Tristayne considered leaving his servant to them. He was a fleshy morsel, and the pack now stalking them would probably rather avoid Tristayne's obvious power and content themselves with the easier prey. That was the logical choice, but Tristayne was angry. His frustration at Waiqar's tutelage had turned to annoyance with himself. He should not have strayed so far. Abandoning Tomaz would be too easy. If the ferrox were foolish enough to threaten him or his servant, he would teach them to regret their choice. He was Tristayne, the Deathless, heir of Count Olliven, Prince of the Black Realm, and he did not flee before anything.

He marshalled his magics, the dark essence of the elemental Mortos now coiling around his body and scythe, visible even to a mortal like Tomaz. His eyes lit with rotting yellow power, a beacon of unholy energy as the last of the day's light faded to black.

"*Nam-úš ki lá inem,*" he roared into the night. "*Inem lugel vost!*"

The gibbering and screeching around rose in response to the challenge. The first ferrox launched itself from beyond the edge of the ruins, claws out, fangs bared. Spitting one last arcane word, Tristayne met it.

CHAPTER THREE

As the creatures attacked, Tomaz hugged his arms around his body and pressed himself back against the stonework.

Tristayne met them head-on. The skeleton was lit by yellowing energies as he swung his great scythe, cleaving the first of the monsters to leap at them from the surrounding dark clean in half. A second and a third followed, then a great rush that Tristayne met with a word rather than a slash of his weapon. The yellow light flared and engulfed them, and they shrieked terribly as their flesh began to melt like wax, sloughing from their bones right before Tomaz's eyes.

He did his best to just stay away from both the creatures and the rancid energies killing them. Being dragged through the festering bog at the behest of a walking corpse had nearly been too much as it was. He had repeatedly felt things tugging at his feet and legs beneath the black surface, and had seen strange deadlights and what looked like predatory eyes gazing at them through the mist.

Tristayne had appeared oblivious to it all, ranting in a scraping voice that seemed to invade Tomaz's mind directly rather than issue from his skeletal jaw. He had felt the briefest glimmer of hope when he had managed to convince Tristayne to turn back, dimmed by his hunger, exhaustion, and the bitter cold that pervaded the marshlands. Now it seemed as though it wouldn't matter. They were going to be eaten and, in Tomaz's case, eaten alive.

The things coming at them were humanoid, but monstrous, their flesh green-tinged, their bodies rangy and daubed in bog filth. Their features were bat-like, and they had raggedy, vestigial wings beneath their arms. It was difficult to focus on anything besides their wicked fangs and talons though.

They attacked the ruin from all sides, Tristayne turning with a great swing of his scythe to behead three of them at once as they came at him from behind. Foul, stinking blood jetted out, almost hitting Tomaz as it spattered up the wall next to him.

He had started daring to hope in the last few days, but that now seemed in vain. Consigned to what he took to be one of the castle's dungeons, he had been brought food and water by a shambling reanimate dressed in the dusty rags of a servant's livery. It had been stale bread and gray meat mostly, but it had taken the edge off his desperate hunger. The skeletal creature he now knew as Tristayne had visited on brief occasions, but this was the first time he had removed him from his cell. He was now wishing he had stayed. In fact, he'd long ago realized he wished he had never become involved in necromancy, or the Death Cult, or even gone to Greyhaven. He wished his father had never reanimated that accursed cat.

Tristayne snarled another string of words that made Tomaz's skin crawl, and a bolt of crackling yellow energy darted from the splayed bones of the necromancer's outstretched hand. It tore like the jaws of a hound through half a dozen of the creatures, bouncing from one to another before dissipating, leaving them in pieces. The scythe took two more, Tristayne tireless as only the living dead could be. Tomaz just stayed down, desperate for the nightmare to be over.

Judging from the rising shrieks around them, it was only just beginning.

Tristayne spun the Black Scythe in his hands, lending it a wicked momentum as he brought it round and sent shorn limbs and torsos flying, adding their bloody remains to the mound steadily forming at the heart of the ruins. They were pathetic, but there were a lot of them, and he was being forced to put everything he had into holding them at bay.

His scythe, at least, was enjoying itself. He could feel its darkness increasing with every kill as it hungrily slaked itself on the shrieking souls departing the bodies of the ferrox, black sludge beginning to ooze thickly down its haft. The creatures were poor fare compared to mortals in their prime, but it was better than nothing. At least Tristayne would no longer have to endure its leeching hunger for a while.

A pair of ferrox bounded over their slain kin and clawed at him, their talons getting tangled in his robes. He cried out in frustration, turning his anger into more death magic, instinctive now, without need for the binding words. He unleashed a razorwind that flensed flesh and muscle from bone, shredding dozens of the things as they swarmed over the walls and each another, reducing them to offal that collapsed, steaming, into the dirt.

And still more came. One managed to rake the back of his robes before it was cut in two, and another vaulted from the top of a section of wall and clattered against Tristayne's side, almost pitching them both over. They grappled for a moment, the necromancer getting a hold on its throat, ripping it out with his bony fingers as the ferrox snarled and bit at him.

That gave the rest more time to close in. Talons ripped at his bones, not enough to break them, but enough to jar him. Up this close he couldn't use his scythe as well, forced to smash the haft into the twisted face of one of the creatures as it lunged for his skull, crunching bones and breaking fangs. He shortened his grip on the scythe's haft, employing it in a flurry of short, hard chops, trying to clear a space around him once again. He needed room to swing and the moment's concentration necessary to unleash the death energies that were visible to his witch-sight, flowing thickly from the bodies all around him.

The ferrox pack seemed endless. He came to the realiz- ation that he was going to die, again. Of course, that held no fear for him. He would rise once more. But how long would it be? In the past his inertia had ranged from hours to the better part of a century. The strange form of immortality, part curse, part blessing, was wholly unpredictable. Waiqar would not wait for him, in fact, he doubted he would even necessarily be able to find him out in the Mistlands' depths. He could claw his way back up from the marshes to find himself replaced by another. Even worse, perhaps Waiqar would finally mount his campaign against Terrinoth. Tristayne would miss it all. It would be intolerable, and his own plans would be for naught.

His scythe took more, growing ever keener as it feasted. Finally, he found the room to swing it properly, loosing a raging howl as he did so.

It seemed for a while as though the display of fury had broken the pack's will. He sensed rather than saw a shift in the creatures around him. The pressure of their writhing, clawing bodies decreased fractionally, and their shrieks and screeches changed in pitch and tone. Now there was a note of uncertainty in them.

Tristayne used the moment to cleave the ones nearest to him to pieces. No more took their place. The ferrox surrounding him had paused their frenzied assault and were backing off, looking around in apparent confusion.

There was a hooting cry from out in the dark and, as quickly as they had appeared, the pack of monstrosities retreated, vanishing back into the marshes.

Tristayne lowered his dripping scythe slowly, letting the energies that had been gnawing at his bones dissipate with a disembodied howl. The blazing yellow deadlights emanating from his eyes and jaw faded down to a dull, bitter glow.

It seemed the pathetic creatures had had enough after all. They had been fools to challenge one as powerful as him in the first place. He would have slaughtered all of them.

He began to stride from the ruins when a whimper made him pause. He thought one of the ferrox was still alive, then realized he had forgotten about the human, Tomaz. He doubled back, finding the desperate creature half buried beneath twitching, bloody remains.

"Up," he ordered him, not deigning to help. Much as he struggled to discern the expressions of mortals anymore, it seemed Tomaz's attention wasn't on him, but on the opposite wall of the ruin, past the piles of dead ferrox.

A sudden, unwelcome sense of vulnerability ran through Tristayne. He turned sharply, scythe at the ready, aware now of a presence that had somehow managed to mask itself until that very moment. A presence that, even by his own admission, was redolent with the power of death, and something even worse. The Ynfernael.

He feared that the bloodshed had drawn a more dangerous monstrosity to them, or had awoken something sleeping within the ruins. The sight was not what he expected.

A figure was perched atop one of the sunken, half-collapsed walls, supporting itself on one arm, one leg resting casually atop the other. At a glance it looked like an elf, with knife-like ears and features that possessed a sharp beauty. What skin was visible was a tainted shade of green and marked with intricate tattoos that Tristayne recognized as arcane wards. The rest of her was garbed in lean, jagged brazen armor, adding to her slender and deadly elegance.

She was the last thing he had expected to be confronted with out in the marshes.

The stranger smiled as Tristayne rounded on her, looking almost amused. He could see the death magics that clung to her, writhing around her like a pack of serpents and making her eyes gleam in the night. She was no lost innocent, but a deadly, ancient being.

"Sorry, am I disturbing you?" she asked.

"I know you," Tristayne said, without replying to her question. He had never encountered her before, but he recognized her from the stories. Every denizen in the Mistlands had heard the tales. He felt an unaccustomed moment of fear, bordering on dread. He fought to suppress it.

"And I know you, Tristayne Olliven," she replied, smiling again. "I hope I didn't interrupt your fun?"

"Zarihell," Tristayne continued, keeping his scythe raised. It rattled in his grip, eager to continue to feed. "The elven witch. Waiqar's fellow prisoner in the days before the Black Rain."

"Ah, the burden of my fame precedes me," Zarihell said in an unnecessarily dramatic tone, slipping lightly down from the wall and dropping in amongst the ferrox bodies. Tristayne took a step back. Of all the encounters he had expected to make after dark in the Mistlands, this was not one of them.

"You should know better than to wander beyond your master's care," she continued. The words stung Tristayne.

"I do as I please," he responded. "And tonight it pleased me to hunt ferrox."

"Hunt, or be hunted?" Zarihell said. She approached him with the elegant threat of a feline closing on its prey and, despite his defiance, Tristayne again retreated, until he was almost backed against the wall Tomaz was sheltering under.

"The ferrox have learned to fear me," she said, stopping just in front of him. "Which is lucky for you, perhaps."

"I would have slain them all," Tristayne reiterated, a little desperately.

"And what would your master think of that?"

"He... He would not care."

"From what I hear, he would not be surprised that you needed assistance."

"How do you hear anything out here, amidst this mire?" Tristayne shot back, trying to regain some sort of foothold in the conversation. "You are an outcast, banished to the edge of the Mistlands, your name reduced to a myth."

"The powerful have their ways, young Olliven," the elf teased, now altogether too close for Tristayne's comfort. He could no longer easily defend himself, and his scythe was practically ripping itself from his grasp in its desperation to hack at the witch. He would have let it do so, were he not afraid that the blow would not be fatal.

"It's such a shame Waiqar doesn't see your potential," Zarihell went on, looking into his burning eyes. "Just between us, I think he is deliberately keeping your studies in check. He fears you becoming too powerful. It's always been the way with him. Trust me, I've known him for a lot longer than you."

"Cease your goading, witch," Tristayne snarled, and

made to drive Zarihell back. Abruptly, he found he could not move. With a speed he had been unable to follow, she had snatched hold of the Black Scythe, gripping its tarry haft.

It should have spelt death for her, ripping her soul from her body and sealing her essence away within the cursed weapon, as Tristayne himself had been once before. But she didn't even flinch. Instead, it was the scythe that ceased to shake, its hunger receding from Tristayne's thoughts. Without a word, without a stirring of magics, seemingly without even thought or effort, Zarihell had tamed the ancient weapon of the Black Realm.

She leaned in and whispered into Tristayne's ear.

"There is more to power than old bone dust. When you grow bored of being Waiqar's servant, seek me out again, here. I would advise doing it before *he* grows bored of *you*."

And with that, she was gone.

CHAPTER FOUR

Waiqar walked the walls of Zorgas, as he often did when the memories became too much of a burden. He was not sure whether it was night or day – such a thing had become indistinct to him long ago – but the mists had returned, swelling like an ocean around the great fortress and rising slowly to strangle it.

The time was drawing close. He could feel it. Centuries of preparation and planning, an interminable wait to guarantee future success. It had been agony, but it was necessary. Time was his greatest advantage. To triumph, he had to make full use of it. Patience in all things.

Since the Night of the Red Feast, he had been reviewing the final preparations. His cult leaders, allies and informants from across Terrinoth had been sending him news by the usual means, capturing an innocent, describing the current situation to the uncomprehending victim, then killing them and sending their souls hurtling to Zorgas. Waiqar would then extract the spirit's memories, gleaning the knowledge that they were unintentionally carrying.

The news was almost all good. To Terrinoth's east the Uthuk Y'llan were stirring in greater numbers than they had for decades. An invasion was brewing, and when it struck, the mortal baronies would find their attentions fixed on the most obvious threat.

The situation of many of the baronies themselves had been deteriorating for some time, a hundred trivial woes – some coincidental, some engineered – adding to the growing instability of the realm. The harvest in Telor had failed for the third season running. A plague had lately swept through Cailn. The heiress to the Barony of Forthyn had recently been killed. Most important of all, the great drake Levirax was continuing to build her power base in the Molten Heath, attracting dragon hybrids from across Terrinoth and beyond. Waiqar had no doubt she would mount her incursion soon, and when it did the baronies would be beset on all sides.

And that was when Waiqar would make his play. He would save Terrinoth from dragon and demon alike, and in doing so reshape it into the kingdom he deserved.

He climbed to the cracked pinnacle of the tower at the top of Zorgas' keep. It was crumbling from almost a millennium of neglect, but it still conformed to the design Waiqar had laid out for it when it had first been built. It was a replica of the same Black Citadel where he had been held in the Darklands, that terrible place that still lived on through his un-life. Nothing, neither living nor dead, was permitted within that particular tower. It was the only truly silent place in Zorgas. When his doubts were strongest, he retreated to its cracked walls, gazed at the shackles that hung about its interior, or climbed the spiral stairs up onto the battlements, where he could look out over the citadel in its entirety.

He did so at that moment, taking in the bristling towers, courtyards and walls of Zorgas below him, a warren-like sprawl of gaunt and jagged masonry. In ages past it had been one of the greatest fortresses in Terrinoth, and Waiqar intended it to be so again. He had still not decided whether, when the baronies crowned him, he would move his capital to Archaut, or remain and demand obedience in the north. He currently favored the latter, intending to show all the might that he had assembled here, the power which so many yet discounted as myth and legend. Still, claiming the old capital of Terrinoth would have its benefits, and bring a satisfaction of its own.

"*Enough*," said the voice, softly, but with purpose. The voice in his head, the one that ensured he kept to the purpose he had been given all those years ago. "You must remain focused."

He chided himself for thinking too far ahead. His plans spanned ages and thousands of leagues, but ruminating on such petty matters was a distraction, and he despised distractions. He could sink into bitter reveries for days, until the voice woke him. What it had said was right, as always. He trusted it. He needed to be focused, now more than ever.

There were plenty of problems still to be solved before the time came. Not all the forces to the south were beset by their own struggles. The elves of the Aymhelin had been marshalling their strength for some time, seemingly aware of the great conflict that would soon befall Terrinoth.

Even more problematic was the defiance offered to Waiqar by the northern barony of Carthridge and its ruler, Baron Zachareth. He was one of the few Terrinoth nobles who gave credence to Waiqar's existence, and was tireless in his efforts to convince his fellow rulers about the rot spreading from Zorgas. Everywhere else the Mistlands slowly advanced, the foul bog spreading inexorably southward, but in Carthridge it had halted. Zachareth had even defeated Ardus. It had taken a great deal of sacrifice and bone dust to reform Waiqar's lieutenant and return him to the physical plane. The baron of Carthridge was defiant, and that was unacceptable.

For his own part, Waiqar only occasionally remembered the mortal pup's existence, though he was still proving to be a greater thorn than his contemporaries. In the past he would simply have waited for such a rival to succumb to the inevitable march of time, sometimes even snatching his soul after his death to toy with, but it seemed that events would force Waiqar's hand while the arrogant baron still lived.

It was no real concern, he reminded himself. The wind was rising, tugging at his purple cape. Zachareth would be dealt with. More pressing were the problems that bubbled and festered within the Mistlands themselves. He had endured doubts before the Red Feast, but that night had confirmed them. The vampire lords of Bilehall had grown indolent at best, and rebellious at worst. Only a few decades ago leeches like Naythen Torvic would never have dared question him openly, within his own hall. He had increased the number of tithes they were required to pay him, yes, but only to test their loyalty. If the bonds that shackled them to his will were weak enough to be strained and broken by that, they would need to have been strengthened anyway. It was the sort of problem that would only worsen with time.

He stalked down to the tower's main chamber, where he pondered the manacles on the walls. Bones littered the floor around them, not the priceless remains of any of his Deathborn, but the desiccated and scattered bodies of wretches who had dared defy him. For some centuries he had imprisoned all who displeased him in this tower, bending all his efforts to torturing them, desperately attempting to inflict the same suffering on them that he himself had endured at the hands of the Llovar's spawn in the original Black Citadel.

Eventually, with the help of the voice, he had realized it for what it was, a madness that was threatening to unmake his mind. He had been trying to replace his own screams with theirs, but it was never enough. Eventually he had found clarity, and now the tower remained unoccupied and silent, used only when he found himself troubled and did not wish to hear the whispers of the dead for a while.

"They will betray me," he said out loud, thoughts returning to the vampiric coven as he stood still in the center of the chamber. "It is the nature of the weak, and they are weak."

"*Perhaps*," answered the voice, its tone guarded.

"I am always betrayed," Waiqar continued, speaking not to the voice but to the bones underfoot. "If I believed in gods or fates, I would think it a great irony. I am reviled as the Betrayer, yet I was the one who was turned upon and abandoned. That truth would unmake the petty baronies. They need to know it. They need to be shown what really happened."

"*You are losing yourself,*" the voice warned. "*You are stronger than this.*"

But for once, Waiqar did not heed it. The memories were coming back, not of the horrors of the Black Citadel, but of a time before it, a time when he had still known hope, and been damned because of it. Suddenly he could feel it all again, the eternal, numbing chill of undeath conquered by the sharpness of his own recollections. The rain, the thunder, the taste of blood, the heart-pounding terror. It broke like a storm over him, consuming him, reminding him of a time at the start.

He knew he should fight the resurgent past, but it was too strong.

Waiqar remembered.

CHAPTER FIVE
Long Before

"If we go any further, we do so alone," Ardus said.

Waiqar did his best not to show his uncertainty. He knew his lieutenant was correct. Three days his army had waited, encamped at the base of the Road of Skulls. The passage into the heart of the Ru Darklands was a winding trail that worked its way between rocky heights, hemmed in by sheer cliffs and sudden drops. It was an arid place where nothing grew, and where the bones of those who had already attempted passage bleached beneath a sky that alternated between ruthless sun and lashing, furious storms.

And now Waiqar faced the prospect of taking the loyal soldiers of his legion, who had fought the cursed Uthuk Y'llan from Riverwatch to the Lothan River, along that same bleak passage. The prize beyond it, the Black Citadel, was great, but Waiqar had been promised reinforcements. To go on with only the soldiers at his disposal seemed more than unwise. It felt like suicide.

Timmorran had sworn he would send his aid, had he not?

"What do you say, Melkor, Karrok?" he asked his other subordinates. The two knights, both veterans of his campaigns through Kell and along the River of Sleep, looked guarded, the way they always did when they thought he was making a mistake.

"It is a long journey, and there is nowhere to replenish our supplies along the way," Karrok pointed out. "We have enough to sustain ourselves as far as the Black Citadel, but if we are forced to surround it, we will not survive a siege."

"Nor has the road been properly scouted," Melkor added, dabbing at his sweat-drenched brow. Even with the lesser amount of equipment Waiqar's host had adopted for their campaigns on the Charg'r Wastes, the temperature was intolerable.

"If we wait longer, we will run out of supplies regardless," Waiqar replied. "Has there still been no word from Lord Timmorran?"

"None of our messengers have returned yet," Melkor said. "Our outriders report no activity to the south or west."

Waiqar forced himself not to curse openly, refusing to show such weakness before his subordinates. Surely he had not really been abandoned? He had begged Timmorran for reinforcements, had tried desperately to impress on him the necessity of striking hard and fast against Llovar, while his hordes were still reeling from their defeat at the battle of the Burning Hills and the subsequent flight of the orcs. He had thought Timmorran was of like mind, yet here they were, days past the anticipated rendezvous and still with no sign of Waiqar's ally and friend. Why was the great wizard still delaying?

A leader could not be indecisive. He had come this far, bent on glory, determined to overcome this final test and strike the blow that might end this war and secure peace in Terrinoth for generations. With his forces in the vanguard, he had fought and overcome three separate hordes of demons and their deranged worshipers. His legion was proud and experienced. He had no doubt they wished to push north and take the fight to the enemy. They awaited only his command.

"We go forward, into the valley," Waiqar said. He signaled the horns to sound the advance.

Death came for them all five days later.

A terrible storm had broken out, shrouding the valley in a perpetual twilight and lashing it with cold, stinging rain. The march had barely started before it was forced to a crawl, horses and wagons struggling as what had been a dirt track became more like a stream of muck, winding between the valley sides.

Death had already started to worm its way in amongst the ranks. On the first day a pair of warriors fell screaming down a precipice that followed the side of the roadway for half a league. That night lightning struck one huddled group of soldiers, leaving their flesh charred and their armor melted to their bodies. The next day there was a small avalanche of rocks and dirt that crushed half a cohort and forced the rest of the column to halt until a path could be dug through. It was as though the valley itself was seeking to repel them.

The real slaughter began on the fifth day.

It started almost innocuously. Against the advice of Ardus and the other knights, Waiqar had taken to riding just behind the column's vanguard. The decision to take the Road of Skulls had been his alone, and it seemed only right that he shoulder the greatest portion of the danger. He was close to the forefront when the drumming of hooves reached him over the incessant seething of the rain, echoing from the rock faces rising almost vertically on both flanks. Moments later a horse appeared, galloping back toward the column.

It was one of the mounts belonging to the outriders, sent to scout ahead along the trail. More worryingly, its owner was nowhere to be seen. It clattered past Waiqar and the other soldiers of the vanguard, bolting past those who attempted to grasp it.

"Order a halt," Waiqar said urgently, his command followed by the pealing of the horn-blower that rode at his side. The sound echoed along the valley, answered by the thud of feet and the clatter of armor as the legion came to a standstill behind him. Abruptly, there was nothing but the noise of the rain, and the soft snorting and jangling of the vanguard's mounts.

Then the howling began.

It filled the valley, followed moments later by the hiss and thud of arrows whipping through the downpour. Waiqar twisted in his saddle in time to see one of the vanguard struck in the throat.

"They are upon us," shouted another, gesturing up the steep slopes of the pass.

He was correct. Dark shapes were spilling over the edge,

totem-standards rising, the terrible, blood-daubed effigies of the Uthuk Y'llan.

"Have the column form on its flanks," Waiqar shouted to the horn-bearer, but the man didn't get a chance to deliver the order – two arrows slammed into his back. Waiqar cursed, turning his horse in a tight circle as several more members of the vanguard pushed their steeds in close and raised their shields for him, protecting him from the deadly hail. They were hemmed in and unable to deploy. It was just what they had all feared. An ambush.

He felt a moment of shame as he realized just what he had led his legion into. He had ignored advice. But where was Timmorran? Why was his host facing this alone? It shouldn't have come to this.

The Uthuk charged, pouring down the steep, rock-strewn slopes on either side, a wild-eyed barbarian tide clad in coarse pelts and daubed in blood and war paint.

Waiqar's legion met them. The veterans wheeled to their left or right, back-to-back, then locked shields and lowered spears. Thunder crashed overhead and was answered from the valley's depths as the Uthuk tide slammed into the column from both sides.

Waiqar drew his sword, but none of the enemy presented themselves. It looked as though they were content to pick off the vanguard with archers on the valley crest while the main body cut off the central part of the column.

"Lord Waiqar!" shouted Ardus. He had ridden forward, arrows lodged in his shield and hooked into the barding of his warhorse. "Lord Waiqar, you must get back! We cannot protect you here!"

"Ardus, pull the column back," Waiqar told him. "Use the rearguard, withdraw a cohort at a time. I won't lose them all here because of my mistake!"

"Lord, it is useless if you fall," Ardus shouted as an arrow whipped between them, so close Waiqar felt the passing spray from its wet fletching.

"You have never disobeyed one of my orders," he snapped, looking his lieutenant in the eye. "Do not start now! Pull the legion back, out of this death trap! Go!"

Ardus hesitated a moment more, then snapped his visor down and wheeled away, back in the direction he had come.

"It's all my fault," Waiqar said to no one. "Gods be damned."

He reached out, delving into the energies that crackled, unseen by most, across the valley. Timmorran had taught him how to harness the fearsome might of the elements themselves, something that had always come naturally to him. The Road of Skulls, in particular, was rife with the sort of power he knew he could draw on with little effort.

He was a student of the greatest wizard to ever live, and he would not be so easily defeated.

"*Sarac tae vos,*" he bellowed, raising one gauntlet to the sky. The storm overhead responded with words of its own, a great rumble. Electrical charge and orbs of light sparked and danced around Waiqar as he closed his eyes, communing with the tempest. He could feel the rage in the heavens, the raw power there, pent up and thrumming.

He clenched his fist and, with a roar, released it.

Lightning struck. A flurry of bolts cracked down into the valley, slamming into the densest masses of Uthuk.

Warriors were flung into the air like discarded toys, flesh scorched, bones charred, pelts burning. The thunder rolled around in the valley, so ferocious it threatened to burst Waiqar's ears.

He clenched his teeth, snarling with effort as electrical energies blazed in his eyes and around his aching fist. The storm was proud. It did not bend long to the will of even the strongest elementalist. If he did not sever the connection soon, it would strike him in turn. He would be annihilated by its wrath.

With an effort that sent a jolt of pain through his entire body, he finally managed to unclench his hand and bring it down. The pounding lightning strikes ceased, but the storm, affronted, grew even worse – rain seethed down, and a wind shrieked along the jagged length of the valley, making the drenched standard stream above the struggling masses.

Waiqar marshalled his strength, trying to find the reserves of fortitude to reach out once more. He drove his consciousness not upward, but into the earth beneath, trying to find other energies there that he could turn to his advantage. The soil and rocks possessed an altogether different characteristic from the broiling restlessness of the storm – the valley itself was heavy and torpid, and shot through with the anguished spirits of the thousands who had perished traversing it across the centuries.

He didn't get a chance to attempt to harness it. An arrow slashed into his horse's neck, the poor animal shrieking and rearing. Caught by surprise, Waiqar fell, experiencing a wrenching sense of dislocation before he met the bitter earth. He grunted and rolled, avoiding his mount as it, too, went down, hooves drumming the cloying earth.

"Lord, they're upon us!" shouted one of the vanguard. Waiqar saw that he was right. It seemed as though the Uthuk had noted his presence. It was likely they had assumed the leader of the column was near its center, but the elemental magics combined with Waiqar's stag's head banner amongst the vanguard caused a shift in the flow of attackers.

They came for him. There was no more time to call upon the essence of the elements. He retrieved his sword, Bitterbite, and grasped the haft of his axe, Doom's Edge, in his other hand. There was no fear now, no despair, no horror at what was unfolding around him. No time for thoughts at all. Now came the killing.

It was desperate, and deadly. Waiqar brought his axe slamming down after using his sword to block the swing of a brute's falchion, cleaving open the Uthuk warrior's skull with a dull, ugly crack. The foe went down, and Waiqar barely had time to retrieve his weapon before the next came at him, jabbing with a half-spear.

The ferocious rush of bodies worked in Waiqar's favor. The Uthuk, bare from the chest up and daubed in crimson, could have run Waiqar through from beyond the reach of his sword, but the frenzied warriors behind shoved him forward. Waiqar was able to take the jab as a glancing blow on his hauberk and trap the haft under one arm before running the Uthuk through the throat with Bitterbite. Blood jetted up the blade, turning instantly pink and running off in great streams as it was caught in the downpour.

Before the body had even collapsed it was being shoved aside by another of the barbarians, a bone axe swinging for Waiqar's head. He parried, Bitterbite chopping through the haft and leaving the half-naked brute defenseless. Waiqar ran him through and kicked him off his sword.

So the killing continued. Waiqar's body flushed with the thrill and fear of it, running on instinct, no time to stop and think. There was no generalship here, nothing to do but meet the enemy blade-for-blade and try to marshal the warriors immediately around him. Dismounted and with rain and lightning lashing down, it was impossible to even see if the rest of the column had been able to pull back, if Ardus, Melkor, Karrok and the other knights had fought their way free. All those considerations were gone now, and Waiqar's world had been reduced to a small pocket of mud, blood and steel.

"Vanguard, to me!" he roared, ripping his sword from the Uthuk's throat and raising it high. His surviving men closed in, shields up as they met a fresh rush of Uthuk tribesmen. Through the clatter of swords and axes and the splitting of wood, Waiqar heard something chilling. It was the bestial snarling and yapping of what sounded like a pack of hounds.

"Flesh rippers," someone shouted. Waiqar realized the warning was correct as the closest Uthuk were thrown violently to one side before they could strike.

The ambush hadn't been sprung by Llovar's minions alone. Demons marched beneath the bestial standards, the warriors of the Ynfernael both mortal and immortal joined in their desire to shed the blood of those who would oppose them. Waiqar had fought such terrors before, including the flesh rippers, terrible part-demons that resembled great hounds – at least, if hounds had possessed ridges of bony spines, raw, skinless hides and talons and fangs as long as butchers' knives.

Their maws were already bloodied – so feral were the demon-spawn that they had been ripping and tearing at the rearmost Uthuk warriors in their need to get at Waiqar and his survivors. Now they flung themselves against the vanguard, their howls rivalling the thunder that still rolled through the valley.

Waiqar plunged his consciousness desperately into the dirt as they leapt, snatching onto the spirits of the stones underfoot and ripping them upward with a string of arcane words that felt like he was choking on mud. There was a cracking sound as a crest of jagged rocks slammed upward from the churned-up mud, into the faces of the oncoming beasts. Bones cracked and for a second it looked as though the sudden barrier would shield the vanguard from the onslaught.

But Waiqar knew demons, knew they were insatiable. In just a few moments the great hounds were scrambling up and over the encircling crown of rocks, drooling blood and spittle, leaping down at their prey.

Waiqar bellowed and drove Bitterbite up into the underbelly of one as it lunged. The steel parted demonic flesh, foul, stinking guts and black ichor spewing forth. The thing bore him down, though, its talons raking his armor, ripping open leather and making him cry out as it found flesh. Even disemboweled it tried to rip out his throat, only ceasing when another soldier of the vanguard rammed his own sword down its gullet, impaling it.

There was no time for thanks. The rest of the rippers were tearing into Waiqar's remaining warriors, screams and blood assailing him. Even worse, a flurry of shards, composed of pure darkness, whipped into the tight little circle, slicing through the rain and flashing through armor as though it wasn't there at all. The man who had saved Waiqar fell, screaming with agony, dropping into the mud and writhing.

Waiqar caught the sulfurous, choking stink of Ynfernael magic. Sure enough, an Uthuk Blood Witch was standing on the parapet of rocks he had summoned, clad in a cape of drenched black feathers and a dripping ram's skull. She raised a staff of bone, spitting more curses at those beneath him.

He fought to heave the flesh ripper's reeking, spiny corpse off him, desperate to get to his feet and reach the witch. He tried to channel more of the elemental energy around him into his body, roaring with effort, summoning the will of rocks and dirt, wind and rain.

It was too late. The vanguard's last stand had collapsed, the formation now gone as flesh rippers and Uthuk tore and hacked at the last few warriors, descending into a frenzy of bloodshed. Waiqar's banner had fallen, trampled in the mud. He stood alone.

This was the end, he knew. He should never have marched into the valley. He should never have trusted Timmorran to send him aid. Cold, bitter acceptance replaced his despair. If it had been betrayal, then he would still die fighting. He couldn't hope for any better now.

One of the Uthuk charged him, screeching praise to her cursed gods. Waiqar turned her blade aside with his sword and chopped her down with Doom's Edge, fury lending him the strength to cleave from her shoulder to her abdomen. The next demon-worshiper to come at him died likewise, and the rest hesitated, even the flesh rippers seeming to sense who he was. The Blood Witch glared down at him, hissing her wicked words under her breath as she drew more Ynfernael energy to her.

"Come then, cowardly wretch," he barked at her, spreading his arms wide, rain and blood drenching him. "I am not afraid to die here. Are you?"

"You would accept this end so easily?" the Witch taunted. "You who were bold enough to march on the Black Citadel alone?"

"Everyone dies eventually," Waiqar snarled. The witch laughed, tipping her head back in the rain, the sound just as stinging.

"Only the lucky ones die, champion," she said, her eyes gleaming red. "Do not forget that."

CHAPTER SIX
The Present

"Waiqar!"

The word was like a hammer-blow inside his skull, making him stumble. Briefly, he remembered what pain felt like.

It receded, and with it, the memories. He was still in Zorgas. The slaughter on the Road of Skulls became a dull, dusty thing once again, barely even tangible.

It was the voice that had brought him back. It snarled now in his head, its ire aroused.

"Cease this weakness. I thought you superior to this. The past has no place here, not now that you are on the cusp of the plans we have laid."

"Yes," Waiqar agreed, feeling a pang of shame at what had happened. "The past is a dead thing. I live on."

"Collect yourself. We have a visitor."

The voice was right. Someone was climbing the spiral stairs to the bone-littered chamber, the flickering light of a mortal soul, albeit one stained by the magics of eternity. It was one Waiqar recognized, and its presence did not surprise him. Mirabelle Trest. Only she would have had the courage to come here seeking him.

She paused in the arched doorway, an austere figure in a belted white kirtle dress, her silver-shot black hair pulled back severely from her scalp and piled high. She carried a staff of black thornwood in one hand, and looked concerned as she spoke.

"My lord? Are you ... well?"

Waiqar regarded her for a moment in silence, seeing the magics that clung to her. They did not cleave instinctively to him when she was in his presence, as they did with Tristayne. She was a strong and talented necromancer, a worthy disciple of death. She had come to Zorgas of her own volition almost three centuries before, forging her path through the marshes and demanding entry at the gate. Waiqar had sent one of his Deathborn to slay her for her temerity, but she had vanquished him and threatened to use the dust of his bones to raise an army and besiege Zorgas. She was the only mortal he trusted.

"Why do you trouble me here?" he asked her.

"The council sent me," she replied. "They believed that since you called for the sitting, you would be present in person."

The council. He had forgotten. He had summoned his inner circle to resolve the matter of Bilehall.

"You were the only one who dared seek me out," he said. It was a statement rather than a question. Mirabelle merely inclined her head.

"Tell the council I am on my way," he continued. "And when they next ask you to find me, tell them to find their courage instead."

Mirabelle smiled tersely and left, her footsteps receding into the terrible silence.

He stood for a while longer, looking at the chains and the bones surrounding him, half-expecting the terrors of his past to resurface. There was nothing now though, nothing but numbness and dust.

He anticipated that the voice would chastise him for lingering, but it was gone. For a moment he felt completely and utterly alone. It was at once terrifying, and strangely liberating. It was not what he was accustomed to. He did his best to shrug off the sensation.

He turned toward the stairs and began to descend.

The Deathless Council had been called to the great hall of Zorgas, and were arrayed around the table that had been returned to the feasting pit. There were six of them in total, and they rose and bowed as Waiqar entered and took to his throne overlooking them.

"Sit," he ordered. They did so, waiting for his permission to begin. On the left were the most senior of his death knights, the commanders of his Deathborn, Ardus, Karrok and Melkor. On the right was Mirabelle, her fellow-necromancer Simon Lond, and the spirit of Lady Falgor. Lond was decrepit and blind, though the phantom orbs that perpetually floated around him whispered the nature of his surroundings in his ear. He was the last surviving founder of the oldest of Terrinoth's Death Cults – besides the traitor Zarihell – and was in effect Zorgas' spymaster. He had replaced Ankaur Maro, a powerful necromancer who had once risen to Waiqar's right hand before mortal champions had slain him permanently.

In life Lady Falgor had also been among Waiqar's most prominent coterie of necromancers, but one mistake had been enough for Zorgas' bitter spirits to tear her soul from her body. She had refused to depart to the afterlife, however, and by an incredible exertion of will not only remained semi-corporeal, but retained her mind and identity, aspects that most souls which stayed in the mortal sphere of existence quickly lost. After Waiqar, it was her commands that the spirits of Zorgas heeded.

"You are all aware of why I have summoned the council?" Waiqar asked of them.

"The aftermath of the Red Feast, lord," Mirabelle said. "It is understandable that you wish it addressed."

"Torvic is defiant," Waiqar said, feeling his ire stir at the recollection of how close the vampire had come to challenging him in his own hall. "I will not stand for it."

"Send me to remind him of his place, lord," Ardus said.

"No," Waiqar replied. "I have allowed this rot to fester for too long, and now it has spread. Only his sister Lucrezia seems to understand that I am not to be crossed."

"Did you have a punishment in mind, Undying One?" Lond rasped.

"The only one that befits those who would challenge me. Annihilation."

Waiqar could see from the way the energy reacted that his underlings were uncertain. It flowed around them wildly, pallid strands of death-magic that twisted one way, then the other.

"Speak," he barked. "I summoned you for counsel, not to sit and hear my decrees."

"You are suggesting making war on the lords of Bilehall?" Lady Falgor asked, her voice a disembodied moan that seemed to speak slightly out of sync with the motions of her ghostly lips.

"I am," Waiqar said. "They deserve nothing less."

"If you do, lord, it will not be an easy conflict," Melkor cautioned. "Our forces far outmatch those of Bilehall, but Torvic's crypt-fortress is strong and well-sited."

"At the very least it would disrupt our preparations for marching upon the baronies," Karrok added.

"Which legions beside the Deathborn have still to be raised?" Waiqar demanded.

"My own and Sir Helow's remain incomplete," Melkor said. "The rites to fully raise and augment the Nightborne and the Iron Bones have yet to begin."

"That still leaves us with sufficient force to strike at Bilehall," Ardus said, ever the war hound. "Give my legion the honor, lord. The Deathborn are ready."

"Perhaps," Waiqar said, not deigning to make the choice just yet. "A slight delay to the opening of our campaign in Terrinoth may be acceptable. What do you know of the movements of the great drake, Lond?"

"Hybrids continue to flock to her," the ancient necromancer said. "Some even dare pass through our lands on their way north and east. Levirax's power swells, but she will not gamble by striking this early."

"The dead say the same," Lady Falgor added, her form shuddering and distorting for a moment. "All the souls I have collected from the Molten Heath know little or nothing about the return of the dragons. They cannot possibly be ready yet."

"Then we still have time," Waiqar said. "And even if we did not, I would order this blow struck. We cannot move on the other baronies with a potential enemy in our rear. Torvic will betray us. He may even try to seize Zorgas while the legions are in the south."

"Are we certain of that?" Melkor dared ask. Waiqar permitted the question.

"I have been betrayed in similar ways before," he said. "I have regretted not acting with greater... decisiveness. I have humored Torvic's arrogance for too long, and it will only worsen."

"But if we attack him without direct provocation, we will be seen as aggressors," Melkor pointed out. "The idea that a lord can turn on his vassal at will cannot sit well with even the most subservient of the other undead nobles."

"Then we shall provoke him," Waiqar said, growing bored with the discussion now. He had wondered if he was going too far, singling out Torvic and his coven for annihilation, but he could see no effective counterargument being put forward.

"I will double his tithes again," he went on. "If Torvic really is loyal to me, then he will accept them. Corpses and thralls will swell our strength even further, and we will be more than ready to march south. And if he decides to refuse the tithe, then he has broken trust with me, and none can deny my right to make an example of him."

"What of Dalibor?" Karrok asked. "Kyndrithul and his brood are closely aligned with the lords of Bilehall."

"Kyndrithul would not dare to aid Torvic against us," Mirabelle said. "He grows ever more reclusive. Some say his grip on reality is slipping."

"Is this true?" Waiqar asked, directing the question at Lond and his murmuring ghost orbs.

"I do not currently have eyes nor ears in Dalibor, at least not close enough to Lord Kyndrithul to report on his state of mind," the necromancer admitted. Waiqar grunted dismissively. For now the other most powerful vampire lord of the Mistlands outside of Bilehall, Kyndrithul of Dalibor, presented no threat. He would be dealt with later.

"It is settled then," he declared. "Ardus, you will send the Deathborn to each of the crypt-fortresses of Bilehall and inform them of the new tithes. The Deathborn Legion will be prepared to march on the vampire lords should Torvic choose betrayal. The muster is to begin immediately, beneath the walls of Zorgas. Is that clear?"

It was. Waiqar dismissed the Deathless Council, all except Mirabelle, who he commanded to stay.

"Does something trouble you, lord?" the necromancer asked, standing now before the dais and its black throne.

"It does," Waiqar said. "And I would trust no other with it."

"Speak it, lord, and I will attempt to alleviate your concerns."

Waiqar pondered the mortal for a moment before explaining.

"It concerns the bone dust of the Deathborn. You know how vital it is to my work."

"Of course," Mirabelle said. "It is the only way by which we might raise new armies of the living dead."

She spoke the truth, but still, it stung. Of all the struggles Waiqar had endured – ending Timmorran's misrule, wresting power from death itself, hunting for the scattered shards of the Orb of the Sky, mastering the death energies and overcoming a thousand challenges from rivals, champions and petty adventurers – no problem had plagued him down the millennia like the riddle of eternal life.

He had spent centuries in research, sometimes not leaving Zorgas for decades at a time as he sought to break what he was convinced was a curse inflicted upon him. He had travelled to the ends of Terrinoth and beyond, from icebound shrines in the snowy peaks of the Isheim to ancient tree-temples in the groves of the Aymhelin. He had trekked tirelessly across the dunes of Al-Kalim to the vast desert crypts of rulers who had lain mummified while the world was still young, and had hacked his way through the sweltering jungles of Zanaga seeking a mythical leonine prophet. He had hunted down ancient relics, treasures and tomes, following a thousandfold stories from cultures and peoples across the known world, searching for any means to break the curse.

Still, he had not been able to find a way. It was not yet possible to reanimate great numbers of corpses with anything other than an Ynfernael-cursed item, or the powdered bones of his own Deathborn Legion. It was possible to leash and puppet the walking dead and snare phantoms and spirits, of course, but creating an army from such miserable creatures was impractical. Mixing even a small portion of the Deathborn dust with arcane rites, however, could create armies of thousands of reanimates. Thus, death withheld the greatest of powers – the control of a vast army of the living dead.

It was a constant frustration to him and, despite his best efforts, it was well known throughout the Mistlands. Until he found a way to raise a host by his own will alone, he could not consider himself all-powerful.

"The dust is the key, yes," Waiqar said. "But I believe that, recently, someone has been stealing it."

Mirabelle was silent, her expression – even the elemental Mortos around her – unreadable.

"How recently, lord?" she asked, perhaps realizing that the concept of "recent" could be very different to one such as Waiqar.

"Within the past year," he said. "I have been watching the crypts closely, but whoever has been taking the essence of my warriors, they still elude me."

"Are you certain any of the dust is missing?" Mirabelle asked.

"Yes," Waiqar said without hesitation. Beneath Zorgas was a vast warren of tombs and mausoleums, a catacomb of death that dwarfed even the fortress that sat atop it. A mortal could easily become lost in the cold, lightless depths, their soul doomed to join the countless others who had likewise strayed and now spent eternity trying to find their way out.

Even Waiqar was not entirely certain how deep the crypts extended, but the most important tombs, those of his Deathborn Legion, lay directly beneath the great hall. There, those members of Waiqar's original host who were not currently serving him slumbered.

Others had had their consciousness destroyed, often in battle, their bones now unanimated but still pricelessly valuable, steeped in necromantic energies. It was from these vanquished corpses that Waiqar created the dust that could reanimate the lesser dead. On certain, dread nights, such as the seventh day of Deepwinter or the full moon during Highsummer, bones would be ground down to powder in the center of ritual circles.

The words of the Black Invocation had to be spoken and channeled, though just how the dust was also employed in the rites varied from one practitioner to another. Some mixed it into a paste with the blood of murderers and executioners, others called upon the howling winds of death to spread it as they cast it into the air, while still more tossed it like seed onto the soil of graves and old battlefields, bringing forth a crop of undeath.

Waiqar had mastered all such means of application. The dust was his to command, the essence of his warriors and servants, and stealing or tampering with the row upon row of bones and skulls that were used to form it in the depths of Zorgas carried the heaviest and most terrible of punishments.

"I know the bones of my legion," Waiqar continued, in defiance of Mirabelle's apparent doubts. "Every last inch.

The tip of one of Sir Agravain's fingers is missing, the smallest on his left hand."

Mirabelle pursed her lips. Even the slight amount of dust such a theft could generate would be sufficient to raise hundreds of corpses, or create several more powerful necromantic monstrosities.

"Anyone taking dust from the crypts of Zorgas would have to be desperate or bold beyond reckoning," she pointed out. "Not to mention skilled, to avoid your gaze and the guards and traps that protect the crypts."

"All the more reason to find them," Waiqar said. "It is yet another betrayal, of that I am certain."

"I will make enquiries, my lord," Mirabelle said, offering him a short bow. "This affront will not go unpunished."

"See to it," Waiqar ordered. "But act with circumspection. I do not wish any of this to become known, even to the rest of the council."

"Of course, lord," Mirabelle said, bowing again.

Waiqar dismissed her, and sat, brooding, upon his throne.

"*She thinks you are mistaken,*" the voice said, eventually.

"I know." As he spoke, he experienced something that, for a moment, felt like regret. Even the ones he trusted most of all feared and doubted him.

But such were the realities of ruling. He would bear such burdens, or he would not be worthy of the true immortality that awaited him.

CHAPTER SEVEN

Lucrezia Torvic stood in the passageway above the great hall of her brother's crypt-fortress, looking through one of the arrow slits and out into the night. The sounds of raucous feasting drifted up to her from below – laughter, exclamations and the last few, plaintive screams made by the dinner.

Blood was dripping slowly from Lucrezia's dress, pooling, unnoticed, beneath her. She had partaken in the early stages of the feast, but had quickly excused herself, not wishing to waste what remained of the night. She found Naythen's inner circle to be boorish and arrogant, except, of course, when confronted about anything. Then they cringed back and scuttled to the safety of their lord, displaying all the characteristics of the vermin they were at heart.

She had read for a while – her brother's library was quite extensive, though it was all for show. Lucrezia doubted he had ever read a book in his un-life. She was considering retiring to the undercroft where she spent the days whenever she left her own keep of Bloodhold to visit her brother, sleeping out the sluggishness that came on in the aftermath of a deep feeding, but something kept her up wandering the halls of the crumbling castle.

Of late, matters had not been progressing to her satisfaction. The Mistlands were growing ever more fraught as Waiqar's power increased. The time to strike against the baronies was drawing near. None outside of Zorgas knew the specifics of his intentions, but the Deathborn Legion would march, that much was certain, and seemingly sooner rather than later. Lucrezia had seen with her own eyes the Deathborn assembled outside Waiqar's deathly holdfast, thousands upon thousands of reanimates standing in eternal readiness amidst the marshland's mire, a symbol of the potency of the Great Necromancer.

Naythen was less impressed. He had always chafed against Waiqar's rule, but of late had been growing ever more restless, bored and indolent with his current holdings. Lucrezia had done her best to remind her wayward brother about his priorities. The safety and furtherance of the Bilehall coven was the most important matter. But Naythen seemed not to care. He only had time for his sycophants these days, not those with the best wishes of the entire vampiric family at unbeating heart.

He was a fool to defy Waiqar, and she had told him as much on numerous occasions. The Night of the Red Feast at Zorgas had almost been a disaster. Lucrezia had been privately shocked when Waiqar had done nothing, but she feared it was only because he intended to make a greater example of the lords of Bilehall at a later date.

It wasn't just recent events that were robbing her of her rest, however. Something in particular was stirring tonight, out in the marsh, and Lucrezia didn't like it. She stood watching as deadlights winked in the darkness, piercing the eternal mist. It was strangely still and quiet, oppressively so. All she could hear was her brother's foolishness below, and the slow, steady dripping of the blood on her dress.

She squeezed some of it onto her hand and licked her fingers idly, her mind still working through the dangers ahead, senses on edge. That was when she felt it. The death magics around the crypt-fortress stirred, imperceptibly to most undead creatures, but enough for a learned vampire like Lucrezia to feel.

Something was coming, something powerful.

At the same time, she heard a dull rattling noise, the clatter of metal chains on stone. She recognized the sound as the main gate's portcullis. It was being raised.

Hitching up her bloody skirts, she hurried to the other end of the corridor so she could look through one of the small windows, providing her with a view of the crypt-fortress' main courtyard. The bailey was quiet, the only figures the statue-like, armored reanimates arrayed on either side of the doors into the central keep. As she watched, however, two others entered the courtyard from under the gatehouse. One of them Lucrezia recognized as Ranwulf, captain of her brother's vampire guard, but the other she did not know immediately. The figure was tall and clad in black robes, the cowl raised.

Lucrezia turned and paced from the window toward the staircase that would take her down to the hall, leaving a wake of blood behind her. Her thoughts were in turmoil. A part of her was sure she recognized the Ynfernael energies that coiled about the new arrival, but her rational side made her doubt. Surely it could not be her? She hadn't been seen in the territory of Bilehall for centuries. Most doubted she even still lived – if, indeed, she had ever truly lived at all.

But if it was her, Lucrezia had to get to her brother first. She had to stop this before things got out of hand.

She reached the hall through one of its side doors. Naythen and his brood were reclining after their meal. A dozen vampires, all blood-spattered, sat or lay on the lounges and seats about Naythen's throne, the remains of the feast at their feet. They let up a dull, drowsy hiss as Lucrezia re-entered the chamber.

"Come back for the scraps, Lady Torvic?" one of her brother's sycophants, Pentageist, leered, drooling blood and spittle. Lucrezia ignored him, kicking aside a savaged carcass as she approached her brother.

Naythen Torvic was blood-drunk. He had a curious affliction, rare but not unknown among the children of the night, that caused him to bloat and distend hideously when he gorged himself on a creature's vital essence. His sallow, flabby flesh had become taut and ruddy, and the oversized nobleman's attire he wore was now straining to contain him. He resembled a gigantic tick, swollen and drowsy in the aftermath of his vile repast.

"Sister," he exclaimed, then pitched partially over the side of his throne and loudly vomited onto the floor. He recovered quickly, baring his fangs in a grin as he used a soiled, fringed handkerchief to dab at his chin.

"I did not think to see you until next sundown," he went on, struggling to find a comfortable position on this throne.

"Look, I saved you the remains of that farm girl. Still warm!"

"We have a visitor," Lucrezia said tersely, ignoring her brother's rambling. "You must refuse to see them."

Naythen frowned, his eyes bleary and unfocused as he tried to take in what his sister was telling him.

"How do you know?" he asked, but Lucrezia was spared the need to answer by a hard series of knocks at the hall's doors.

"Turn them away," Lucrezia urged, but Naythen's attentions were now on the hall's entrance. With a gesture he impelled the reanimates guarding the doors to swing them open.

Captain Ranwulf entered, leading the figure Lucrezia had seen outside. Being in the same room, its power was even more apparent. Lucrezia felt her skin, still warm from the recent feeding, prickle, and even the most addled of her brother's brood roused themselves from their stupor.

"Who is this?" Torvic demanded of Ranwulf, part alarmed, part intrigued. The captain paused at the edge of the gathering and offered a short bow.

"My lord, forgive the interruption, but Lady Zarihell has come to speak with you."

Naythen's sycophants gasped and murmured. Lucrezia clenched her fangs, resisting the urge to lash out. Her fears had been confirmed, and the rumors were true – the cursed witch elf again walked abroad in the Mistlands.

"Did you think it wise to bring her into my hall without informing me she was at the gate?" Naythen demanded of Ranwulf. As he spoke, Zarihell lowered her hood, revealing her beautiful, wicked features, a slight smile on her lips.

"You must forgive my imposition, Lord Torvic," she said, offering a curtsy. "I'm afraid your brave captain here didn't have much of a say in the matter."

If she blinked, Lucrezia could briefly see the energies Zarihell was harnessing, black, stinking Ynfernael coils that were holding Ranwulf in their grasp, like a puppet.

"You dare enchant the captain of my guard and walk into my crypt-fortress without my leave?" Naythen snapped, swallowing loudly as he fought back another upsurge of fresh blood.

"I just felt it was more dramatic that way," Zarihell admitted.

"Release him," Naythen ordered.

"Perhaps later."

In all her centuries, Lucrezia had never seen another being stand, alone, with so little apparent concern before a brood of feasting vampires. But then, she had never encountered Zarihell in person before.

She knew the stories, and thus far she seemed to be living up to them. She had been a fellow prisoner with Waiqar before the Second Darkness, held captive in the Black Citadel by Llovar and his demon-worshipping Uthuk Y'llan. When Timmorran had finally freed Waiqar, Zarihell had been saved as well. She had served Waiqar – or, at the very least, fought alongside him – in the wars of the Second Darkness. There had even been rumors of courtship between the two but, at some point, they had parted ways. Zarihell had become almost a myth, a capricious sorceress who roamed the Mistlands, her will unknown, her intentions a mystery.

Until now.

"What do you want with us?" Naythen demanded. Lucrezia could sense the fear that had penetrated her brother's post-feeding haze, despite the fact that he was a lord in his own hall. It was with good reason. Even one not attuned to death energies or the Ynfernael in general could have sensed the terrible potential at Zarihell's fingertips. She was redolent with dark magic. Lucrezia had only felt its like while in the presence of Waiqar.

"I came to test the hospitality of the greatest lord of Bilehall," Zarihell said, her humorous tone at odds with the tension in the blood-drenched chamber. "I am, after all, but a humble traveler."

"This castle does not play host to any outside my coven," Naythen growled, shifting awkwardly again on his throne. "Not unless you are an emissary of Waiqar, and somehow I doubt you are here tonight to do his bidding."

"Would that the same could be said of you, Naythen Torvic," Zarihell replied. "I have heard the shackles that bind you chafe more and more. It is a tragedy, that a grand fiefdom like Bilehall must pay such outrageous subservience to those who are, in truth, no more powerful."

"Do not cast aspersions," Naythen said, though there was hesitation in his voice.

"She seeks to beguile you, brother," Lucrezia said, fixing Zarihell with a glare that would have frozen the hearts of the mightiest of champions. "Whatever your intentions here, witch, you will not cast your spells upon me or my brother. I see your power, every strand of it."

"Forgive me, I thought this was the hall of Naythen

Torvic, not Lucrezia," Zarihell said, meeting her gaze with one every bit as cold and unyielding. For a second energy surged, and dark lightning crackled and darted between them, causing the nearest members of Naythen's coven to scramble back or tumble from their seats.

"Sister, please, restrain yourself," Naythen cried out, trying and failing to pull his bloated body up out of the throne. Lucrezia snarled, but snatched a hold of her magics before they could clash with the intruder's. Despite her anger, she knew that to try and face an ancient creature like Zarihell – a *Daewyl* no less – would not end well for her. As much as she railed against the interloper in their midst, she could not fight her head-on, not without the rest of the coven.

"I come here in good faith, Lord Torvic," Zarihell addressed Naythen once more. "Matters are now in motion that will define the future for you and your household. The Betrayer grows ever more arrogant. Many within the Mistlands would see his power checked. I am here to offer my help in doing just that."

"What you speak of is treason."

"A bond of fealty works both ways," Zarihell countered. "Waiqar long ago broke the one that exists between Zorgas and Bilehall. He views you as nothing more than parasites, and treats you even worse."

The vampires around Zarihell hissed, but the elf seemed unconcerned. She advanced right to Naythen's throne, ignoring the bloodied predators that surrounded her, standing tall before the swollen nobleman.

"Hear my counsel, lord, and if you do not wish to heed it

then no harm has been done. But I have much to offer, and you should listen to what I have to say before I depart. For the good of Bilehall, and the Mistlands as a whole."

"She will seek to deceive you, brother," Lucrezia said loudly. "She serves only herself."

"You think I am so easily beguiled?" Naythen demanded, not taking his eyes off Zarihell. "I would hear her out."

"Not with her here," Zarihell said, half-turning to exchange another dangerous glance with Lucrezia. "What I have is for you alone, my lord."

"She will bend you into making war on Waiqar," Lucrezia said urgently, yet again cursing the fates for making her subordinate to her older brother. She could not endure much more of his foolishness. "She seeks only to further her own goals!"

"I seek only to end the despotism that we all languish under," Zarihell said. "It is time that the Mistlands were free of the Betrayer's shadow."

"Sister, if you will not calm yourself I will have you removed from my hall," Naythen declared. He was still blood-addled, sluggish after gorging himself so deeply.

Lucrezia looked around for support. Her brother's cronies, all as drunk as he was, looked thoroughly cowed by the elven witch, cringing back from her and avoiding even Lucrezia's eye contact. She could not rely on any of them to come to her aid. They were all cowardly wretches, and the only other vampire in Naythen's coven that she would have trusted to speak wisdom, Ranwulf, was currently little better than a drooling puppet on the end of Zarihell's dark strings.

Lucrezia realized that she had to get out, before Zarihell

properly appreciated just how vulnerable she was. In her own crypt-fortress at Bloodhold she would be able to marshal her power, consult with her brood-kin. Unlike her brother, she had learned that the blessings of near-immortality allowed for a more cautious form of strategy.

"You need not remove me, brother," she told Naythen coldly. "I know the way out."

"Regardless, perhaps the captain of the guard should see you gone," Zarihell suggested, smirking. Ranwulf took a step toward her.

"Lay a hand on me and I will rip your fangs from your jaw, whelp," Lucrezia hissed, baring her own wicked canines at the commander of her brother's bodyguard. Even ensorcelled, Ranwulf hesitated.

"Leave her be," Zarihell said, clearly enjoying the supremacy she had gained over the assembled vampires. "I think this hall has seen enough violence for one night, don't you?"

Ranwulf stepped back, and Lucrezia locked eyes with Zarihell.

"Bilehall will not become another pawn in your schemes, witch," she said. "I will pluck out your eyes, rip out your tongue and feast on your withered heart if you dare to betray my family."

"I shall bring your family glory," Zarihell replied as the vampire turned to leave. "But you shall know none of it, Lucrezia Torvic."

CHAPTER EIGHT

Waiqar was communing with the spirits when one brought him the news he had been waiting for.

The hall of Zorgas was filled with souls, shimmering, pale deadlights whose features twisted in and out of definition as they howled and thrashed. Waiqar had bound them all and was interrogating what they knew. They bore word from across the baronies, knowledge that Waiqar prized. He needed to know all the pieces that were in play. Only then did plans become reliable and probabilities more assured.

He stripped out the memories of an apprentice painter, who had been murdered by the Arch Mortificer of the cult loyal to him in Tamalir. Before killing him and sending his soul to Zorgas, the Mortificer had imparted news about the cult's latest efforts, information that the terrified victim would have been unable to comprehend, but which it now delivered to Waiqar via the memories that he pillaged from it.

He saw a vision of the cultist standing over his bound

victim, ritual knife in hand. He spoke of the efforts to acquire the cursed portrait of Baron Harrow, which was said to contain the soul-essence of the long-departed nobleman, a prize that Waiqar had coveted for some time. The painting had been located in the collection of a reclusive collector, and the cult was closing in on "acquiring" it. Another soul would be sent with more news on the Moonday of the next month.

Waiqar relinquished the spirit that had delivered the information, allowing it to dissipate with a final groan. He was about to turn his attention to the next, when he realized that one of the souls in the great hall was not an unwitting message-vessel, but one of his servants. The phantom, dressed in the incorporeal remnants of his livery, dared drift closer, spectral eyes averted.

"A mortal is at the gates, Undying One," the thing whispered. "It bears an item you seek. It craves an audience and… recompense."

"Send to the Deathborn to bring them here," Waiqar commanded, dismissing the spirit and momentarily locking the ones he had been interrogating in place, silencing their wails and binding their maws with a spat curse. He felt a stirring of anticipation, tempered by rare doubts. Mortals were nothing if not unreliable. Still, if one had made it this far, and was bold enough to seek entry into Zorgas, there was a reasonable likelihood that they did indeed possess what he currently sought.

A Deathborn guard entered, accompanying a woman who was disgustingly alive. Unlike most of the mortals who came to Zorgas, she did not wear the black robes and bindings, or one of the skull masks of the Death Cults, nor was she merely one of the cattle that crammed the citadel's slaughter pens. She was wearing comfortable leathers and a travelling cloak, and her clothes were spattered with the muck of the Mistlands. Her face was hard and scarred. Waiqar's witch-sight could detect the barest hint of death energy around her – she had killed before. Still, he was not impressed.

Without prompting, the woman went down on one knee and averted her eyes. Waiqar wondered if she had been to Zorgas before. He could not recall. He struggled to remember faces, and the mortal essences visible to his witch-sight – fear, disgust, hatred – had long ago started to meld together. The dead were so much easier to read.

This one was an adventurer, one of the countless mercenaries, wanderers, vagabonds, and sellswords who plied their trade across the baronies. Waiqar had plenty of dealings with her like. Mostly, those dealings involved slaying the misguided fools who came to the Mistlands hunting treasures, relics, or knowledge, but at times he or his lieutenants made use of the less scrupulous ones. The Death Cults were numerous, but not always wholly competent. Conversely, there were many rogues across the baronies who specialized in locating and retrieving specific artefacts. Waiqar had sent out a demand for just one such artefact some months ago.

"You have what I require?" he demanded of the woman, seeing her flinch at the raw power in his words.

"I do, lord," she said, not raising her eyes and she fished into a pouch at her waist and drew something out.

Without a word, Waiqar compelled the Deathborn who had brought her in to retrieve the object and hand it to him.

It was a stone, innocuous at first to anyone without a connection to Mennara's magics. He turned it over and noted the marking on it, an arrow with a point at both ends.

It was a runestone, a shard of rock imbued with magical properties. Even one not versed in the many ways of magical manipulation would be able to utilize it.

This one was known as the Soulbinder, and it was exceedingly rare. Waiqar had been hunting it for some time. Having it now in his grasp gave him a rare moment of satisfaction.

"You have done well," he told the adventurer, before commanding the Deathborn to run her through. The woman, still kneeling and bent forward, gasped as the rusting blade punched through her back and out through her chest, blood drizzling down onto the foot of Waiqar's throne. The Deathborn put his boot on her back and slowly dragged the sword free.

Waiqar clenched the runestone in his fist and stood, holding it over her. With a thought he activated its dormant power, the runic marking on it becoming luminous as its energies latched onto the mercenary.

She screamed, but the noise did not come from her throat. Her spirit, visible to Waiqar, surged up from the fatal wound, but became snared around the runestone in his grip, like a fly in a web. It twisted and thrashed back and forth, but could not break free.

Waiqar's mind assailed it. He drove into its terrified consciousness, almost immediately identifying a flurry of the memories he sought. He pieced together how she had found the runestone, learning rumors from a seller of arcane antiques in the Free City of Riverwatch, then onward to a trek through the Howling Giant Hills. She had overcome the treachery of one of her fellow hunters and the animated statues that had guarded the Soulbinder's final resting place, in the abandoned and forgotten shrine of a hero from the days of the Third Darkness. Then she had journeyed here, itself a perilous route that few would have survived.

Waiqar almost found himself impressed after all. But more importantly, he was sure that the stone he held was the one he sought. It was the true Soulbinder.

He held out his other hand so both were above the woman's body. He began to chant. The spirit shivered and pulsed, the screaming growing even louder, and then it did something it was not supposed to do. It started to recede.

It was not the dissipation of a soul that had escaped to the afterlife. Rather, it was being forced downward, back into the body it was fleeing.

"You will remember nothing of this," Waiqar said, driving his consciousness deep. He found the soul's living memories the way he had found those of the spirits he was sent by his emissaries. He crushed all recollections she had of her death, and discarded them.

The soul was wrestling, struggling with him, like a body near the surface that naturally strives to rise back up. He snarled the words of power, not those of death, but of another plane entirely, one that he rarely had use of, but which he still recalled being taught by the Timmorran of old.

The woman's soul, wiped of its most recent memories, was driven back, piece by piece, into her body. Waiqar worked his own magics while channeling that of the runestone, invoking incantations rarely witnessed in Zorgas. It was a spell of healing, something anathema to Waiqar's very essence. The magics that usually clung to him roiled and rebelled, but he was powerful enough to keep them at bay until the magics were completed, his form rigid with effort and concentration.

Finally, it was done. The spirit had been returned, and the mortal wound healed. With a gasp, the woman sat up, panting and shaking. In shock, she dared look up at the Undying.

"Arise, and go," he ordered, releasing both her body and her soul. "Your fee for this will be paid to you at the gate."

"Y-Yes, lord," she stammered, fear overcoming her obvious confusion.

She departed, shaking and stumbling. Waiqar flexed slightly, bones crackling, easing himself as he allowed the elemental Mortos to take hold once more. He settled back into his throne, gazing down at the runestone still in his hand.

"*It works as it should,*" said the voice in his skull.

"It does," Waiqar agreed. "Now the next phase of our plan can begin."

He turned his attention to one of his Deathborn guards.

"Bring me the mortal, Tomaz."

•••

Sir Ulthor of the Deathborn Legion rode in through the gate of Naythen Torvic's crypt-fortress at midday. Such an arrival was a calculated insult – Ulthor knew that the vampires would have to be roused from their slumber and, even with the sun hidden behind the Mistlands' perpetual fog and brooding clouds, they would be sluggish and uncomfortable.

In fact, neither was true. As Sir Ulthor reined in his mount before the steps of the fortress' keep, Naythen Torvic strode down to meet him, pausing just before he reached the bottom so that he remained above Ulthor. The vampire's body had largely drained of the blood it had recently consumed, returning to its gaunt, sagging state.

More notably, Lord Torvic was garbed for war. He wore crimson plate armor that clicked as he descended to meet the black knight, and had a broadsword at his hip. A clutch of his brood kin followed him out into the weak daylight, likewise armored. Among them Ulthor noted a hooded woman who stayed just behind Torvic. The assembly would have been fearsome, but Ulthor cared not. His consciousness was bent wholly to the task he had been assigned, the delivery of his master's message.

"Another of Waiqar's fleshless puppets," Torvic said as he glared down at Ulthor, the words ringing through the courtyard. Thralls and lesser vampires clustered in the shadows of the walls or leered out from the windows and arrow slits all around.

"Has your master nothing better to do than disturb my slumber?" Torvic went on.

Ulthor did not answer the jibes. He had come to deliver an ultimatum, nothing more.

"Lord Torvic of Bilehall, I bring word from your liege-lord, Waiqar the Great, the Undying, Master of Eternity, the Rightful King of Terrinoth."

The Deathborn knight reached into a moldering saddle pouch and drew out a small glass vial, filled with a smoky substance.

"Your lord, Waiqar, decrees that henceforth your tithes shall be doubled. Payment is due at Zorgas by the first Runeday of the next Icetide, delivered by you in person. The specifics are as follows."

Ulthor shattered the vial against his shield. A shrieking filled the courtyard as the bound phantom within was released. It coalesced before Torvic and began to scream at him – the exact specifics of the enhanced tithe that was expected of him, right down to the number of bone-arrows and charnel wagons. Throughout it all Torvic said and did nothing, though his jaw was clenched, and his gauntlet shook slightly where it gripped the hilt of his sword.

Eventually, with its litany complete, the spirit-messenger ceased its screaming and began to dissipate into the mist, its soul now free. Torvic waited until the last wisps had faded before stepping down the last few steps toward Ulthor.

"Do you submit?" the Deathborn asked him.

Torvic glared up at the knight for a moment and then, without warning, snatched at the desiccated throat of Ulthor's skeletal steed and ripped the necromantic construct's head clean off. Its magics disintegrated immediately and Ulthor fell as it collapsed into a pile of bones, rags and barding.

Vampires, especially powerful ones, were lightning-quick, but so were the warriors of the Deathborn. Ulthor was on his feet in an instant, and the crash of steel on steel rang around the crypt-fortress' courtyard as the swords of Waiqar's herald and the vampire lord met.

The onlooking coven shrieked and hissed with excitement as the sudden duel swept across the courtyard. Torvic was relentless initially, but Ulthor recovered rapidly, his methodical style of combat parrying strike after strike before he went on the offensive and drove Torvic back toward the keep. He was Deathborn, and even the surprise ferocity of such a betrayal would not cow him.

It looked as though the black knight would corner the red until, abruptly, a purple glow suffused Torvic's sword. There was a crash as it met Ulthor's and shattered the Deathborn's ancient blade, abruptly rendering him defenseless.

Torvic took the moment, cleaving through Ulthor's arm and kicking his legs out from under him. With a clatter Waiqar's emissary fell to the courtyard's dirt and was pinned there by Torvic's foot.

The purple energy that had briefly suffused the vampire's sword faded. He looked back toward the gathering on the steps, where the figure in the cloak and cowl lowered her hand, the purple light still glowing in her eyes.

"I promised you assistance, lord," Zarihell said. "This is just a foretaste of the advantages I offer."

"Treachery," Ulthor hissed up at Torvic.

"Yes," the vampire responded. "And it's about time."

With a splitting crack, the lord of Bilehall brought his heel down on Ulthor's skull, shattering it to pieces. There was a howl as the Deathborn's spirit, bound to its body for a millennium in defiance of the natural laws of Mennara, was finally torn away to the realm beyond.

"See how easily the minions of the Great Betrayer are bested?" Torvic demanded of his onlooking coven, reaching down and retrieving a shard of Ulthor's skull.

"He has mocked Bilehall for the last time," the vampire lord roared, voice ringing back from his fortress walls. "No longer will we suffer the affliction of Waiqar's misrule! From this day forth, Bilehall answers only to us!"

He crushed the shard in his crimson gauntlet, steel grinding bone. Then, screaming the words of the Black Invocation, he cast the dust to the wind, scattering it over the courtyard.

What little sunlight there was darkened to a premature twilight. A moaning sound filled the bailey, playing counterpoint to the grating of rocks and soil. The trampled dirt started to split open as shapes began pushing their way up to the surface.

At Torvic's command, the dead rose. Long-deceased warriors of the Bilehall holdfasts ripped their way free from the mass burial pit beneath the castle, clutching at old spears or hauling up swords and shields. They found their feet, moving jerkily, but with greater purpose as the necromantic magics of the Black Invocation grew accustomed to puppeting them. The rest of the coven watched on in awe as, rank by rank, the reanimate host assembled itself before the keep. Eventually, with a final clatter, they came to attention, dirt cascading from their bones and armor. Crimson witch-fire ignited in a thousand hollow eye sockets.

Torvic brandished his sword and bared his fangs in a wicked grin, his triumphant words ringing out into the night he had summoned.

"Bilehall marches to war!"

PART TWO

BILEHALL

CHAPTER NINE

Tristayne had been death-walking.

It was an affliction which plagued almost all the living dead, or at least all those who retained a tolerable level of independent awareness. Most had no need of sleep, and even the concept of rest had along ago fallen by the wayside. Nevertheless, it seemed consciousness could not endure for eternity uninterrupted. Every so often Tristayne would slip into a fugue state, a period of mental dullness which could last anything between hours and years. Unless someone awoke him, he would remain in this state until it ran its course, only vaguely aware of his own surroundings and thoughts.

Some claimed these incidents occurred more and more as the centuries wore on, and without someone to wake them, a reanimate would eventually slip into semi-consciousness permanently, reduced to a shambling dullard or left unable to even rise from tomb or throne. Like all such immortals, Tristayne had spent decades searching for a cure, but to no avail.

There was only one who seemed to have overcome death-walking. Of course, it was Waiqar. He had refused to share how, but Tristayne had never caught him in a state of unawareness or wandering the halls of Zorgas mindlessly. It was as though he had a voice in his head that snapped at him to wake up every time he slipped away. It was yet another simmering point of jealousy that Tristayne felt toward the Undying One.

Such emotions did not occupy his thoughts right now. Indeed, very few did. He was dimly aware that he was standing outside a door somewhere in Zorgas, stooped forward, leaning on his scythe. How long had he been here, comatose? Days? Weeks? Nothing had disturbed him. He should do something, urged the tiny spark of sentience that still flickered weakly in his skull.

His body responded only with the greatest reluctance. It was as though he was able to see his surroundings and what he was doing, but was unable to actually act on his own will. His hand reached out to the door and unbolted it before pushing it open.

He shambled inside, struggling to walk, the scythe feeling heavy in his hand. It was pitch black within, but that was no trouble to one such as he. More pressing was the confusion that still clouded everything. Where was he? How had he gotten here? How long had he been shuffling around the crypts and corridors on his own?

The room was small. That much he managed to discern. There were no windows. Something stirred at his feet. The motion elicited a response from his torpid body. He raised the Black Scythe.

"Master?" croaked a voice in the dark.

Life. He could feel it. Hideous, tangible, squirming life, laid out there at his feet. The death energies refused to touch it. It was anathema. He had to extinguish it, before it infected him with its warmth, its pulsing, sweating, stinking, lice-infested, breathing, blinking, swallowing, quivering filth.

He swung his scythe. The blow was clumsy and ungainly, and it missed. Sparks struck from stone where the wicked, cursed steel rebounded from the floor.

The life shrieked. It recoiled. It screamed. It just made him want to snuff it out all the quicker. He reached for it with his other hand, trying to strangle and choke, feeling that detestable warmth in his grasp.

"Master, please!" the life screamed. "Please, no!"

Finally, the words brought him back. They snapped Tristayne from his dream state. With a shriek, his yellow deadlights reignited.

He stood deadly still, looking down at what he was grasping. The worm, Tomaz. Understanding dawned. He had entered Tomaz's cell and now, apparently, he was trying to choke him to death.

For a second, he was tempted to continue.

Instead, he forced his digits apart, letting the bedraggled oaf fall to the floor, crying and whimpering.

"Why…" Tomaz managed to whine, crawling back to the far wall.

Tristayne glared down at him dispassionately for a few moments.

"A test," he said eventually. "I… wanted to test you."

Tomaz said nothing, rubbing at his neck. Memories flared dangerously through Tristayne's mind, the phantom of the noose's tightness fastening once more around his throat, making him gag. He pushed it away.

He went and sat down against the wall next to Tomaz, laying his scythe on the floor beside him.

"I despair," he said.

Tomaz said nothing. Tristayne could feel him still trembling beside him. The mortal disgusted him, but he was such a welcome change from the walking dead and phantoms that infested Zorgas. The former were merely reanimated puppets, and the latter morose or locked in perpetual terror or despair at their ethereal existence. Waiqar's Deathborn were more coherent, but were bonded utterly to the Great Necromancer. Tristayne didn't trust any of them. But then there was Tomaz, largely uncomprehending, innocent, an outsider thrown into a world of horror that he was still trying to come to terms with.

"Waiqar frustrates me," he told the mortal. "We languish in this crumbling fortress, the rest of existence oblivious to us, while he teaches me tricks. Instead, he should be divulging the last of the secrets I need to realize my full power. I am no petty bone-raiser! I am Tristayne Olliven! Prince of the Black Realm, Terror of Greyhaven! I cannot be killed! Strike me down and I will rise again! Imprison me and I shall be freed! I am Deathless!"

"Yes, lord," Tomaz mumbled.

"When did Waiqar last walk abroad from the Mistlands, in spirit or in body?" Tristayne went on. "When did he last command a host in battle? He gives us nothing to strive for. He does not share his plans, just as he does not share his arcane knowledge. Why would he free me, take me on as his apprentice, if he did not wish to see me grow my abilities?"

He hissed in frustration, clutching the Black Scythe once more.

"He has promised to take me on a journey of enlightenment, though he refuses to say where," he said. "He mocks me, as though I am some sort of child that he can beguile with the promise of treats."

Tomaz did not reply. Tristayne sat and festered.

Waiqar frustrated him, refusing to allow him to use the precious dust of the Deathborn to its full potential. More and more, Tristayne had found himself thinking back to his encounter in the Mistlands ruins. He had told no one that he had met the legendary Zarihell, but her words continued to haunt him. Could there really be a way to raise the dead without the dust? Could it be done with will alone, and not some tome or artefact tainted by the Ynfernael? It was a question all necromancers craved an answer to.

Had any other claimed to have such knowledge, Tristayne would have dismissed it as lies or fantasy, for there were none superior in the necromantic arts than he and Waiqar. But if any other stood a chance of solving the ancient riddle, then surely it was Zarihell? It was said that she had shared the same tortures as Waiqar in the original Black Citadel, before his ascension. Some of the souls Tristayne had lately consulted with had even whispered that she was more powerful than the Undying One.

She was a *Daewyl* elf, one who cavorted with the hell-plane known as the Ynfernael, a place infested with demons that Tristayne himself had courted. The Ollivens had a long history of connection with that nightmarish place – all bar his fool brother Rylan – and Tristayne had spent decades wandering the Black Realm, a warped un-reality somewhere between the Aenlong and the wider horrors of the Ynfernael kingdoms. It was where he had bound the powers of his stolen scythe, and where he had made pacts that had ensured his immortality. Demons craved dominion over mortals and undead alike, and there were none more fickle than their kind, but their powers were at the root of the same magics employed by necromancers. The elemental Mortos was ultimately another form of Ynfernael magic. Demons thus made for potent allies, and none communed more closely with them than the *Daewyl* elves.

Tristayne had weighed all of that when considering whether or not to return to the ruins where he had met Zarihell. She had long fallen out of favor with Waiqar, and stories about the rivalry between the grim king of undeath and the capricious and deadly queen of the witch elves abounded throughout the Mistlands and beyond.

For Tristayne to deliberately seek her out was to dabble in his own destruction. He had no idea what motives she had for aiding him, beyond the fact she no doubt sought a powerful ally. And yet, if he combined the power he already held with the promised ability to raise the Mistlands' countless corpses without recourse to the remains of Waiqar's minions, he was certain it would leave him powerful enough to seize Zorgas, to overthrow the tyranny of the Betrayer and anoint himself as the true Undying One. He could not be killed, after all. Whenever he was struck down, his spirit rose again, his body reformed. Surely, he was already more powerful than Waiqar, more deserving of the titles that old betrayer had usurped?

"I must seek out the elf," Tristayne said. Tomaz managed to muster up a response.

"Is that wise, lord?"

Tristayne was too surprised to react with anger.

"You know of whom I speak?" he demanded.

"You have… spoken of her before," Tomaz mumbled. "Many times. In your rage you… you say she will give you the power to…"

"Do not say it," Tristayne hissed, afraid his idiot servant was about to speak the treason he was considering, and thus doom them both.

"It is a risk," the necromancer admitted, more to himself than Tomaz. "But if Waiqar will not teach me, I must find the knowledge elsewhere."

"What if he intends to grant you what you seek soon?" Tomaz asked. "You said he is going to take you somewhere soon? Somewhere… enlightening?"

Tristayne pondered the suggestion. What Tomaz said was true, though Waiqar's obfuscation continued to frustrate him. Would whatever Waiqar intended to show him really make a difference? Could Tristayne trust it not to be some other foolish or petty trickery he was trying to teach?

"If it is not worthy of you, then perhaps you can seek the help of others," Tomaz dared continue.

"You urge caution," Tristayne said, hardly believing he was listening to the advice of some mortal slave. "Probably just so you don't have to go out into the marshes again, hmm?"

Tomaz began to stammer something, but Tristayne overruled him.

"You will go out regardless. I expect Waiqar to summon me for whatever he has planned. You had best hope the journey is worth it, for your sake."

He stood and shook out his musty robes before hefting the Black Scythe. It hadn't fed in long enough. It yearned for Tomaz's soul. He brought it back under control, leaning on it as he walked to the cell's entrance.

"I do not know how long I was death-walking," he admitted to the clueless Tomaz. "I must discover Waiqar's whereabouts. When we are ready to depart, I shall return for you."

Without waiting for a reply, he strode out, the reanimate guard barring the door behind him.

Tomaz still lived, though sometimes he doubted it. He did not know how long it had been since he had been taken from Greyhaven. His world seemed to have been reduced to a perpetual night, and he had long ago given up on hoping for the dawn.

At some point the horror he had felt at what was befalling him had turned to a kind of numbness. He only rarely wept anymore. He even managed to sometimes snatch occasional bouts of sleep. Walking corpses and ethereal shades no longer made his flesh crawl and his heart freeze.

Sometimes he actually tried to talk to the one who brought him food and water, though it never replied.

There came a point, he realized, where the mind came to accept even the worst of circumstances. It was a matter of survival, of self-preservation. That, or he had simply become broken. He welcomed either alternative as preferable to the perpetual nightmare of his initial stay in Zorgas.

His master, Tristayne, still held a terror for him, though it was largely due to his mercurial nature. The only times Tomaz was permitted out of his cell was when the necromancer visited. Sometimes they walked the marshes, as they had done when Tomaz had first arrived, though thankfully never again at night. On other occasions they would go up onto the crumbling battlements – where carrion birds pecked at the still and silent sentinel-corpses that gazed sightlessly out into the marshes – or down into the crypts, where Tomaz had gazed in dark wonder at the thousands upon thousands of remains that seemed to buttress the ancient, cursed holdfast. Always, Tristayne ranted, normally about matters Tomaz had no comprehension of, the necromancer's disembodied voice ringing angrily in his head.

He had managed to piece together some of Tristayne's complaints though. It seemed as though he served Waiqar as an apprentice in the magic arts, but was growing ever more dissatisfied with his tutelage. Tomaz had no real idea as to why, beyond the fact Tristayne seemed to think he was not being educated at a quick enough pace.

Tomaz himself had long given up pondering the irony of the past and the pathetic desires he had once harbored regarding the magics of death. To think that he had fancied himself a reanimator of the dead, too! He had been a different person, then. An innocent whose mind hadn't been bent to breaking point. Those who had kidnapped him, his former friends in the Death Cult – he struggled to remember their names – seemed like less than petty fools now, with their black robes and skull masks and worthless, ineffective incantations.

One of the few hopes Tomaz clutched onto was that one day they, too, would be brought here, and would see what he had seen, and suffer what he had suffered. Then their own petty dabbling would be shown for what it was. They were as much like the creatures that inhabited this place as a baby scrawling gibberish on a page was like a learned bookkeeper and lord master of Greyhaven.

Desire for revenge reminded Tomaz that he yet lived, and that his mind was not yet completely numb. At times, though, even that was not enough. He knew that there were sights yet remaining that could reignite the fear he had felt when he had first been thrown in among the dead. When Tristayne came back for him and brought him to Zorgas' main courtyard, he realized he was going to experience one such place. This would be no walk in the marshes, not this time.

He stepped into the open, blinking in the pallid sunlight. The walls of the fortress soared around him, none higher than the central keep that dominated one side of the courtyard. Tristayne had called it the Black Citadel, a vast cluster of crooked towers and hanging parapets, a jagged crown that sought to pierce the low, dark clouds overhead.

After so long in dank tombs and his festering cell, it made him dizzy.

The courtyard's center was occupied. Waiqar was there, sitting astride a great, undead steed. Tomaz had seen him in passing again on several occasions, though never as close as the night he had first been brought before him. Simply laying eyes on him brought his body to a standstill, his living flesh refusing to obey him anymore, refusing to approach any closer. It was as though death itself, raw and icy, radiated out from the hulking skeleton, chilling Tomaz's blood and making his skin prickle and shiver.

"Move yourself, wretch," Tristayne hissed, snatching the shoulder of Tomaz's ragged robes and dragging him forward.

Waiqar was not alone. There were half a dozen other riders, skeletal brutes in heavy black armor, undead knights similar to the ones which had first brought him to Zorgas. One was clutching a black and purple banner bearing the white skull and antlers sigil. They were the Deathborn, he knew, Waiqar's personal legion, the remnants of the warriors who had sworn their fealty to him in life, when he had served as a general and apprentice under the great wizard Timmorran.

Waiqar shifted slightly in his saddle, turning the burning sockets of his skull slowly toward Tomaz. The mortal whimpered and flinched.

"Here," Tristayne demanded, practically carrying Tomaz the last few paces. "You can ride, can you not, flesh-worm?"

He showed him to a mount that did not yet have a rider. It was one of two, both the rotting remains of horses.

Their ribs and elongated skulls showed clearly through the vestiges of flesh and innards that still clung to them, their bodies in tatters. Their eye sockets had been pecked clean and the remnants of their manes were lank and patchy but, grotesquely, they still shivered and pawed the packed dirt of the courtyard with their hooves. The stink of decay, ever-present in Zorgas, was almost overwhelming next to them.

Tomaz tried to answer Tristayne's question, but just moaned instead.

"Mount it," Tristayne hissed. "And quickly! You're embarrassing me!"

Trying not to think about what he was doing, Tomaz clutched the saddle and set a foot in one of the stirrups before pulling himself up and throwing a leg over. He was shaking uncontrollably, and couldn't stop himself from crying out as the festering thing twisted beneath him and clacked its jaws.

"It is repulsed by your living essence," Tristayne told him. "But I have bent it to your will. Do not antagonize it with your heartbeat, and it will not eat you."

Tomaz was too terrified to ask for clarification about how he could stop his heartbeat from antagonizing it. He sat astride the living carcass, gripping the remnants of its reins and saddle for support. Tristayne climbed onto the back of the second corpse-mount, slinging his scythe and arranging his robes about him.

Without warning, the undead steeds set off, Waiqar and his knights in front. There was a rattling sound, and Tomaz saw the wicked portcullis in Zorgas' vast gatehouse beginning to slowly rise ahead of them. Dolorous horns brayed out, and the reanimated horses found their stride as they clattered out of the gateway and down the steep path that led from the great crypt-fortress' crag into the surrounding marshes.

Being taken on what seemed like a formal outing with Waiqar both surprised and terrified him, but for the first time he found himself taking a small bit of solace from Tristayne's presence. Wouldn't he protect him? Just where were they headed?

Their route took them down into the mist and the bogs, where the unliving steeds ploughed on tirelessly, the marshland seeming to yield a path for the dread riders. Tomaz focused on clinging on and not tumbling into the muck, certain the others would not stop for him.

Slowly, the land around them began to change. The hooves of the corpse-mounts struck firmer ground as the marsh started to recede. The turgid flatness also gave way to more uneven terrain, impressions of hills and valleys visible through the shifting mist. Boulders and stones grew more numerous, until the riders were passing between jagged spurs of black rock and frozen ignis, a volcanic landscape where the remaining stretches of bog bubbled and popped, as though something was broiling underneath the surface. Still, however, the air remained cold.

Tomaz spotted ruins amidst the unyielding landscape. They rode in amongst them, until they were surrounded by the remains of what he assumed was some manner of settlement. The nature of it or who built it was impossible to tell, as only broken and tumble-down walls remained, roads long subsumed and the buildings themselves crumbled and decayed. Still Waiqar and his servants did not stop, the cantering of their deathly steeds echoing along the lost remains of streets that had been abandoned eons before.

A shape became discernible in the distance, looming up out of the fog. It was a great mound, standing proud of the shattered city that surrounded it. As they drew nearer Tomaz recognized that it was, in fact, a vast barrow, an artificial rise of turf that had been heaped up by hands unknown. Set in its flank were two vast menhirs of black stone that stood either side of a rough-cut hole, a route that led directly through the slope and into a void-like darkness.

The sight did not bring Tomaz any comfort. The group halted at the foot of the barrow and dismounted, simply leaving the corpse-steeds standing. Tomaz practically fell off his own, scrambling away as it nipped at him.

The others were already moving up the slope toward the entrance, Waiqar in the lead. Tomaz dragged himself up the slope, desperate not to be left behind on the edge of the cursed and forgotten city.

"Stay close," Tristayne told him. "Do not listen to the whispers, nor follow the lights."

As ever, there was no further explanation. Tomaz hurried in the necromancer's wake as he, too, climbed toward the menhirs.

The entrance between them yawned, redolent with dread. Tomaz fought the urge to beg Tristayne not to go in, knowing it would do no good. Practically clutching the tails of the necromancer's robes, he followed him past the weathered, lichen-encrusted standing stones.

The darkness swallowed them whole.

It was bitterly cold beneath the barrow. The tunnel Tomaz found himself in was illuminated by the flickering witch-fires that burned within the skulls of his companions. The air was stale and fetid yet, despite the temperature, it smelled oddly sulfuric.

They hadn't journeyed far, the downward slope of the tunnel becoming increasingly notable, before Tomaz caught a sound above the shuffling and scuffing of feet. It was a ticking noise, slow but regular, almost like the sound made by the great astronomical clock on the Celestial Observance, sitting at the top of Winding Hill in Greyhaven. But what purpose could a clock serve down here in the dark?

Abruptly, the barrow tunnel ended. Tomaz stepped through it in Tristayne's wake and found himself in a larger, more natural-looking passageway. The rock around him was jagged and dark, like the volcanic spurs he had seen on the surface.

They carried on. The space wound away uncertainly ahead, at times so low and narrow it required the party to stoop in single file, at others so wide and high it seemed almost cavernous. Sometimes they passed by dark openings leading to other, branching tunnels. Twice, they took forks along the route, still led by Waiqar. The only constant was that they were always going downward.

The ticking was still present, and it was growing louder.

A susurration now accompanied it, like voices murmuring to one another just out of earshot. It made Tomaz's skin crawl.

The screams, when they started, were worse. The first one was almost imperceptibly faint, so much so that Tomaz put it down to his fevered imagination, but soon the desperate wailing was undeniable, drifting up from the branching tunnels all around them. It sounded to Tomaz as though he was being brought down into the pit of Ynfernael damnation itself.

The feeling was heightened by the fact that the temperature now seemed to be oscillating between frigid and hot. Still the ticking came, grating on Tomaz's shredded nerves. The susurrations playing counterpoint to the distant screams had risen to a definite murmur.

Tomaz caught movement. There was a light drifting down the tunnel toward them, bobbing irregularly. It was pallid and cold, and as it drew nearer, he saw that it was a spirit orb, a little sphere of ghostly luminescence that floated serenely past the group. Tomaz had seen them before in Zorgas. Tristayne had always warned him not to let them touch him. He scrambled to give it a wide berth as it passed.

"That is good," Tristayne murmured. "We're on the right path."

On they went. More of the orbs passed them by. Tomaz noticed that the unliving flames that burned within the skulls of his companions were now brighter and stronger as well. They moved less stiffly, too, as though the magics that bound their skeletal bodies, that acted as invisible flesh, muscle and sinew, had grown stronger the deeper they travelled.

They took a tunnel branching off to the right. The whispering was so loud now Tomaz was convinced he could make out individual words. He saw another shape ahead, a figure this time, clad in robes, hood raised. It walked down the passageway toward them, hands clutched before it, hidden in the sleeves of its garment. Tomaz was surprised when the others didn't react to it. They didn't even pause. But when the figure encountered Waiqar, it simply passed through him without breaking stride, doing likewise with the rest of the party, one after the other. Tomaz practically threw himself aside so that the apparition didn't walk through him as well, but it didn't even seem to be aware of him. It passed by and on up the tunnel, disappearing into the darkness that crept steadily after them.

"Did… Did you see that?" Tomaz dared to whisper.

"Silence," Tristayne hissed back.

Tomaz didn't dare press the matter. He had only gone a dozen or so paces when an unearthly shriek made him cry out in terror. Another shape burst from one of the branching side tunnels, a woman clad in rags, her feet bare. She screamed in abject terror as she dashed across the breadth of the tunnel, seemingly fleeing from something at her heels. When she reached the far wall of the passage, however, she simply vanished through it, disappearing as quickly as she had appeared.

Tomaz moaned in fear. The tunnels were infested with the dead, with phantoms and their echoes. He practically latched onto Tristayne's back as they progressed, the others oblivious to the specters, or simply not caring. They walked past a man crouched over, his head in his hands, sobbing, as he rocked back and forth in the dirt. Another went by them in the opposite direction, dressed like a farm laborer. He whistled as he went, seemingly unconcerned, the noise of his jaunty little tune echoing down the tunnel and ringing away weirdly in his wake. Yet another sat upon a stool and wrung out laundry into a bucket. This one looked up, locking eyes with Tomaz. He yelped, but she simply cackled and went back to her eternal work.

There were bones underfoot now, and the whispers, rising from the other tunnels and branches, reached him in full, calling out to him quietly.

"Where are we?"

"Are you lost, little one?"

"Stop and rest."

"Have you seen my children? Where are my children?"

"Out! Let me out, by the gods! I've got to get out!"

And still there was the constant tick, tick, tick, like the grim, relentless counting of some eternal clock, beating down the seconds that led to death, when Tomaz's soul would be forced to wander these volcanic depths with the rest of the tortured spirits.

Abruptly he noticed a light up ahead distinct from the ghost orbs that continued to float past them. It flickered like a flame, though it was too pallid to belong to natural fire. As they advanced, he realized it was indeed some sort of witch-lantern, attached to the end of the pole that was clutched in the bony grasp of a black-robed and hooded figure that sat upon a spur of volcanic rock. It was overlooking another branch in the tunnel. Unexpectedly, the group stopped. Tomaz heard Waiqar speak, making him shiver.

"Which way this time, watcher?" the Great Necromancer asked.

The shrouded creature sat still for a moment longer then, with a dull crunch of bones, slowly raised its free arm and pointed along the left-hand corridor. The group set off down it. Tomaz didn't dare look at the thing as he passed, but he found himself snatching a glance back afterward, seeing it still sitting and pointing, its ghostly lantern flickering. As he watched, it snuffed out suddenly, and the darkness rushed gleefully after them.

This tunnel was different from the others. Now bones were not simply scattered at their feet, but were inset into the walls as well, forming a catacomb of remains. The other tunnels that branched off were full as well, not of bones but of people, old and young, human, elf, dwarf and orc. Some watched him solemnly, others screamed and pleaded, yet others still smiled or laughed. None came out into the main tunnel though. Tomaz couldn't tell if they were living or dead. He fought not to start sobbing.

The ticking was oppressively loud now, drowning out the constant, cursed whispering and even the screams. The tunnel had become completely clad in bone, femurs and ribs, skulls and spines creating an ossuary of morbidity. The air stank of the moldering grave. It was still swelteringly hot one moment and bitingly cold another. He felt as though he was close to collapse.

Finally, the tract ended. Now there was a fiery glow

ahead, the molten wrath of the raging depths. Tomaz stepped out into a vast cavern, screams and the ticking ringing in his ears, the stench of sulfur and charred flesh choking him.

There, he beheld the most terrible sight he had ever seen.

CHAPTER TEN

"At last," Tristayne murmured as he stepped out of the tunnel's end. A cavernous space opened up before him, larger than any king's hall. At its far end the rock face was split and cracked, and great streams of blazing lava poured forth, running thick and heavy down into the back of the mighty construction that dominated the cave.

It stood as high and as wide as the gatehouse at Zorgas, a machine crafted from black iron and fused bone. Its flanks resembled a vast ribcage, through which its internal workings could be glimpsed – massive cogs and wheels, and ducts that channeled the lava that poured from the wounds hacked into the earth, cooling the streams amidst the mass of bone and flesh that was constantly fed into the machine. To keep its parts churning, hundreds of figures toiled on either side to turn the wheels within, working at dozens of axles. They were reanimates, the dead who worked tirelessly, bound to their stations. The carcasses continued to labor, until eventually the very bones themselves collapsed and turned to dust, and another walking corpse took its place.

The pinnacle of the machine was a great dragon's skull, each fang as long as a man was tall, gleaming amidst the broiling clouds of sulfur and the hellish glow of the lava. A wheel like that of a mill was set between the open jaws of the long-dead drake, and as Tristayne watched, it turned slowly, churning within it the brilliant heat of the geothermal streams that sustained the machine. It was from its cursed axle that the dreadful ticking emanated, a slow, steady click that seemed to echo around within the necromancer's skull.

As Tristayne watched, a fresh clutch of souls poured from the wheel as it turned, shrieking, writhing phantoms that materialized from the magma within and soared through the cavern or rose up to circle its heights, where a great flock of spirits, freshly born from the nightmare creation, swarmed and screamed in never-ending torment.

"Bow before the Everliving Engine," Waiqar exclaimed.

Tristayne rarely knelt down with any true feelings of contrition, but he did so now, throwing himself to the dirt and bowing his head, scythe clattering beside him. The other Deathborn did likewise. The great engine seemed to respond to their genuflecting, the magma flaring all the brighter, the shrieks of the souls above rising to a fever pitch.

It was glorious. Tristayne's soul thrilled, his withered essence feeling fresh and renewed. It was the power of the Engine, he knew. He realized absentmindedly that Tomaz was screaming, overwhelmed by it all. Tristayne slapped him and snarled at him to show respect. Instead he collapsed, unconscious. Tristayne sighed. He would have left him for the machine, but he couldn't simply abandon Waiqar's gift while he was with him. He would have to carry him out.

"Rise," Waiqar commanded. They did so. Tristayne stared at the machine, trying to take in its majesty, its raw power.

It was the Everliving Engine, and it was the source of so much of the elemental Mortos in Mennara. Tristayne had heard the legends, had even searched for it at times, but now, at long last, he beheld it in all its majesty. Waiqar, he knew, claimed to have built it, though it seemed hard to fathom how any mind that had once been mortal – even one that had since conquered death – could conceive of such a construction. The fact that Waiqar had brought him into its presence felt like an affirmation of his own potential. His old doubts and fears fled, replaced by exaltation.

"Now you will witness the true potency of the power of undeath," Waiqar declared. "Archlich Revik!"

The last words were addressed to a figure approaching them from the direction of the machine. It was skeletal, though its skull still bore long, white hair that hung down its back. It wore fine robes of black and purple, and carried a staff in one hand tipped by a shard of amethyst. Around its brow was a slender circlet of gold inset with another amethyst stone. Both seemed to glow with a light that pulsed in time with the ticking of the Everliving Engine.

"My lord," the undead figure rasped as it halted before the group and bowed to Waiqar. "I hope your journey through the catacombs was not overly taxing."

The Deathborn bowed toward the creature, and Tristayne

quickly did likewise. This then was Archlich Revik, the legendary keeper of the Everliving Engine. He was the being appointed to oversee its function, who monitored it day and night, and had done for millennia. He alone was said to understand its purpose and how it worked, perhaps better than even Waiqar himself.

"I have brought my apprentice, Tristayne, to witness the miracle of the Engine," Waiqar declared. "I thought seeing it in person might spur his studies."

Tristayne remained bowed before Revik.

"It is an incalculable honor to be in the presence of both you and the machine, Archlich," he said.

"It senses you, Tristayne Olliven," Revik replied. "You who cannot be killed. It favors you."

Tristayne struggled to maintain a sense of humility as he dared raise himself up.

"Then I am blessed indeed," he said. "It is a sight I had long ago given up any hope of seeing."

"Come," Waiqar said. "Explain the Engine's purpose as we inspect it."

Revik beckoned Tristayne to his side with one bony finger, and along with Waiqar they walked along the edge of the cavern, leaving the Deathborn and the unconscious Tomaz at the tunnel mouth. A gantry had been built to one side of the Engine, allowing observers to overlook it. Tristayne climbed it, gazing down in awe upon the vast machine, ignoring the desperate, shrieking spirits that soared around them the higher they went.

"It is the root of all our powers," Revik said, his staff tapping the gantry's creaking wooden boards as they went.

"A miraculous device that returns life to those long dead. Can you feel its power within you?"

"I can," Tristayne admitted. He was moving more freely, and the aches that haunted his old bones had disappeared. He felt revitalized, his thoughts sharp, strong in both body and mind. Waiqar seemed even more potent. Tristayne could see energies of death physically flowing from the machine's maw and surrounding him, while a host of spirits keened for his attention. His eyes blazed with purple flames, more vigorous than Tristayne had ever before witnessed.

"It is the Everliving Engine that churns much of the magic of death out into this mortal plane we inhabit," Revik went on as they stopped at the gantry's highest point, across from the great dragon's skull and its nightmarish wheel. "Long ago a gap was torn in these caves between this reality and the other side."

"But how is it kept open, in defiance of all natural laws?" Tristayne asked, not even trying to hide his wonder. Of course, it was possible to pierce the veil between life and death. All necromancers did it to a greater or lesser extent, from dabblers tentatively calling upon the souls of the departed as part of a seance or fortune-reading, to the likes of Waiqar, who could plunge into the ether and drag forth an entire army of phantoms. The holes torn, however, never lasted. Offended at such defilement, existence itself repaired the damage, keeping life and death separate and restoring the balance and order of the planes of existence.

Here, however, the wound in reality was being kept open, and on a truly industrial scale.

"Your master was an elementalist before his ascension

to immortality," Revik said in answer to Tristayne's earlier question. "By his design the Engine perpetually draws on the volcanic energies of the depths. It is this which powers it, which enables it to continue to defy the world's order."

"It must still be fed though," Waiqar pointed out. "The Engine's power keeps the conduit between this realm and the other side open. It is part of what subverts the natural energies of the lava and draws forth the energies of Mortos in its place. Instead of the flames of the deeps, the chill of death howls forth."

"From here comes much of the power that gives life to the dead across the realms," Revik said, picking up the account. "Its glorious, ceaseless workings are a beacon, drawing more souls to the mortal plane. The magics that see departed spirits haunt their places of rest, or the dead spontaneously rise from their graves, the whispers heard in the dark in old mansions and castles, or the knocking at the door on a Deepwinter's Moonsday eve, so much of it is drawn into being by this device."

"So the stories were true," Tristayne said in wonderment. "I feel its power in my bones."

"All who harness the power of death sense it," Revik declared. "When the engine turns at its strongest, even the dead in far-off Al-Kalim or the rainforests of Zanaga stir."

"It is my greatest work," Waiqar declared. "One day it shall be only one of many though. All across Terrinoth and beyond, these machines shall tear down the detestable barrier between life and death, and then there will be no more of either. Immortality will be the common currency of all."

Tristayne could scarce imagine such a future. It was glorious, like the promise of an afterlife that had been truly realized. It almost made all he currently endured seem worthwhile.

"What of the Ynfernael?" he asked, seeking further answers, clutching greedily to all the knowledge he could glean. "The death energies are related to it, after all. If this becomes but one rip of many, what will stop demonkind from invading this plane of reality, as they have tried to do before?"

"This is just one of my experiments," Waiqar said, sounding terser than he had before. "I am conducting many others. I intend to seal the Sphere of Death off from the wider Ynfernael. Once that is done, the demons I strove against while I still lived will have no access to souls, either living or dead. They will become powerless, divorced from the blood and veneration of mortals, that which gives them power. They will become inconsequential things. Perhaps, once immortality is secured, I will take the armies of this reality into that other, hellish place and conquer the Ynfernael itself."

From anyone else it would have sounded like madness but, for a moment, Tristayne believed him.

"Thank you for showing me this, master," he said, genuine emotion getting the better of him. "Thank you for deeming me worthy."

"I hope it serves as a reminder that you still have much to learn, my apprentice," Waiqar said. Tristayne bowed his head rather than allow himself to be lured into a retort.

"I will show you the workings in detail," Revik said,

the Archlich seemingly enjoying the opportunity to demonstrate the device he had overseen for so many centuries. The trio descended from the gantry and walked in among the columns of prisoners being herded into the Engine, the bedraggled, terrified-looking mortals flinching and scrambling back from the three terrible beings. Tristayne barely noticed them, gazing up at the deathly contraption as it loomed over him. Bloody and burning, organic debris occasionally drizzled down, churned out by the maw-wheel that now towered above them.

They were about to pass along the toiling souls working at the axles when Waiqar raised a hand. The gesture was small, but Tristayne still found himself unable to move, both he and Revik stopped in their tracks.

"Is there a problem, sire?" Revik asked, making no effort to fight the will-force that had halted him, unlike Tristayne.

"There is a presence in the chamber," Waiqar said, half-turning. "Someone seeks me."

Tristayne also gazed around, confused and annoyed at the fact that his tour was being interrupted. He soon saw why. A shape coalesced before the trio, its ethereal form eventually becoming recognizable. It was Mirabelle, one of Waiqar's advisors. As a fellow necromancer, Tristayne had always considered her a rank amateur, too loyal by half and too cowardly to properly throw off the shackles of mortality that still clung to her. She had done so for the time being though, and had spirit-walked all the way down to the Everliving Engine, a feat of bravery and skill that he would not have credited her with.

"Mirabelle," Waiqar said as the ghostly figure bowed

before him. "Why do you seek me? I told the council I was not to be disturbed."

"Yes, lord," Mirabelle's vision said, her voice sounding distant and faint, as though she was calling from far away. "But a matter of particular importance has arisen at Zorgas."

She seemed to hesitate, but Waiqar bade her continue.

"Speak freely," he said curtly.

"Fell news has reached Zorgas, my lord," the necromancer replied. "Word has come from Bilehall that Naythen Torvic has risen in rebellion. When Sir Ulthor rode to demand the new tithes, Torvic slew him and has used his remains to raise up his retainers, and a great host besides. He has declared war on Zorgas."

Tristayne felt an unexpected thrill at the shocking news. There had been rumors about unrest among the covens, and Tristayne had witnessed it for himself firsthand when Naythen Torvic had come within inches of speaking out directly against Waiqar during the Night of the Red Feast. He had never expected the craven creatures of Bilehall to follow through with their bluster though. The fact that they would challenge Waiqar pleased him on two levels – his master's arrogance would be checked, while the cretinous vampires would likely be annihilated.

"Have all the lords of Bilehall joined Torvic?" Waiqar asked, seemingly without emotion.

"Almost all. Wandering spirits from the marshlands and the sight of our razorwings show that the Pelacosts and Lord Vorun'thul are answering the muster call and marching toward the Red Keep from their own retinues.

There has been no movement from Bloodhold though. It is unclear if Lucrezia Torvic backs her brother's rebellion."

"And what of those beyond Bilehall?" Waiqar asked. "Has the rot spread to Dalibor as well?"

"There has been no word of Kyndrithul or his thralls joining Bilehall. Sir Vortigern delivered the terms of the new tithe and Kyndrithul reportedly accepted them and reaffirmed his oaths."

"That is welcome news," Waiqar said. "Nevertheless, send Melkor and a cohort to the Dalibor estate. Make it clear that any hint of sedition will be met with immediate retribution. I expect Kyndrithul's experiments to remain firmly within Kyndrithul's estates, and for our outposts along the border to remain undisturbed."

"Of course," Mirabelle said, her phantasmic form bowing.

"I will return to Zorgas immediately," Waiqar said. "Make ready the summoning fields and begin the rites in the upper crypts."

"Yes, lord," Mirabelle said, her form dissolving as Waiqar dismissed her. The vision had barely dissipated before Tristayne was speaking.

"My lord, allow me to accompany you to the summoning fields," he said, seizing his chance. This was exactly the sort of moment he had hoped for, an opportunity to display his full potential to Waiqar, to prove to him that feats of power trumped petty intrigues with spirits and phantoms. "With both of us combined, we can raise a mighty host in a matter of days and crush these parasitic upstarts before their rebellion can spread."

"You presume to suggest strategy to me, apprentice?"

Waiqar asked, and Tristayne abruptly realized that his lord was in no mood to humor him. He had hoped, given the goodwill evident in permitting him to visit the Everliving Engine, that he could press Waiqar into further concessions. That now felt like an unwise assumption.

"I will summon the Deathborn Legion to put down this insolent insurrection," Waiqar declared. "And you are not yet equipped to lead even a single cohort of that host. Or do you think my own abilities are not sufficient anymore? That I am not a worthy judge of my apprentice's progress?"

"Of course not, master," Tristayne said hastily. "I merely hoped that–"

"Do not put your trust in hope, Tristayne," Waiqar interrupted. "Trust in me. Your time will come. Until then you will return to Zorgas and continue your studies in my absence."

Tristayne felt a surge of fury so potent he almost lashed out. The Black Scythe rattled in his grip. Waiqar didn't seem to notice though. He was already busy giving instructions to Archlich Revik.

"Intensify the output," he ordered. "I will see more cattle delivered here. War is once more upon us, and the dead shall abound. I would show these vampiric parasites the true power of Zorgas. We will crush them, slowly and surely. If need be, I will tear down the Red Keep with my own hands, stone by stone."

CHAPTER ELEVEN

Waiqar climbed the steps to the battlements of Zorgas' gatehouse and gazed out upon the summoning fields. It was night, and for a while the mists had fled, revealing a sickle moon that seemed to leer down upon the Black Citadel. He could feel the power in the air, the rising power of death as it was slowly but surely drawn to him, turning everything ice-cold and bringing the murmur of unheard voices on the wind.

The Great Necromancer gazed past the parapets, at the great expanse of marshland that stretched away from the crag of Zorgas. Directly below, figures were moving in lines through the bog, swathed in black and purple robes, bent over as they sifted dust into the muck, like rows of seed-sowers planting their fields. They were the minor acolytes and junior necromancers of Waiqar's cult. Each had spent the last day and night preparing the bone dust with blood and rite-words, under the watchful gaze of Mirabelle, Lond, and the other more senior practitioners.

Now they spread it over the summoning fields at Waiqar's command, preparing a crop that he would soon call forth.

While they worked, the Deathborn Legion marched. The hard, rhythmic tramping of their iron-shod boots rang about Zorgas and echoed out into the marshes as cohort after cohort passed from the Black Citadel, through the main courtyards and down the crag. The column of skeletal warriors stretched away beneath Waiqar, their ragged banners catching the wind as they passed beyond the gatehouse, the purple deadlights in their skulls burning brightly, a river of witch-fire stretching away into the night.

Ardus sat on his great corpse-steed at the foot of the crag below, taking the salute of the cohorts as they passed him. Karrok was already somewhere out in the darkness, marshalling the front of the Deathborn column. Waiqar had raised the Legion in its entirety, something he had not done for almost a century. He had walked through the layered crypts beneath Zorgas, chanting the Black Invocation, waking his warriors from their slumber.

The effort had left him feeling drained, but he would not stop now. While the Deathborn were his best, his personal guard, Waiqar intended to demonstrate his power in full. The increase in tithes had ensured Bilehall had been goaded into rebellion for the purpose of displaying his strength and securing unity for the campaigns to come. He would not stop at half measures. To the Deathborn would be added the myriad undead hosts that lay awaiting his summons in the marshes around Zorgas, as well as the spirits and phantoms that infested the ancient fortress itself. He would crush Naythen Torvic, slowly and surely, and all of the insolent vermin who had dared to join him. Only then could he turn his attentions south, to the baronies. He would be safe in the knowledge that no traitor would rise up to usurp him when he departed Zorgas. He could not resume his hunt for the shards of the Orb while fearing for the safety of his seat of power.

The hour was nigh. Waiqar pushed back against the fatigue brought on by raising the Deathborn, reaching one hand out to act as a locus for the death energies surrounding him.

"*Nu ed šar,*" he said, hand extended, once again speaking the familiar, bitter words of the Black Invocation. "*Giš ní-ĝu inem, ug gud, ug éren.*"

The night stirred. The wind picked up, howling around Waiqar, whipping at the stag banners that hung on either side of him atop the gatehouse battlements. The silvery moonlight seemed to dim. Below, the marshland shifted.

Waiqar's eyes blazed. His witch-sight could see the dead, as well as the energy as it surged out, splitting into a thousand individual, luminescent orbs that dived down like meteorites, into the muck of the summoning fields. There they met with the bone dust, electrifying it, creating a consciousness where there had been nothing. That consciousness, directed by Waiqar's arcane words, sought out and attached itself to the vessels beneath. Sinews of raw magic took hold of old bones and ragged skin, tugging and pulling, dragging them slowly forth from their graves.

The dead rose. Waiqar roared the final words of the incantation, defiling the night with them, and as he did so Zorgas itself seemed to answer with a shriek. From arrow slits and cracks in the crumbling walls, and broiling up from the caverns in the crag beneath, came a swarm of souls, thousands upon thousands of the apparitions that haunted the ancient place. Some were forced out by the raw strength of Waiqar's will, others came of their own volition, hungry to feast upon the powers of death and the promise of more to come. They followed the pathway of necromantic energies that Waiqar had launched out into the night, streams of hundreds of gheists that flocked toward where Lady Falgor acted as a beacon for them to assemble above the summoning fields, like a pale, flickering star. With a howl that would be audible from many leagues around, the army of phantoms joined the host of walking dead that was slowly churning itself up from the mire, ripping skulls and limbs out of the ooze that had entombed them.

Slowly, awkwardly, but with ever greater purpose, the necromantic energies dragged them into a semblance of formation, forming ranks and files as the mud of the Mistlands dripped and oozed heavily from ribs and eye sockets and ran from the notched, rusting blades of swords and spears. Horn-blowers and trumpeters who had not sounded their instruments for many centuries gave forth an ugly, braying cacophony that reverberated from the sheer walls of the Black Citadel towering above. Little by little, the reanimate host assembled before their king, the Deathborn having already halted in their cohorts beyond them, standing silent in serried, heavily armored formations, their banners fluttering in the icy wind.

Waiqar slowly lowered his hand, realizing that it was shaking. Even with the assistance he had been given, summoning so vast a force so quickly had almost been too much. The death magics gnawed at him, making his bones ache, spreading through them like a cancer, until he wished once more for the dull numbness that was his regular existence. A summoning such as this was a feat no other necromancer could have hoped to achieve. But there were no necromancers like Waiqar the Unliving.

The last of the newly risen reanimates shuffled into position. Their eye sockets lit, a constellation of deadlights that spread below Waiqar and out into the night. He managed to raise his hand again, and even the shrieking of the spirit host was stilled.

In the bitter, grave silence that followed, he spoke a single word, laced with all the imperatives of his death magics, so that it echoed around in each skull and seared itself onto each consciousness below.

"March."

"My king."

The words were a whisper, breathed from a fleshless throat. They penetrated Farrenghast's consciousness slowly, his mind unwilling to leave the embrace of his long slumber quite yet. There was no coldness there, no pain in his joints or brittleness in his bones. There was only the drifting thoughtlessness of an eternal rest, free from the crushing weight of age that assailed his deathless body and mind.

"My king."

The ritual of awakening had been completed. He could feel it, tugging on his spirit, coaxing it back into his crumbling body. He rebelled against it, like a child who refused to rise from his bed, silently kicking and screaming. But it was no use.

Every time he awoke it took longer. Every time he rose, it was with greater difficulty, his mind sluggish, his body struggling to bear him up. He felt as old as the world itself, and in many ways he almost was.

"My king, can you hear me?"

"Yes," Farrenghast Penacor croaked. "A curse upon you, Yolland, I can hear you."

"Do you need assistance, my king?"

"No," Farrenghast snarled. He forced his limbs to respond. There was a dull crunch as bones that had not stirred for hundreds of years cracked back into motion, disturbing the grave shrouds that had lain over them. The dead king clutched at the side of his sarcophagus with unfeeling fingers and, with a bellow of effort, hauled himself up, leaving dust and cobwebs behind.

He sat for a while – days, perhaps – there in the bowels of his tomb, struggling to hold onto true consciousness, moaning as he tried to make his ancient, skeletal body obey his will. Finally, still spurning any help, he rose and dragged himself out onto the floor of the crypt, almost collapsing as he did so.

"My king, you are risen," Yolland said, stating the obvious, as ever, as he bowed and scraped. Farrenghast's chief retainer was only partly corporeal now, so old was his body. Despite the binding magics, some bones had crumbled away entirely, the space now occupied by their ghostly twin. Yolland's left forearm and hand were missing, their phantoms beginning where the broken bones ended;

likewise, the left upper part of his skull, including his eye socket, was a ghostly apparition, the physical bone long ago shattered and lost. It was a testimony to his own seemingly eternal desire to serve that Yolland's mind was able to project an ethereal form even as, down the slow, inexorable millennia, his physical remains slowly failed him.

Farrenghast managed to right himself fully, and rasped at Yolland to rise. He did with just as much difficulty, facing his king of old.

"What is the meaning of this?" Farrenghast demanded. "Why have you awoken me?"

"My king, it was not without all due consideration," Yolland said, voice a dry, wizened whisper. "Matters are at hand beyond the keep, and within it now as well. We have a visitor."

"Someone has dared disturb my slumber?" Farrenghast demanded.

"A bearer of great tidings, my king," Yolland said. "A *Daewyl* elf. Her name is Zarihell."

"Zarihell," Farrenghast rattled softly, pronouncing each syllable slowly. "Za-ri-hell. Do I know this name?"

"You do," Yolland said. "It is the witch elf who once served Waiqar."

"Do not speak of him," Farrenghast bellowed, a sudden surge of anger adding vigor to his decrepit body and mind. "Do not speak to me of the Betrayer!"

"No, my king, no," Yolland groveled, doing his best to bow with a crack of bones. "But this Zarihell, she has long railed against the Betrayer, cursed-be-his-name. She has come to us now seeking our aid in destroying him."

"Fool," Farrenghast bellowed, his wrath shaking dust from his bones. "The King Penacor gives aid to no one! I will not grant an audience to one of the Betrayer's witches, whether she be loyal to him or not!"

"But she brings fortuitous news," Yolland dared to continue. "The Betrayer is weaker than he has been for many centuries! There is a rebellion, in Bilehall!"

Farrenghast had been considering silencing his undead servant with a blow, but the words checked his hand.

"Those verminous blood-addicts have finally found the courage to defy him?" he asked. Yolland nodded so hastily his spine made an ugly crunching noise.

"The vampires seek to throw off his shackles. The Betrayer has raised the entirety of his legion and now marches from Zorgas to bring them to heel."

"All of his legion?" Farrenghast asked disbelievingly. There was no force, when combined, that was more potent in all of Terrinoth than the Deathborn Legion. That Waiqar would bring them all together – and risk them on one campaign – was something Farrenghast had rarely seen before, and he had been battling the so-called Great Necromancer for supremacy in the Mistlands for millennia. Farrenghast was the oldest undead lord that yet endured, and he was certainly the mightiest still independent of Waiqar's will.

Farrenghast had been the first true undead king, and had long claimed an unfulfilled dominion over the whole of the Mistlands. Waiqar was a mere upstart, but Farrenghast knew he could not match the Great Necromancer when he was at his most powerful. There were always opportunities, however. He found his thoughts, still sluggish from the slow awakening, growing more keen.

"The elf claims Deathborn cohorts are assembled in full," Yolland said. "And so many spirits follow the host that their luminescence lights up the sky to the north. I knew you would want to question this account in person. That was why I ordered the ritual of awakening to be completed."

"I will never ally myself with the parasites of Bilehall," Farrenghast said, speaking to himself now more than Yolland. "But if that treacherous young pup has marched all of his forces east to crush them..."

"Then the Everliving Engine will be almost undefended," Yolland finished.

Farrenghast glared at him, as though he was about to chastise him for daring to utter out loud what he had been thinking. The Everliving Engine was the key to a vast reserve of elemental Mortos. With it, he would be able to finally replenish his forces, armies that had been slowly withering away down the centuries. He gave a series of terse commands.

"Awake the rest of my household and have them bind me in my royal shroud. Then bring my staff and crown. I will not speak to this *Daewyl* traitor still heavy with tomb-dust. King Farrenghast Penacor walks again, as he did in days of old, and both the living and the dead shall tremble before him!"

CHAPTER TWELVE

The morning mist was hanging low about the marshes, leaving the bloody stonework of the Red Keep looming up out of the miasma, a jagged crown in a sea of gray. Waiqar watched as, in the distance, a slab of stone the size of a small barn collided with the parapets of the citadel's curtain wall, throwing up a billow of dust and sending a cascade of broken masonry crashing down into the ditch surrounding the castle's southern and eastern flanks. The cracking sound of the impact and subsequent, partial collapse reached him seconds later, ringing out over the flat marshland between the wall and the siege works.

It was the best strike there had been for days. Over a month had passed since Waiqar's host had marched from Zorgas. Deepwinter's chill had descended, turning the mist bitterly cold, filming the black bogs with a layer of ice and leaving the marsh grasses brittle. The Bilehall lords, when they witnessed the size of the forces at Waiqar's command and how quickly he had raised them, had chosen discretion as the better part of valor. Naythen Torvic had scurried back to the Red Keep, and although some of his coven had abandoned him, none had yet found the courage to come to Waiqar in person and crave forgiveness. Waiqar had carried on with the plan and invested the Red Keep, though the subsequent siege had been slow.

Waiqar had consulted with his engineers and masons, and had settled upon a methodical approach. It had been some time since he had commanded a siege, and he took the opportunity to reacquaint himself with the nature of such a systematic style of warfare. The Red Keep and its defenders presented a moderately challenging opposition. Crushing them was only a matter of time, but Waiqar didn't intend to waste a single soul that he did not need to. Other necromancers were profligate with their servants, but not he. Even a clutch of common reanimates represented a grain or two of Deathborn dust, and in that sense they were precious. His time and resources were vast, but they were not quite yet unlimited, and he did not intend to make the mistake of treating them as such.

Another of the trebuchets launched its projectile into the cold morning air, sending the stone streaking away toward the jagged parapets and towers of Torvic's lair. The siege engines were made from the bones of the vast carcasses that dotted the Mistlands, the remains of primordial creatures that the foul swamp had dredged up over the eons. Dozens of them hemmed in the Red Keep along its open southern and eastern walls, maintaining a tireless bombardment. Sections of parapet had been staved in, one tower had come crashing down and two others were practically ruinous, but as of yet Waiqar's forces had been unable to fashion a practical breach in the curtain wall.

Such were the realities of siege work. Torvic's forces were contained and, while Waiqar suspected they had sufficient cattle penned in their dungeons for the vampires to endure their hunger for some time, their defeat now seemed inevitable.

Ardus and a few other members of the council had urged him to mount a grand escalade of the walls, to attack from all sides with ladders and siege towers and overrun the Bilehall traitors with sword and spell. He had considered it, of course, especially as it would end matters more quickly, but it was not worth the bodies – or, more accurately, the dust. Torvic's slow annihilation was sending out just as potent a message, even more so the fact that other members of his coven, including his own sister, were content to leave him to his fate. All in the Mistlands would be aware of what was happening at the Red Keep. Any other dissenters would think twice before turning on Zorgas.

Another trebuchet missile whickered away, slamming into the gatehouse, sending broken masonry and dust cascading past the portcullis. Another followed just after, arcing up over the walls and crunching down somewhere in the main bailey. Waiqar wondered how long it would be before the forces within attempted to sally out. Ardus was itching for them to do so – he and a cohort of Deathborn knights had been armed and saddled since the start of the siege, ready to meet them the moment Torvic and his vampiric host poured from the gate. Waiqar suspected it would be some time yet. The supposed lord of Bilehall would still be coming to terms with the fact that he was trapped and helpless.

That was never an easy thing for an immortal to endure. He remembered Tristayne, who had once been trapped by a band of Terrinoth heroes in his infamous Black Scythe. The necromancer was unkillable, always rising back eventually to un-life. This fact was fascinating to Waiqar, but it had confounded those who had sought to defeat him until they had been able to turn Tristayne's own dark magics against him and seal his soul away in the ever-hungry scythe. Waiqar, when he had discovered it, had freed him, but it had been years before Tristayne had recovered from the derangement brought on by his imprisonment.

Waiqar had almost felt sympathy for him. To be shackled and confined was the worst fate he could imagine. After all, it was the same one that had befallen him. Even though it had been a millennium past, the echoes of the fear and pain that had beset him in Llovar's Black Citadel still echoed back to him, more haunting than all the phantoms that stalked Zorgas' crypts and corridors.

Abruptly, he found himself sliding once more. He knew he should fight it, but he had been standing for too long, undisturbed, watching the siege progress. Days had passed. His thoughts had locked onto the memories he had buried so deep, that he had plunged into the icy depths of his soul in the hope that they would drown. Now they were rising back up to choke him again.

He remembered.

CHAPTER THIRTEEN
Long Before

Screaming woke Waiqar. After a while, he realized it was his own.

He forced himself to stop, whimpering at the effort. Pain and fear made him shudder, the manacles binding his wrists biting deep and drawing blood.

It was dark outside, a single bracketed torch on the wall giving a fiery light to the hellish scene that had been Waiqar's constant companion since he had been brought to the Black Citadel. He was in a tower, a circular chamber, built from the dark, volcanic stone of the Ru Wastes. Fellow prisoners were ranged around the walls, thirty-three in all, most of them stripped almost bare. Most were humans, but there were a few dwarfs and an elf among them.

Two of them were his own soldiers, Kalesandra and Sir Naimen, both from the third cohort of the legion. They had been captured during the ambush in the valley. Neither knew how the wider battle had gone, whether or not Ardus and the rest of the legion had been able to hack their way clear.

Waiqar had tried to be strong for both of them, but it was difficult when the barbarian torturers dug into his flesh, and equally difficult when he saw them suffer in turn. They, like almost all the others, were close to breaking.

All except the elf.

She alone endured with an almost gleeful defiance, seemingly unaffected by the cruel blows her lean, tattooed body had suffered. She spat and laughed at her jailers, and warned them that the fate that awaited them was far more dreadful than the one that was currently being inflicted on her.

Waiqar could no longer find it in himself to show similar defiance. The pain had become too much, and the horrors of what he had witnessed being done to the others had only added to the burden.

One hope remained, one slender thread that he grasped at, praying that it would hold. Timmorran would come for them. Had he not promised before marching into the valley that he would send reinforcements? Surely now, when news of the disaster reached him, he would come with his full host, and unleash his arcane might upon the Black Citadel. He would tear down the walls and break the shackles, and the agony would end.

That was what he tried to tell Kalesandra and Sir Naimen, and all the others. Every time he said it, it rang hollower and hollower. Eventually, he stopped making the claim. Eventually, he stopped being able to even look his fellow prisoners in the eye.

No one was coming to save any of them.

"Wake up."

The command was accompanied by a jolt of power, a magical imperative that yanked him forcefully from a fevered dream. He moaned out as the pain of his wounds returned, but the voice made a shushing sound, as though trying to soothe him.

"Suffer quietly, my human friend," whispered the elf. "Or our jailers will come back and make you cry louder."

Waiqar slumped against his chains, casting a bitter glance at the woman. It was the depths of the night, and the braziers within the tower chamber had burned down to red embers. The elf's eyes were bright though, alert with magical power. Waiqar had sensed it in her before, just as he suspected the elf could feel his own aptitude for magic. It did neither of them any good – the rune-carved walls of the tower, dense with Ynfernael energy, stifled anything but the merest magical prod.

"Why?" Waiqar croaked, his throat as rough and dry as desert rock. "Why wake me?"

"You are the leader, are you not?" she whispered. "The one who commanded the host that was ambushed in the valley?"

Waiqar managed to nod. The words felt like an accusation, another sting to add to his pains.

"Your last warrior is dead," the elf said, nodding across the chamber to where Sir Naimen had slumped against his own bonds. Kalesandra had passed a few days before, her body eventually unshackled and dragged out by pelt-clad brutes. Waiqar closed his eyes, feeling a profound sense of despair. He had told them he would get them out. He had told them Timmorran would come for them.

"I suppose you want to join them?" the elf asked. Waiqar didn't answer. He had long given up on the will to live. Time itself was becoming meaningless. He didn't know how long it had been since he had first been hauled to the tower. He couldn't even accurately recall who among the prisoners had been present when he had first arrived, and who had been brought in and shackled since.

It was a blur, an unending nightmare from which snatched moments of sleep offered the only fraction of respite. Even the tortures themselves had grown worse. He had seen brutalities he could not have conceived of before meted out, seemingly for no reason other than the amusement of their jailers. He had seen demons summoned from the blood and life-essence of the prisoners, horned, snarling, otherworld monstrosities that made his skin crawl.

He had seen Llovar himself.

The ruler of the Uthuk Y'llan, the mortal champion of demons, had visited the tower when he had first been imprisoned. Waiqar had expected the gigantic, fur-clad barbarian king to interrogate him, to demand to know Timmorran's plans and the state of the realm's preparedness. Instead, and to his surprise, Llovar had asked for his fealty. Swear a blood-oath and the pain would end. He would be inculcated into the ranks of the Uthuk Y'llan, and know power and riches far beyond the petty rewards he had received thus far from Timmorran.

Waiqar had found it in himself to refuse, one last flare of

defiance. There had hardly been a day or night since when he had not regretted that act. He had begged with his jailers and torturers, had pleaded with the manifesting demon-things, had sworn them an eternity of service, continual praise, all the secrets of Timmorran, all of his heart, mind and soul if they would only make it all stop. None had listened. Llovar had not returned. He had been abandoned, and in this foul citadel he feared that even death would not be a release.

"You do not have long left, I think, human," the elf said. Waiqar glared at her again.

"How can you endure so much?" he demanded hoarsely. The elf let out a little giggle, a sound utterly alien in the bleak and bloody chamber.

"Oh, I serve a power far higher than that adored by our captors," she said. "Their desperate cravings for attention from the Ynfernael are like the pestering of little children. Quite inconsequential."

"Who then?" Waiqar asked. "Who do you serve?"

"Myself, firstly," the elf said, still sounding amused, as though she were subtly making fun of him. "And then a few others. They will be most displeased with these barbarians once they discover what they have done."

"And you are content to endure all this until then?"

"These bonds I wear were not the first to shackle me. I have broken far more potent restraints."

"Then how did you come to be captured?" Waiqar asked, not believing her.

"Perhaps I wanted to be," the elf pointed out. "Perhaps it sounded like fun."

The mere mockery alone made Waiqar feel sick.

"If you have the power, then break these bonds," he begged her, his voice sharp and desperate in the half-darkness.

"I cannot yet," she admitted. "But still, I have hope. Who was it you used to say would be coming? Timmorran?"

The name was as bad as another hot knife against his skin. He snarled.

"No one is coming," he said. "I have been betrayed."

"Perhaps," the elf said lightly. "Betrayal is subjective. Still, I'm impressed you've lasted this long. There's something about you. I think you impressed Llovar."

"Cease your cruelty," Waiqar hissed. "I have endured enough without it."

"I speak only the truth. They are growing more inventive with you. Soon you might even start to hear voices."

"I do not care if I lose my mind. It would be a reprieve."

"I said nothing of losing your mind," the elf pointed out. "What is your name, human?"

Waiqar hesitated. Timmorran had taught him how knowledge of a name could give those with arcane abilities power over the one who bore it. Still, it hardly seemed to matter anymore.

"Will you tell me yours?" he asked.

"Of course," the elf exclaimed, her eyes like those of a predator in the dark as she smiled.

"I am Waiqar," he told her, even his own name sounding strange now that so much else had been stripped from him.

"Waiqar," the elf repeated, several times, as though testing it on her tongue. "A strong name. Worthy of a leader. Of a king."

"And what is yours?" Waiqar demanded, suspecting she was mocking him again. She looked at him and smiled once more.

"Zarihell."

Waiqar endured. Through the pain and misery, he lived on, though often he did not wish to. He developed a habit of speaking to Zarihell during the night, when it seemed that even demon-worshipers and their masters slept. She was enigmatic and her moods were capricious, but their conversations provided the only respite from the relentless brutality.

They talked of their pasts – though Waiqar sensed the elf left much unspoken – and of their upbringing. Zarihell had belonged to the Deep Elves, who made their homes amidst the roots of the Dunwarr mountains, but she claimed to have spent time in the Aymhelin, that great southern forest that others of her kind called home. Waiqar tried repeatedly to gauge her age, but could find little certainty beyond the fact that she was far, far older than she appeared.

Then, one night, a voice spoke to him that wasn't Zarihell's. It sounded like that of a man, rich and deep, and it started him awake by speaking his name.

"*Waiqar.*"

He looked around, thinking at first that it was one of the newer prisoners, one whose screams he had not yet grown to recognize.

"*Do not look for my coming. I am already here.*"

With a chilling sensation, Waiqar realized that the voice

wasn't emanating from anywhere in the dark chamber. It was inside his head.

"Calm yourself. I mean you no harm."

He looked at Zarihell, but for once the elf appeared to be asleep. He didn't dare raise his voice to wake her, knowing that doing so might attract unwanted attention, either from the guards or the other prisoners.

This was what the elf had warned him about. Voices in his head.

"What do you want with me?" he hissed, reluctant even to address the presence.

"Only your company," replied the voice. *"I have long lacked stimulating conversation, and I believe you might be able to change that."*

"What are you? Why are you in my head?"

"I am a fellow prisoner. A trapped echo, if you will."

"You are a demon," Waiqar surmised. "I have seen enough of your kind since I was chained here. You are not the first to try and twist my mind."

"My dear Waiqar, would that I had the power to twist anything. A child of the Ynfernael I may be, but I long ago lost my hold over anything, including my corporeal form."

"So you want mine instead?" Waiqar snapped. "I am not yet wholly broken, demon. I will not become your host."

"That is not what I've heard, Waiqar. I've heard your begging. I've heard my kin ignoring you. They've mistreated you, I'll grant you that."

"How do you know my name?" Waiqar demanded.

"I listen."

"Zarihell told you? She's betrayed me?"

"Not yet she hasn't."

"Tell me your name, demon, or we will speak no more."

There was a pause, and briefly Waiqar wondered if the disembodied entity had left his head, abandoning it as quickly as it had appeared. Its next utterance dispelled his hopes.

"I am Baelziffar."

"Leave me, Baelziffar," Waiqar said. "I have no need for the company of the Ynfernael."

"Will you still say that tomorrow, when the torturers return?"

Waiqar baulked. He knew he would not. He knew he would say anything then to make them stop. But he knew also that they would not.

"But they might," Baelziffar's voice whispered, taunting him. *"I could make them stop."*

"Get out of my thoughts," Waiqar shouted, clutching at his head and making his chains rattle. Several of the other prisoners stirred and cried out.

"I told you to be calm, Waiqar. I told you I mean you no harm. We will get to know one another, you and I."

Abruptly, Waiqar found himself crying. This was more than he could bear.

"I just want this to end," he moaned, sniffing. "I want all of it to end."

"Some of it will, if you wish. If you accept my help."

"At what cost?" Waiqar demanded, his voice raw.

"Does it matter?"

Waiqar thought for a moment, then shook his head slowly, wearily.

"No."

"Then we have our first accord. Splendid."

"What do you want of me?" Waiqar asked. This time, there really was no reply. He repeated the question, over and over, until he was screaming it and the other prisoners were shouting at him, and the guards were storming in, bellowing. One struck Waiqar, and he remembered no more.

The next day, he wondered if it had all been a dream. He had endured stranger and more terrible nightmares. The voice – Baelziffar – did not come back to him.

After tormenting one of the newer prisoners to Waiqar's left, two of the torture-mongers approached him. They were hulking, muscle-bound brutes wearing nothing above the waist bar dark leather aprons, stiff with old blood, like some foul parody of a pair of butchers. Their faces were masked by tusked, pig-like grotesques made from crudely beaten brass, fashioned to resemble the bestial demons that had visited the prisoners on a number of occasions. Black spittle oozed thickly from the gurning mouth slits of the masks as the duo loomed over Waiqar, reaching into their apron pockets to retrieve their rusting tools.

Waiqar shivered despite himself. It was not so much the pain anymore, though he was still not inured to it. The worst thing was the fact it seemed there was nothing he could say or do to stop them. It appeared they wanted nothing from him, only his suffering. It was a waste of time even asking them to kill him.

One leaned over him, then paused abruptly. Waiqar braced himself, shaking, trying to find the courage and defiance that had been slowly cut out of him.

The torturer grunted something to his companion, then turned away. Waiqar remained taut, convinced this was some new form of mockery, that they were toying with him. But instead of returning with his knives, the brute scooped two fingers into a pouch at his waist. He smeared a black, tarry substance over Waiqar's mutilated chest, daubing a symbol there. It stung and made him moan.

To his disbelief, the torturers moved on. As the screaming of another prisoner rang out, the voice returned to Waiqar's head, making him gasp.

"See. I told you I could help you."

"What did you do?" Waiqar whispered.

"You have been marked for better things. I cannot stop all your suffering, but you will bear less of it from henceforth."

"T-Thank you," Waiqar managed, still disbelieving. At that moment, the fact that he was conversing with a demon meant nothing. All that mattered was that, for once, the pain he had anticipated hadn't come.

"What's their name?" Zarihell asked him one night. Waiqar didn't attempt to obfuscate the question.

"I shouldn't tell you."

"Sworn yourself to them already, have you?" the elf said mockingly.

"Baelziffar," Waiqar answered. It was the first time he had uttered the name out loud since that first night. It seemed to struggle to leave his tongue, as though even the blighted, stinking air of the Black Citadel felt like the place where it belonged.

Zarihell didn't speak to him for the rest of that night, nor did the demon.

A fever took Waiqar the next day. He shivered, still bound against the wall, hugging himself as his skull throbbed and his thoughts burned up.

"*Endure a little longer, and all will be well,*" Baelziffar soothed him.

"I... I cannot," Waiqar whispered. "I have nothing left to endure with."

"*You have everything. You are strong. You are noble, and courageous. I speak as one king to another.*"

"I am no king," Waiqar croaked.

"*Oh, but you shall be, Waiqar,*" said the voice. "*And a king, what's more, whose reign shall endure forever.*"

"I want none of it, if I must suffer here any longer."

"*You will not. You will be free, and free from more than just these chains, or this tower. The pain of flesh and blood will haunt you no longer.*"

"What must I do?" Waiqar asked, finding a moment's clarity.

"*Do not fear. When the time comes, I will show you,*" said Baelziffar.

The Black Citadel shook.

Waiqar was only dimly aware of it. The fever still held him in its grip, leaving him shivering and sweating, his mind clouded, every thought a struggle.

One realization pierced the veil of sickness. Llovar's stronghold was under attack.

The tower quaked again, and there was a cracking sound from somewhere outside, as something slammed into the exterior wall. Many of the prisoners remained slumped like Waiqar, too ruined by the work of the torturers to either know or care about what was happening around them, but a few looked up in confusion. Zarihell stood from where she had been sitting cross-legged, drawing her chains taut.

It continued. After a while there was more than just the shaking. There were voices.

The sound of them made Waiqar moan and raise his head, looking past his long, sweat-streaked hair as the door to the chamber burst open. A clutch of Uthuk Y'llan swept in, iron-shod boots clacking on the stone floor. Two of them were the pig-like torturers, in their bloody aprons and grotesques, but the others were warriors, clad in furs and leather armor. They were daubed in red slaughter-paint, the mark of an Uthuk about to enter combat. They carried notched blades and axes, fully drawn.

One particularly large one, her head shaven and crisscrossed with ritual scarring, gesticulated angrily at the prisoners and barked something at one of the torturers. He replied in a tone that was just as angry, the Uthuk's tribal tongue full of guttural snarling and spitting.

Several of the other warriors murmured, looking to their leader. She jabbed a finger at the torturer's chest and leaned in to growl something in his face, before turning abruptly and heading for the door. Her warriors followed her, clattering back down the spiral stairs. The torturers remained.

"She wanted to kill us all," Zarihell murmured to Waiqar. "But our boorish friends claim Llovar forbids it. They will risk defending us from those who would rescue us."

Rescue. The word failed to reach Waiqar properly. He leaned back against the wall, shivering uncontrollably, his head throbbing.

Other sounds drifted up from lower in the tower, screams and the clash of steel on steel. The noises grew steadily louder. The torturers hauled the door to the chamber shut and barred it, grunting at each other in their bestial language.

Abruptly, the sounds of fighting ceased. For a short while, nothing stirred. Now all but the most brutalized prisoners were looking up, confused and afraid; also bar Zarihell, who was picking dirt from under her nails, apparently bored with the wait.

Waiqar felt a sudden stirring, a surge of magical energies that he hadn't felt for a very long time. It roused him from the fever, giving him a sudden moment of clarity. He managed to stand up.

The magic grew. The dark runes daubed or chiseled into the stonework all around them were glowing, the Ynfernael curses they spelled out battling with the sorcery being channeled from just outside the chamber. They were struggling to hold it back, to nullify it the way they nullified the abilities of both Waiqar and Zarihell.

But they weren't strong enough. With a flash they ignited, and were seared away, overwhelmed and burned out by the raw power of the one beyond.

The torturers exchanged a glance, expressions unreadable behind their terrible masks.

The door to the chamber exploded inward. Blue light, redolent with the power of the Verto Magica, surged, and a figure stepped through it, laden with arcane wrath. Waiqar shied away, unable to look at him. A terrible combination of relief and loathing rose up inside him, overwhelming in its intensity. After all this time, he was here. Yet it was late. Much too late.

The twin torturers charged, bellowing, knives drawn. The figure extended an arm, wordlessly. Two bolts of blue brilliance spat from his fingers, earthing into the broad chests of the brutes. They both dropped instantly, their cries cut abruptly short.

Waiqar peered at the intruder. The rest of the prisoners stared, some open-mouthed. Slowly, the blue energy began to recede, showing the being at the heart of it, the one who had such power to command. He was tall and lean, with a chiseled, noble face and long, dark hair, pulled back from his scalp. His eyes continued to play with actinic light. He wore flowing robes of blue and purple, and there was a curved sword with a bejeweled hilt still sheathed at his hip, held in place by a golden sash.

Waiqar knew him, indeed, he had known him since he had felt his magical presence outside. It was Timmorran.

The greatest wizard to have ever lived surveyed the grim chamber, his expression set. Behind him his warriors in blue and white livery hurried in, panting, their swords bloody. They had fought their way this far.

"By the gods, Llovar will pay for this," one of them said as she took in the sight of the bedraggled, bloodied prisoners, the stench of the room causing her to raise a gauntlet to her mouth.

"He will, when we catch up with him," Timmorran agreed, pacing to the chamber's center, the bottom of his robes brushing across the blood-encrusted stones underfoot. He gazed around once more, from one prisoner to another, as though searching for someone.

Waiqar tried to say something to gain his attention, but could only manage an ugly croak. It was enough though. The wizard turned and looked at him directly.

"Waiqar," he breathed. He rushed to him, reaching out to catch him just as the last of Waiqar's strength left him, and he collapsed.

Timmorran held his emaciated, bloody body close as Waiqar whimpered, consciousness threatening to desert him.

"You came," was all he managed.

"Forgive me, my friend," Timmorran murmured, bowing his head over him. "Forgive me that it took until now. The road has been long and the battles hard."

He spoke an arcane word, and the shackles fell from Waiqar's wrists, clattering to the floor. The sudden weightlessness felt surreal, dream-like. Timmorran lifted him in his arms.

"The others," Waiqar breathed, his head swimming. "The others too."

"They will all be freed," Timmorran assured him, his soldiers already moving to break the bonds that held the remaining prisoners. "They will come with us. None of you will know this horror ever again. It is over."

Over, but too late. Far, far too late. His consciousness fading, Waiqar felt a deep pang of bitterness.

"Will you leave me?" he whispered.

"No," Timmorran said, voice firm, as he began to carry him from the chamber. "Never again, friend."

But the words had not been meant for Timmorran. And, heard only by Waiqar, Baelziffar whispered back his own answer.

"I will be with you from this day on, Waiqar. Every step of the way, from here, to eternity."

CHAPTER FOURTEEN
The Present

The crash of stone brought Waiqar back.

He started, and watched as, in the distance, a section of the Red Keep's gatehouse came down, dust broiling up into the leaden sky. The sudden return to the present made him shudder, his bones cracking.

How long had he been lost to his memories this time? Mere minutes? And yet the day seemed darker than it had been before. Perhaps he had spent the better part of it standing mindlessly, a thrall to his past.

He turned his gaze from the distant walls of Torvic's citadel, looking to see if any of his lieutenants were in his presence or had noticed his malaise, but none were in sight. The host that he had summoned stood arranged around the Red Keep, rank upon rank of reanimates, their deadlights smoldering. Crows and other carrion pecked at them, occasionally rising in great, squalling flocks. Waiqar had loosened the necromantic strings that puppetted many of his warriors, knowing that there was no need for him to maintain absolute control over the entire host for the time being. If Torvic did try to sally out, his Deathborn would be sufficient to contain them.

The siege would continue.

With a flutter of wings, Pentageist swept through the open balcony into Lucrezia Torvic's hall and collided with a crunch against the stone floor. He slid, leaving blood in his wake, thrashing and mewling as he morphed from a razorwing back into his human form.

Lucrezia had sensed his approach. She had half considered sending up her own flock of razorwings to tear the fool apart before he could even make Bloodhold's keep, but she had thought better of it. His arrival was as fortuitous as it was pathetic.

Disaster was looming. Something had to be done to save the coven, to save the very existence of Bilehall itself. That was always her priority. Without a true brood family, she had always believed vampires became something lesser than they should be, like the cretin Kyndrithul.

Sometimes, protecting the family meant sacrifices were necessary.

There was an ugly crunch of bones as the vampire finished his metamorphosis. He was left hunched over and bare before where Lucrezia sat upon her throne, his pale body grimy and emaciated. He hissed instinctively, but forced himself to bare his throat in the vampiric gesture of submission, gazing up at her from between strands of lank black hair.

"My lady," he said.

"You escaped then?" Lucrezia demanded dispassionately, as her retainers closed in around the crouching vampire, swords and pole arms poised to butcher him on her command.

"Yes," Pentageist rattled, struggling to articulate as his body continued to recover from its transformation. "Your brother... sent me."

"Did he, or did you flee of your own accord?" Lucrezia asked. "Even among those who cleave to my brother's shadow, you have always been counted a coward."

Pentageist was in no position to respond angrily to the accusation.

"He sent me," he reiterated. "To find you."

"To beg," Lucrezia said. "To bring my host to the Red Keep and lift the siege."

"Yes," Pentageist said. "You are his sister. Closest of his brood. Second in the Bilehall coven. You must help us."

"I must do no such thing," Lucrezia snapped, feeling her ire stir. All of this had been so predictable. Her brother truly was a fool. Still, by sending Pentageist, he was providing an unwitting way out of this entire mess.

"What became of my brother's determination to throw off the shackles of Zorgas?" she demanded, indulging her anger for a moment. "What of the mighty host he raised with the dust of Waiqar's minions?"

Pentageist began to respond, but Lucrezia cut him off, leaning forward in her throne, her eyes turning blood-red with anger as she bared her fangs.

"What of the witch who tricked him into this foolishness? What of her supposed power, of the aid she promised?

Does she languish with the rest of you in your master's encircled citadel?"

"She does not," Pentageist admitted, failing to meet Lucrezia's furious gaze. "She disappeared after Lord Torvic refused to meet Waiqar in open battle."

"She deceived you," Lucrezia said, sitting back. "As all knew she would. All the stories agree that she is a trickster, a meddler. She seeks to sow discord and undermine everything associated with Waiqar. She cares nothing for us or our brood, much less the independence of Bilehall."

"We did not expect the Betrayer to react as swiftly as he did," Pentageist groveled. "He raised all of the Deathborn in a single night!"

"You underestimated him," Lucrezia said. "I did not. I refuse to receive the same punishment that you all deserve. To that end, I will show you mercy. I will end you here, and save you the terrible fate of falling into Waiqar's hands."

"You cannot," Pentageist stammered, "I am your brother's favored! We belong to the same coven!"

"Which is exactly why your death will serve a purpose," Lucrezia said, before sending a single imperative to her guards.

"Behead him."

Pentageist's shriek was cut brutally short as the blades of the reanimates struck home. Dark, rancid blood, the essence of the beings he had last drunk from, spurted across the flagstones at Lucrezia's feet. The body began to shrivel, the blood-magics binding it unravelling. The severed head was picked up by one of the reanimates and presented to Lucrezia on bended knee.

"In your true, final death, you will prove far more valuable to House Torvic than you ever were before, Pentageist," she told it.

News Waiqar had not expected arrived on the same day that the Red Keep's gatehouse finally collapsed.

It fell with a crash, a pall of dust billowing up to momentarily shroud the walls on either side. Waiqar stood, patiently waiting for it to clear, knowing that Ardus and the others would plead with him to be allowed to begin the assault.

A part of him was tempted. And yet, reducing the crypt-fortress of Naythen Torvic to rubble without the unbinding of a single of his own reanimates was a far more potent display of strength. That would come to pass, or Torvic would sally forth before long, and his Deathborn would get the battle they craved.

He felt the simmering energies surrounding him stir, sluggish, like a sleeper lately awakened. He looked back, and found Mirabelle approaching. A reanimate had gathered up the train of her white kirtle dress and was following her so that it did not trail in the marshland's muck.

"My lord," she called out. Waiqar could tell from the way the death essences were taut around her that she had ill news.

"You are disturbing my musings," Waiqar warned her. She halted and bowed.

"My apologies, Undying One, but we have received word from the south. Unexpected tidings, and unwelcome at that."

Waiqar wondered what Mirabelle was talking about. What had he missed? What variable in his plans had gone unaccounted for?

"Speak then," he said brusquely.

"Reports indicate that Farrenghast Penacor has risen from his tomb," Mirabelle said. "He is gathering his warriors and marching from the Misty Hills."

That was indeed unexpected. Waiqar had wondered if news of open war between Zorgas and Bilehall would tempt the ancient king to try his hand. Even by the reckoning of immortals, it had been long since the fallen Penacor had last attempted to defeat Waiqar.

It only further confirmed his suspicions. There was something working against him in the Mistlands, something that was attempting to unite all his enemies. He had been right to try and root it out before marching on the baronies.

"He comes against us here, or to Zorgas?" Waiqar asked, suspecting the latter.

"It would seem neither, lord," Mirabelle said, and now she truly did seem concerned. "On his current route, he is bound for the ruins of Kelipa."

"The Everliving Engine," Waiqar hissed, feeling a surge of anger. Suddenly, it made sense. Farrenghast, the oldest undead lord still in existence and the only one in the Mistlands who still did not owe Waiqar some form of allegiance, was attempting to capture the Everliving Engine. Normally the ruins it lay beneath, at Kelipa, were within striking distance of Zorgas, but with Waiqar's host raised and invested in Bilehall, the great, precious machine was almost undefended.

"*The Engine cannot be allowed to fall into the hands of the Penacor,*" said the voice of Baelziffar. It had been some time since the demon had last spoken to Waiqar. He suppressed a moment of bitterness, the urge to ignore the presence in his mind.

"If we raise the siege here, Torvic may build his forces," Waiqar said, not caring about Mirabelle's look of surprise. From her perspective, it seemed as though Waiqar was holding a conversation with himself.

"The vampires who have not yet joined him may be emboldened to throw in their lot," he continued. "They may see our withdrawal as a sign of weakness."

"*So demand their assistance,*" Baelziffar hissed. "*No matter your quarrel with Bilehall, you know how Penacor hates the vampiric broods. He would never ally with them, and if he gains control of the Engine then Bilehall will be short-lived. Once he has Zorgas, Farrenghast will next march upon the Red Keep. Torvic's fate would be even more thoroughly sealed than if this siege continued.*"

What the demon said was true. A direct alliance between Penacor and Torvic was inconceivable. The Everliving Engine could not be abandoned – with it Farrenghast, who had fought against Waiqar even before he had ascended to undeath, would finally be able to supplement his host, and Waiqar would be cut off from both the spirits that joined his army and the greater flow of elemental Mortos churned out perpetually by the machine and its sacrifices. After more than a millennium in Waiqar's shadow, trying to usurp the Mistlanders, Farrenghast would suddenly have the power he craved.

The Red Keep would have to wait. But first, Waiqar needed to send word to Torvic and the rest of his brood. This was no withdrawal. The balance of power in the Mistlands was at stake, finely balanced. Victory for the old Penacor king would be as much of a disaster for Bilehall as it would be for Zorgas.

"Find Lady Falgor and have her bind and prepare two messenger-spirits," Waiqar ordered Mirabelle. "Order them to be sent to me, and I will imprint what I need upon them. I have a proposal for Naythen Torvic."

"Are you sure about this, master?" Tomaz asked, scratching his neck.

Tristayne glared at him, wondering if he had shown the mortal too much leniency. Permitting him to speak occasionally when Tristayne was voicing his discontent was one thing, but now the worm was actually questioning him? It seemed as though since visiting the Everliving Engine – and surviving – his confidence was growing, and that was not something Tristayne particularly wished to encourage.

Perhaps the servant merely wished to save his own skin? For a second Tristayne almost empathized with him. It had been a long time since the necromancer had felt true, tangible fear, but he suspected this was close to it. To be seeking out a being of such power was one thing, but doing so in defiance of the wishes of his equally powerful master seemed beyond dangerous. Tristayne knew what fate awaited him if he was caught, or betrayed. It was almost enough to make him falter.

Almost.

"I did not give you permission to speak," he snapped at Tomaz, overcoming his doubts. The die was cast. They were already out amongst the marshes, Zorgas long swallowed up by the mist at their backs. They were hunting, and Tristayne had resolved not to turn away until he had found what he sought.

Waiqar should have taken him to Bilehall. He had not even included him in the summoning rites. He had been confined to his studies in Zorgas' crypt-library, a place he had long ago exhausted of arcane knowledge. The powers at play beyond, the exertion of vast, raw necromantic magics, had made his bones ache and his soul itch, but he had partaken in none of it.

It was a final insult, forming a pinnacle atop all the others that had been heaped upon him. Waiqar had refused to let him call upon the Deathborn or even dredge up the lesser reanimates and ghosts that augmented the dread legion. He had refused to entrust him with even a single grain of grave dust, and had denied him a place on his war council once he had set out for Bilehall. He was to remain in the Black Citadel and study ethermancy, spirit-walking and half a dozen of the petty little runestones Waiqar had allowed him to pick from the vaults under the castle. Rune magic, of all things! The lowest of the low. Did Waiqar truly think he was still some foolish little student from Greyhaven? It was intolerable!

And so, after Waiqar and the Deathborn Legion had marched from Zorgas, he had resolved to go into the marshes, and seek once more the ruins where he had encountered the *Daewyl* elf, Zarihell. Tomaz had dared voice his concerns, but there would be no turning back. Tristayne had become convinced that Waiqar was deliberately stymieing his progress and seeking to hamper his abilities. The visit to the Everliving Engine had been a false hope. Tristayne could feel power at his fingertips, just tantalizingly beyond his grasp. He needed it, and if Waiqar would not be the one to let him have it, perhaps Zarihell would. It now seemed his best hope, and with Waiqar gone from his fastness, why should he hesitate anymore?

Impossibly, the witch was waiting for them. She sat astride one of the ruined walls, as she had when Tristayne had first seen her. She spread her arms as they rode close on their corpse-steeds, letting her hood fall back to reveal a beauty that seemed far removed from the festering foulness that surrounded her.

"Master Olliven, I was beginning to wonder whether I would see you again," she said.

"You made me an offer when last we spoke," Tristayne replied, in no mood for Zarihell's teasing. "You spoke of a way to raise the dead without Waiqar's dust. A means of truly mastering the Black Invocation."

"Perhaps," Zarihell said, lowering her arms. "Perhaps you dreamed it, Tristayne."

"Show me," Tristayne demanded, gesturing with the Black Scythe.

"I can take you to a place where you will learn more," Zarihell said. She slipped down off the wall, and with a snap of her fingers, summoned her own undead steed from deeper within the ruins.

"It may be a long ride," she pointed out, looking past Tristayne at the fearful Tomaz. "Will your little companion be able to endure it?"

"His steed will, and he is strapped to it," Tristayne said, doing his best to mask the thrill he felt. He should have taken up the elf on her offer before. If he wasn't being misled, this could change everything. "Where do you intend to take us?"

Zarihell smiled.

"To Dalibor."

CHAPTER FIFTEEN

Dalibor's domain lay beyond Deadwood Forest. The former woodland was now a dense, tangled mass of long-deceased timber that rose up to the west of the Bilehall marches and spread in a great arc almost to the foot of the Karahesh. Even for the Mistlands, it was a dark, accursed place. The old, twisted trees sighed and creaked in the wind, and there were all manner of chilling noises, just on the edge of perception – the odd, distant howl or scream, a dull rattling sound, the abrupt snapping of twigs, a soft growl.

As ever, Tomaz followed close behind Tristayne, daring to urge his undead horse on a little. He had realized that it was best not to look around at his surroundings. Night was falling, and the marsh mists were coiling about the gaunt, leafless trunks and branches, reaching out as though to hold them in an ethereal grasp. Repeatedly, he caught movement amidst the thickets to his left and right, but he forced himself to avoid glancing to one side, keeping his eyes fixed ahead. He had learned that at times the best way to endure horror was just to pretend none of it was happening.

He had hoped Tristayne would not seek out the elf. He had hoped that, if he did, Tristayne would not take Tomaz. Yet here he was, once more being dragged in the necromancer's wake. He still hadn't fathomed just what his purpose really was, or why he had been kidnapped from Greyhaven in the first place. If he was to be Tristayne's servant, there was very little he aided him with; indeed, there was very little the necromancer had need of at all.

Like all those returned from the dead, he did not seem to eat or sleep, did not need to wash or change his garments, and always had his dreadful scythe close at hand. On several occasions he had commanded Tomaz attend him in Zorgas' library, having him fetch and carry tomes. Even that mundane act had been fraught with terror – the shelves were haunted by unliving librarians, and one of the books he had been tasked with retrieving had tried to steal his soul, while another had attempted to drain his blood.

Still, besides that he did nothing other than languish in his cell or follow his master on his nightmarish expeditions. Since enduring the hellish sight of the Everliving Engine, he had found himself becoming numb to it all, his fear losing some of the dreadful edge it had possessed when he had first been kidnapped.

This was his existence now, and he was almost accepting of it.

Sometimes he felt as though he was only there to lend an ear when Tristayne launched into one of his rants. He had no true appreciation of necromantic magics, knew nothing of Waiqar besides the legends and the brief glimpses he had endured of him, and could barely conceive of the relationship between the pair, but from what he could understand Tristayne was his apprentice, and was perpetually dissatisfied with what Waiqar was trying to teach him. He raged at Tomaz rather than dare confront the Undying One. It alarmed Tomaz, though at times he was thankful of it, as it seemed to be the only thing ensuring he was kept alive.

This, however, seemed like a step beyond student dissatisfaction. The elf – Tristayne had called her Zarihell – appeared dangerous, even by the standards of the creatures that inhabited the Mistlands. She was enigmatic, and her playful tone and smile hid something cold and terrible. Tomaz had dared speak against seeking her out again, but of course, Tristayne had not listened. As far as Tomaz understood, the necromancer believed Zarihell could teach him what Waiqar couldn't, or was refusing to. That seemed like an exceptionally dangerous thing to believe. Even from their brief encounters, the elf seemed untrustworthy and inscrutable. The fate that awaited Tristayne and, by extent, presumably Tomaz didn't bear thinking about if Waiqar discovered just how his apprentice had been tempted by another.

So they rode to Dalibor. Tristayne had told him that it was one of the two fiefdoms controlled by the vampire covens, alongside Bilehall. Tomaz had thankfully had little dealings with vampires since that terrible night when he had first arrived at Zorgas, for they rarely visited the Black Citadel. That at least was a small mercy. Some of the terrors of the Mistlands had started to become almost familiar to him, but the predatory threat of vampirism still chilled him.

Tristayne had complained to him repeatedly that Waiqar had not seen fit to take him on his campaign against Bilehall, who it seemed had risen in rebellion. Dalibor, apparently, had not joined them, though the fact that Zarihell was now leading them there did not bode well. Tomaz did his best to adhere to what he had learned – keep looking straight ahead, remain close to Tristayne, and try not to think of the myriad ways he might meet his end in this accursed forest.

Unexpectedly, he saw a light in the distance. It was not one of the pallid ghost orbs that haunted the marshes or winked in between the corpse trees on either side. It glowed yellow, like a true flame, a pinprick in the gathering dark.

It was joined by several more. As they drew closer, Tomaz understood what he was seeing. It was firelight glowing through the windows in a vast and crooked manse. It rose up out of the forest, a grand structure of stone and timber, with a tower framing both ends. It seemed to stand warped, almost bent over, likely having partially subsided into the marsh since it was first built. Still, its sheer size would have put the residences of many of Terrinoth's nobility to shame.

As they drew nearer, further signs of the mansion's dilapidation became apparent. The roof was sagging and the timbers rotten. The dozens of windows, most of them dark, were filmed with grime, and seemed to be watching them like rheumy eyes as the trio approached down the long path between the corpse trees. There was an air of brooding threat about the place, but also melancholy. If once it had housed a happy and respectable lord, it had not done so for a very long time.

Tomaz scratched at his throat as they came to a halt before the building's heavy wooden doors. It had been itching a lot, recently. He had seen Tristayne do similar before, rubbing at the bone of his spine, as though there was still flesh and blood there to be soothed. Tomaz wondered if he was unconsciously imitating the necromancer.

He dismounted with the others, putting rapid distance between himself and his undead steed before it could nip at his rear. The doors stood ahead, framed by statues that had long ago become too time-worn and broken to be decipherable. The first lords of Dalibor, Tomaz assumed, now long forgotten.

Zarihell led the way, opening the doors with a gesture. They creaked slowly apart, to reveal a gloomy hallway beyond. Before he crossed the threshold, Tomaz glanced up at one of the windows illuminated by the candlelight within. A figure stood there, a gaunt silhouette, watching them as they entered. Tomaz almost froze with fear.

The entrance hall was dark, but Zarihell once more issued a wordless command, and braziers along the walls ignited. They illuminated a dusty, decaying place, its grandeur faded. The floor was covered with threadbare carpets, the walls with old wooden paneling. A great staircase dominated the center, leading to a landing that branched to the left and right.

There was no sign of anyone else, either living or dead.

The air was not completely still though, but seemed to thrum gently, in time with a faint vibration that Tomaz felt running through the decrepit building.

"Does he know we are coming?" Tristayne asked Zarihell.

"He will soon enough," the elf replied without looking back, beginning to climb the stairs. They creaked heavily, and as Tomaz and Tristayne followed, the mortal was convinced they were about to collapse beneath them.

Zarihell turned to the right-hand flight where they branched away from each other, more braziers igniting as she passed, one by one. Tomaz saw portraits hanging upon the walls, but they were so thick with dust and cobwebs, and their varnish so darkened by age, that it was impossible to pick out a single detail. The thrumming grew more noticeable.

The stairs led to a corridor overseen by a skeletal figure in full plate armor. Tomaz expected it to bar their passage with the halberd it carried, but it showed no signs of sentience. A strange curiosity caught hold of Tomaz, and he paused to peer through the thing's vizor, standing on his tiptoes.

Whatever was wearing the suit, it wasn't the skeleton of a human, at least not any Tomaz had ever known. He stared at it with a mixture of fascination and revulsion, until Tristayne snarled at him.

"Don't dawdle, you whelp! And don't touch anything either!"

Tomaz scurried after him as Zarihell led them down the corridor. Though the walls were paneled like the entrance hall, the floor was bare stone. Tomaz could feel the air practically vibrating now, and tremors running beneath his feet. There was a whirring noise coming from somewhere up ahead, and the crooked doors that ran along the corridor rattled in their frames.

Tomaz shuddered, not knowing what awaited them at the far end. He had terrible recollections of the great engine of bone and black metal he had witnessed in the volcanic depths beneath the barrow city. Terror, or perhaps the benevolent hand of some deity, had robbed him of consciousness that time, and he had awoken in his cell wondering if it had been yet another nightmare. He had been too afraid to ask Tristayne about it. Now he feared he was being led to something similar.

A room waited at the end of the corridor. The door was ajar, and a strange, foul green light was spilling through, pulsating. Tomaz hung back as Zarihell stepped into it and pushed the door fully open, the light outlining her slender form.

He dared follow Tristayne as the necromancer went after her, entering the chamber.

Here the last trappings of a stately home had been completely laid aside. At first glance it almost looked like one of the practical teaching rooms where Tomaz had learned the art of the runestones. The floor and walls were cracked stone, while the wooden beams of the ceiling were sagging or split, with large gaps in the roof above. Rows of benches occupied the space, weighed down by vast amounts of paraphernalia. There were mounds of books and scrolls, beakers and test tubes, vials and glass orbs and contraptions of brass levers and cogs that Tomaz couldn't fathom. There were also body parts, and not just bones – all the stages of decay were present, and the stink of rotting flesh made Tomaz retch as he took it all in.

A pair of objects in the room's center seemed to be the source of both the vile light as well as the thrumming charge that filled the air and vibrated through the whole manse. Two brass spheres stood on poles formed from fused spinal columns, attached by a series of copper wires to a flat, circular metal plate between them. The plate was befouled with layers of blood and viscera, and charred remains filled its center. As Tomaz watched, a bolt of green lightning arced between the brass spheres with a crack, kicking out sparks and filling the air with actinic energy.

The whole chamber reeked of derangement. Tomaz could fathom none of it, but a weight of morbid curiosity made him move after Tristayne as the necromancer and Zarihell walked around the edge of the room, giving the crackling contraption in the middle a wide berth.

While the strange machine was clearly functioning in some capacity, there appeared to be no one present overseeing it, or working amidst the clutter. That was, until Tomaz's route took him toward the far side of the chamber, and he spotted the figure hunched over behind one of the benches in the corner.

It became aware of the interlopers just as they became aware of it. There was a snarl as it turned, still crouched, and lowered what it had clutched in its claws – a huge rat. The creature had been eating it.

It was, Tomaz realized, a vampire. He thought he recognized him from the first night in Zorgas, but it was difficult to tell – the creature was filthy, his gray flesh covered by a patina of old grave dirt and the fresh blood of the rat, which glistened darkly over his chin. His clothes, robes of russet brown and black, were similarly befouled. He was emaciated, and his claws were as long as Tomaz's fingers. His fangs, unlike the others Tomaz had seen, weren't as enlarged as his incisors, which he now bared at the intruders. Tomaz found that strange, though he also found himself wondering at the fact that his life had changed so dramatically that he was now mentally noting the physical differences between vampires.

Zarihell raised a hand before the creature could either attack or flee.

"Do not be concerned, my lord Dalibor," she said. "I bring you friends."

"Friendsss," the feral creature rattled, blood-red eyes locking onto Tomaz. "Or... food?"

Tomaz quailed behind Tristayne. Zarihell let out a little laugh.

"Friends for now, my lord. May I introduce Tristayne Olliven, the Deathless, apprentice to Waiqar, and his flesh-servant."

Dalibor emitted a strangled shriek and skittered back into the corner, still clutching his disgusting repast in one hand while pointing a grimy claw with the other.

"You bring Waiqar's apprentice here! You betray Dalibor!"

"Not yet, my dear, bloodsucking genius," Zarihell said. "None of us are here at the behest of Waiqar. I simply thought Tristayne might be able to assist us. He has great potential, potential that the Betrayer knows but refuses to utilize. Tristayne has grown tired of being held back, have you not?"

The question was directed at Tomaz's master, who seemed to hesitate before answering.

"I came here because of certain claims, certain promises," he said, obviously guarded. "I was told you had made great strides in the necromantic arts, Lord Dalibor."

Right now, it was difficult for Tomaz to imagine the creature before him making great strides in any sort of art, unless it was using blood for finger wall-daubing. Kyndrithul's eyes darted from Tristayne to Zarihell and back, his wicked incisors still bared, drooling the rat's viscera slowly onto the floor.

"He is still blood-drunk," Zarihell said to Tristayne, sounding almost apologetic. "His diet is… not the healthiest."

"I can hear you," Kyndrithul hissed.

"Good," Zarihell said, smiling. "Then take us down below. Tristayne is a dear friend, and he wishes to see the experiments."

"The experiments," Kyndrithul said, seeming to find a moment's clarity. "I must check on the experiments! But first… I want that one."

He pointed at Tomaz. The former student of Greyhaven felt his heart nearly stop. The terrible silence that followed seemed to last an age, as he stood rooted to the spot, convinced Tristayne was about to give the bestial thing leave to feast on his flesh.

"This living worm was a gift," Tristayne said eventually. "From Waiqar. You do not wish to rouse the Betrayer's ire, so I am sure you understand why I do not wish to either. You may not have him… not yet, anyway."

Tomaz's sense of relief was short-lived. Kyndrithul made a hideous, gargling moan of disappointment, but Zarihell spoke over it. Her words were charged with the arcane now, and even though they were not directed at him, Tomaz felt his body shudder and twitch, caught up in the force of her will.

"Time runs short, and I tire of your foolishness," she said, voice deep and riven with power. "You will take us to the depths of the manse, and you will do it now, Kyndrithul Dalibor."

The vampire obeyed.

The host of Zorgas broke the siege around the Red Keep and marched east.

Waiqar divided his forces into three, knowing it would make his arrival at Kelipa all the quicker. The columns of undead infantry and cavalry wound their way through the bogs, their deadlights a flickering stream of fire that glimmered faintly in the bitter, eternal fog.

When Waiqar's legion had first marched from Zorgas to Bilehall great packs of barghests and swarms of razorwings had flocked to the column from the surrounding marshes. They were drawn by the dark power of the Great Necromancer and his host, but when the campaign had turned to siegecraft many of the undead beasts had slunk back to their lairs. Now, however, as the host of Zorgas retraced its steps, they returned. Even without the opportunity to gorge themselves on the flesh, blood and bones of the cattle that Torvic kept beneath his keep, the promise of battle between armies of undeath was a potent means of attraction.

Waiqar leashed the creatures to his will and dispersed them ahead of his march, using them as his eyes and ears as he sought to put himself between the barrow mound of Kelipa and the oncoming heir of the Penacor kings.

He was aided by Farrenghast's age. Even forcing his march by channeling all his power into propelling his reanimates forward, the ancient undead ruler was not capable of covering ground as quickly as Waiqar. He was further hampered by the marshlands themselves, the spirit of which Waiqar had long ago tamed through the elemental arts he had learned under Timmorran. The Misty Hills were Farrenghast's fiefdom, the ground his to command, but beyond them the bogs would drag at the legs of the Penacor's warriors while yielding firmer paths for the winding columns of the Deathborn.

Even so, the abruptness of Farrenghast's march from the Misty Hills almost led to disaster. Waiqar sent Ardus and his cavalry ahead to try to force a presence in Kelipa before Farrenghast's own outriders reached it. The Deathborn were capable of their own forced march, but Waiqar was required to sink considerable amounts of energy and concentration into keeping the rest of his reanimates moving at pace, willing their own basic functions to move with more alacrity. Soon he was able to sense the barghests and razorwings he had leashed clashing in the distance with Farrenghast's own creatures. Not long later, a spirit orb arrived, moaning and gibbering news that he had hoped for – the soul had been sent by Ardus, who had repelled the head of Farrenghast's column just south of Kelipa.

Waiqar rode with the rest of the Deathborn Legion into the ancient, ruined city. He had his standard planted atop the barrow mound at its center and called a council of war.

CHAPTER SIXTEEN

Down Kyndrithul Dalibor took his visitors, through the manse and then further yet, to dank, crumbling cellars and crypts. Beyond even those was a warren of narrow tunnels, burrowed into the dead soil beneath the mansion and spreading like a hidden infection under the surrounding forest.

Tristayne had never journeyed to the Dalibor estate before, and he had little expected what awaited him. Kyndrithul was known as a dabbler in experiments, an unstable genius according to some, but what Tristayne had seen so far defied comprehension. He was on his guard, wary of betrayal at every turn. Zarihell had shown clear influence over Kyndrithul, but how far did it extend, and did she intend to use Tristayne in the same way? There were greater schemes at play, he was certain, and yet still the ultimate, tantalizing prize lay just before him, drawing him on. Power without recourse to the Deathborn dust or any other petty artefact or demon-curse. An ability currently beyond any in Terrinoth.

Dalibor, at least, became more coherent the further they walked. The worst of the blood haze left him, though he continued to carry the dead rat in one hand, and would occasionally gnaw on it. The vampire walked with a stooped gait, and seemed to have abandoned all the tarnished trappings of nobility that so many of the other vampire lords clung to pathetically. Tristayne wasn't sure whether to be disgusted or intrigued by the strange figure.

"You must forgive my caution," Kyndrithul said as he led them down a set of dirt steps and through an uneven, sloping tunnel ankle-deep in brackish water. "These are difficult times. You all must know of the Bilehall brood's rebellion?"

"Of course," Tristayne said, using the haft of the Black Scythe to help guide him through the muck. "Many in Zorgas were surprised you did not throw your lot in with your kin."

"Kyndrithul's experiments are far more important than Torvic's petty power struggles," Zarihell said, seemingly speaking for Dalibor. "Isn't that so?"

"Of course," Kyndrithul said. "Naythen Torvic's arrogance is second only to that of the Betrayer. Both will become insignificant once my work here is complete."

"And just what work is that, Lord Dalibor?" Tristayne asked pointedly. The vampire replied through a mouthful of half-chewed rat.

"You shall see soon enough, necromancer."

The tunnel became wider, held up, it seemed, by the dead roots of the corpse trees that protruded in knots and bundles across the ceiling and along the walls. There were doors now as well, to the left and right, dozens, built from timber but daubed with warding sigils and binding magics. They began to rattle as the group passed by, and an unearthly shrieking went up, filling the corridor.

"My children are hungry," Kyndrithul said, casting a glance back toward Tomaz. Tristayne deliberately blocked him.

"You will show me these experiments," he told the vampire. "And explain to me the merit of your work. I am in no mood for games or riddles, not anymore."

Dalibor grimaced and turned to Zarihell, but the elf offered him neither support nor instruction. The vampire gestured curtly to the nearest door.

"See for yourself then, Deathless One."

Tristayne stepped up to the door and peered through the slat in it. He could feel death energies beyond, held in check by the markings carved and daubed onto the wood.

The thing inside howled at him. It was a monstrosity, a misshapen conglomeration of flesh, bone, and bared muscle. It had two heads, one canine and rotted to the bone, the other that of a human woman, but blinded. The torso was swollen and grotesque, with extra, grasping limbs that had been grafted with wicked claws and spiny protrusions. The lower half was little more than a long sleeve of flesh, like the tail end of a great worm, that thrashed and writhed as the monstrosity flung itself at the door, clattering at it furiously as it shrieked from its suture-lined throats.

Tristayne didn't so much as flinch. The abhorrent creature, along with bone constructs, were among the easiest things to give un-life to. The fact that Kyndrithul had filled the underbelly of his estate with them was hardly surprising. Clearly, they gave him an opportunity to indulge his crazed passions for anatomy and cadaver-sowing, but it was far from impressive. He was simply a vampire with an imagination, and too much spare time.

"Is this all you have to show me?" Tristayne demanded, feeling a keen sense of disappointment. Did they think him a fool? Were they mocking him? To his surprise, Kyndrithul let out a wet little chuckle.

"Patience," he hissed, warding Tristayne away from the door before opening it.

Tristayne assumed the flesh-and-bone horror within would rip the vampire apart, but he was to be disappointed. Instead of clawing its way to freedom, it ceased its screaming and dragged itself out placidly, both heads bowed. Kyndrithul extended a hand and it nuzzled into him, like a grotesque parody of a faithful hound. Then, seemingly almost as an afterthought, the vampire tossed it the gnawed remnants of his rat. The thing yapped and gurgled as the two heads fought over the remains. Tristayne watched the display dispassionately.

"Come," Kyndrithul rasped, though whether it was to the horror or the others was unclear. They all followed, the abhorrent dragging itself along in Kyndrithul's wake, Tristayne trailing behind, refusing to sully himself by getting too close to it.

They reached the end of the tunnel, where a chamber was waiting, dug into the dirt and rock, an earthy, festering, dank space far removed from the black stone and volcanic wrath Tristayne had lately experienced when he had journeyed to see the Everliving Engine. It was arrayed similarly to the laboratory they had already seen in the manse itself, though here there was an even greater profusion of clutter and strange, arcane devices. A larger version of the two brass orbs he had seen in the manse had been set up here, their poles made from fused, moaning corpses, green lightning crackling back and forth endlessly and casting lurid, unnatural light across the chamber. It seemed as though the floor was composed entirely of skeletal remains, thousands upon thousands of bones packed hard together to create a jagged, crunching surface.

There were more abhorrents too, malformed, stitched-up nightmares of all shapes and sizes, kept in cages and pens all around the room's edges. They let up an unseemly clamor as Kyndrithul and his companions entered, like some cursed menagerie. Tristayne felt a surge of utter revulsion. Most of the creatures were more alive than dead, and their beating hearts and squirming flesh were utterly repulsive to him. He stomached his disgust as best he could, focusing on Kyndrithul as the vampire approached the lightning contraption.

He bade the pet he had brought from the tunnel shamble its way in between the two orbs. The vampire then splayed his long, talon-tipped fingers, and planted his hand on one of the devices. With a hissed word, it spat an arc of green energy across to its twin, transfixing the abhorrent as it did so.

The creature exploded.

Tristayne stared for a moment at the carnage, before slowly wiping a gobbet of steaming offal from his brow.

Tomaz had managed to leap behind him just in time to avoid the ugly shower.

"Is this a joke?" Tristayne demanded.

Neither Zarihell nor Kyndrithul replied. Tristayne was considering storming out when he realized something was happening. The floor was moving.

The space immediately around the brass orbs was starting to shift. With a dull, grinding noise, the bones that comprised the floor had started to raise themselves up. The shapes they were knitting together were far from certain, yet there was no doubting that some sort of sentience existed there. Tristayne could feel the electrical charge that gave them life, and the elemental Mortos responding. But where had it come from? There had been no bone dust involved.

Dalibor had removed his hand from the orb and had raised both, chanting. It was the Black Invocation.

Tristayne experienced a moment of awe. The dead were rising. The forms they were taking on were not especially humanoid – they were bone constructs, rivalling abhorrents as the lowest form of necromantic summoning – but they were aware. They dragged themselves up all around the twin orbs, ghastly conglomerates clattering and rattling as they were puppeted by the foul magics.

He had done it. Somehow, Kyndrithul Dalibor had discovered how to raise the dead himself.

And then, abruptly, it all came undone. Pierces of bone began to fall away, skulls, femurs and pelvic bones cracking as they bounced back down to the broken floor. The constructs lost what little coherence they had, their waking motions growing sluggish before ceasing altogether. Kyndrithul's chanting continued, but it became ever more strained and desperate. He was fighting the tide, Tristayne saw, struggling in vain to maintain the conduit of death energies to his new creations. The very matter of the constructs seemed to rebel at being used this way, snuffing out the unnatural un-life that Kyndrithul was trying to drag into existence. Whatever Kyndrithul had done to raise the dead, it was not enough.

The vampire gave up on the Invocation, screeching with raw frustration. The last of the constructs fell apart, their remains rejoining the carpet of bones underfoot. Tristayne gazed at where they had once stood, then at the orbs, for some time. Eventually he looked at Dalibor, who was panting, baring his long fangs in anger. Tristayne said a single word.

"How?"

The vampire seemed loath to answer. Zarihell spoke for him.

"The abhorrents are the key," she said.

"In what way?"

"They were created in part using bone dust, liberated from the depths of Zorgas."

"So there is still bone dust required?" Tristayne asked, feeling cheated. "We are not truly any closer to being free from Waiqar's minions."

"We are," Kyndrithul said, taking over the narration, seemingly stung by Tristayne's tone. "I need the bone dust no more. It is only necessary for the first generation of these creatures to be imbued with it. After that their spawn remain redolent with it."

"Their spawn?" Tristayne said.

"We are capable of producing more," Kyndrithul said, speaking slowly, as though he thought Tristayne incapable of understanding him.

"And those offspring remain potent with the potential carried by the bone dust," Zarihell added. "We can create a legion of these creatures, the remains of which can in turn produce countless reanimates."

"All that is necessary is the charge of the orbs," Kyndrithul said. "That electrifies the blood of the abhorrents and gives it potency. It is where the consciousness of the newly risen originates from, rather than relying purely on the elemental Mortos."

It all sounded ridiculous to Tristayne, and yet there was a perverse reasoning behind it all. If the necromantic potency of the dust was now carried on through the bloodlines – and literal blood – of these misbegotten creatures, then the need for the bones of the Deathborn had truly been severed. Yet, problems remained.

"They are not stable," he said. "The constructs you sought to raise with the blood. You could not maintain them. Reality has cut their strings."

"Which is why I have brought you here, Tristayne Olliven," Zarihell said, ignoring Kyndrithul's glowering expression. "Whether Waiqar knows it or not, whether he appreciates it, you are a potent practitioner of the necromantic arts. By combining your abilities with those of Lord Dalibor, we may yet break through the resistance of the natural laws and create something… permanent."

"True enough," Tristayne allowed. There were none

more potent than he, save Waiqar himself. Now Zarihell's reasoning became clear.

"Bring out another of your abhorrents, Kyndrithul," he told Dalibor. "And I will lend you my abilities."

Dalibor seemed less than thrilled at being told what to do, but his twitching excitement at the prospect of a breakthrough overcame his arrogance. One of the chamber's cages was opened and another hissing, lumbering monstrosity was lured out and directed in between Kyndrithul's charged device.

The orb's energies annihilated it. As stinking blood rained down, Tristayne grasped the Black Scythe in both hands and cracked its haft into the bones before him, his head bowed. Tomaz edged away, clattering into one of the detritus-heaped tables, ignored by all else in the chamber bar the hungering abhorrents that lashed and rattled their cages around its edges.

Tristayne focused his mind, feeling the power that had once again been unleashed around him. The blood of the abhorrent, charged with the orb's energies and that of the dust, was trickling down into the charnel pit that formed the base of the chamber, running like life-giving water toward seeds of consciousness. It took root and began to grow.

Tristayne started to chant, earlier than Kyndrithul had. He bent the familiar words of the Black Invocation to his will, summoning the magic of the realm beyond and sending it surging down through the blood, trying to lash it onto the rising sentience.

He succeeded. The tortured bones began stirring once

more, put together piece by piece by Tristayne's magics. Kyndrithul picked up the incantation, the potency of the dark powers being called on so great that even an uninitiated mortal like Tomaz would be able to see the elemental Mortos as ghost lights and streams of pale, luminescent ectoplasm.

Again, the dead rose, though this time there was more coherence, more certainty. They were not merely constructs either. Tristayne's chanting had bound together ribs and spines and skulls properly, forming true reanimates. There were over a dozen, their bones red with the blood of the abhorrent.

They stood before Tristayne. He could feel the tremulous nature of their binding, how the natural laws fought against them, sought to unmake them even as Tristayne put them together. The bone dust rendered such resistance mute, and while he could still sense some of its presence in the bodies before him, it was altogether more difficult to hold them together against nature's wrath.

He used the Black Scythe as a locus, something he had not done for a long time, opening himself to the power of the unholy realm it was linked to. A thick, tar-like substance began to ooze not only from the scythe, but from Tristayne's body as well, drooling thickly from between his clenched teeth and pouring out of his nose. He could hear the screaming of the souls trapped within the scythe, souls whose essence he ripped and defiled, pillaging them for their energies.

He slammed what they gave him into the foul words he was spitting, no longer aware of what was happening in the rest of the chamber, of Tomaz or Zarihell or even Kyndrithul and his own version of the incantation. Every ounce of his mind, body and soul was being channeled into raising up and holding together the reanimates. They remained standing before him, though they shook and rattled.

Tristayne let out a snarl that rose steadily to a roar of effort. Finally, with a surge of exhilaration, he saw deadlights flare into life in their bloody eye sockets, a sign of true consciousness. The flames were the same sickly yellow as his own.

The dead lived, though not for much longer. Binding and awakening them had almost burned him out, maintaining them now would surely be too much. The dark bile of the Black Realm was choking his throat and pooling amidst the other remains still at his feet. He felt his own bones starting to crack and split under the strain. Finally, howling, he let go.

There was a crash, a shockwave of death magic shrieking out through the chamber. Like puppets whose strings had been abruptly snapped, the reanimates standing before Tristayne clattered apart, the lights in their skulls snuffed out. Some of the bone shards crumbled entirely, reduced to dust by the weight of the magics they had been imbued with.

It did not matter. Tristayne had done it. He had raised the dead with his own will and, for a few precious moments, had felt their awareness, their ability to follow his commands. Never before had he accomplished that, summoning reanimates without the bone dust or some arcane artefact. And if he had done it once, he could do it again, and again, for longer and with more.

He began to laugh, a dry, rasping sound that echoed around the subterranean chamber as it settled in the aftermath of the howling deluge of dark magics.

Now, finally, everything would change.

CHAPTER SEVENTEEN

Upon the barrow mound of Kelipa, amidst the eternal, faint ticking of the Everliving Engine, Waiqar laid out his strategy.

Karrow, Melkor, and Mirabelle were all present, along with the other cohort commanders, a wedge of death knights that stood arrayed around their master, black and purple standards fluttering above them. Waiqar did not consult them. He had already formulated how the battle was to be conducted. He simply needed them to understand.

"Ardus will command the cavalry," he explained. "On the left wing." The Deathborn lieutenant was the only senior warrior absent, charged with maintaining a screen of riders out among the ruins of Kelipa, to disrupt Penacor's forces if they arrived with speed.

"Karrow, you will marshal the right and Melkor the center," Waiqar continued, the witch-fire of the Deathborn flaring with understanding as he spoke. "I will hold the reserve here, atop the crest of the mound."

"We are to fight defensively, lord?" Karrow said. "It may be that we outnumber the Penacor."

"We do not, and besides, numbers are immaterial," Waiqar said, silencing Karrow, not appreciating the interruption. "All that matters is standing between Farrenghast and the route to the Everliving Engine beneath us. That is why he is here. If he wishes to claim it, he must attack."

The discussion was interrupted by the sound of distant horns. Waiqar had felt the presence of Farrenghast looming closer all the while, but now as he turned, he was able to see the actual army of the last Penacor king emerging from the mist.

They came in a column at first, a long block of spears and standards that loomed jagged from the mist, passing around and through the ruins to the south. The lead contingent wheeled to the right, while the main body carried on, only halting when it was almost at the foot of the barrow mound. The rearguard turned left, and the column became a line, facing up toward the barrow hill.

A shape materialized ahead of the front ranks of the Penacor host.

Ardus was approaching, mounted on his rotting steed. Loping alongside him was a wolf-like creature that Waiqar initially took to be a barghest, before he recognized it as Farrenghast's emissary. It rose onto its hind legs and walked as it drew closer, its shaggy black pelt receding slightly while it assumed a more human aspect.

"Farrenghast sends his dog to parley with us, lord," Ardus said, pulling up his mount before Waiqar and lowering his axe to block the beast before it could get any closer to the Great Necromancer.

"On your knees before the Undying, animal," the undead knight snapped.

The shapeshifter glared from Ardus to Waiqar, its lupine gaze showing no fear. His name was Voldart, and he had been bound to serve the Penacors for as long as records existed. Legend claimed he was one of the first men, and had been cursed with a bestial aspect when he had committed the first murder. Waiqar did not believe such tales, though his apparent immortality was, in itself, intriguing.

Wisely, Voldart knelt.

"You bring word from your master?" Waiqar demanded.

"King Penacor wishes to parley," the beast snarled, his fangs making speech difficult. "Between the lines."

"Farrenghast exposes his weakness," Waiqar observed. "I see no reason to parley."

Voldart grunted, cuffing drool from his distended maw on the back of his forearm before continuing.

"You are without your vampire pets. You are out-numbered. Speak to my king, and perhaps your slaughter will be averted."

"Shall I cut this wretch down, lord?" Ardus asked Waiqar, visibly burning with the desire to behead the creature.

"Go back to your dusty master," Waiqar told Voldart, ignoring his lieutenant's question. There were times when it was good to face an enemy head-on, to assess their strengths and weaknesses in person. He wanted to see if the Penacor was still the weak old fool he had been when he had last challenged Waiqar. "Tell him I will see him at the foot of the barrow."

Voldart rose and turned, departing without another

word. He bounded down the barrow's slope, dropping onto all fours, his wolf aspect taking hold once more as he loped back to his master.

Waiqar considered the message he had borne. It was unusual for Farrenghast to want to talk. More than any other in the Mistlands – perhaps more than anyone in all of existence – he despised Waiqar. The wayward son of the Penacor kings of old, it was said he had made a pact with a demon who had sworn to save him after his father imprisoned him for his crimes in the dread tower of Nerek. The creature had neither freed him, nor interceded before his hanging, but after his corpse had been laid to rest the Ynfernael had reanimated him and his followers. The demon had granted him a great host of reanimates with which he had carved out his fiefdom in the Misty Hills. His power had been greatest during the rise of Timmorran, when he had threatened to overthrow the Daqan lands.

While still living, Waiqar had been sent with his legion to stop the undead Penacor. They had met in a great and desperate battle at Black Bog, on the edge of what eventually became the Mistlands. It was the first time Waiqar had encountered the living dead. The horror he had felt at the time had long faded into oblivion, but he still remembered the desperate slaughter, as the tide had swung one way and then another, both sides battling for control of a ridge line amidst the teeming rain.

Eventually, Ardus's cavalry, held in reserve, had made it up the slope and crushed Farrenghast's left flank. The undead host had collapsed, and the living had triumphed. Farrenghast had withdrawn to his ruinous keep in the Misty

Hills. The pressures of the war with the Uthuk Y'llan had stopped Waiqar from pursuing – fate had instead drawn him to battle at Timmorran's side in southern Talindon, and then on to the doomed expedition to Charg'r and the Black Citadel. Farrenghast had been left, forgotten in his bleak hills, to lick his wounds and slumber in his ancient tomb.

How ironic it was that, while he slept, events played out that would eventually result in Waiqar joining him in undeath. After the slaying of Timmorran, the Black Rain and the defeat at the hands of the combined armies of humans, elves and dwarfs, Waiqar had withdrawn to the Mistlands to recover his own strength. Farrenghast had awoken, initially mocking Waiqar for having become the same unliving monster he had once battled against.

The mockery had not lasted long. Waiqar's grasp of necromancy was far superior to Farrenghast's, and the ancient Penacor had suffered a second defeat to Waiqar's legion, now in their guise as the Deathborn.

Farrenghast had tried many times to overthrow Waiqar's mastery of the Mistlands since then. Waiqar could not easily recall how many battles had been fought down the millennia. Always, Farrenghast had failed, driven back to his stronghold in the Misty Hills. Waiqar in turn would occasionally attempt to seize the crumbling citadels and fastnesses along the Mistlands' bleak south-eastern border, but the cost to the Deathborn was always too great to pursue a campaign to completion. He could not waste their priceless bones, nor risk Farrenghast acquiring them.

It had been some centuries since the Penacor had last

roused himself. Waiqar had wondered if the ancient king had slipped into some final, eternal rest. He hadn't anticipated his sudden reappearance, let alone the aggressive lunge of his host toward the Everliving Engine. The Ynfernael energies that had raised Farrenghast and his host could not be replicated or channeled reliably, and by capturing the Engine the Penacor would finally be able to reinforce his withered hosts.

That was surely his goal, but there was also something more at work behind Farrenghast's return. It was not just mere opportunism, brought on by Bilehall's rebellion. A hidden hand was stirring up all the forces that had opposed Waiqar in the Mistlands.

In a way, he was thankful for it. Everything was progressing as he had planned.

"*Penacor is weak,*" said Baelziffar, unbidden. "*The one who raised him has long abandoned him. His magic grows ever fainter. Every time he summons his host, fewer of his warriors rise from their crypts. This may be his last opportunity to challenge Zorgas. To challenge you.*"

"The old fool will crumble into dust before he claims the Mistlands from me," Waiqar assured the demon.

"Indeed, lord," Ardus said, clearly thinking Waiqar had been addressing him. Waiqar turned his attention to the Deathborn.

"We shall see what the fallen Penacor has to say," he decided. "You and Mirabelle shall accompany me, and your cohort. Melkor will have command of the rest of the legion in my absence."

•••

Waiqar rode to the foot of the barrow at the head of a phalanx of Deathborn knights. Each was a mighty warrior of yore, clad in battered and scarred black armor, plates and barding clattering and scraping as they rode. Their shields and tabards were emblazoned with the black and purple of Zorgas, and great weapons hung at their sides or were clutched in their steel gauntlets, their notched edges bearing old and bitter curses of biting and cutting. Ardus and Mirabelle led just behind Waiqar, the former bearing Waiqar's great standard, streaming like a specter in the mist that closed in around them.

Waiqar rode at the fore, the very air around him suffused with the moaning of the spirits that were dragged to him by the sheer force of his subconscious will. He halted his steed as ahead the Penacor delegation emerged from the mist.

Two lich priests led the way, holding ceremonial staves bearing the ancient bronze insignia of the Penacors. Behind came a palanquin borne up by a dozen bone constructs, their bodies fused and bent beneath its weight. The majority of it was composed of Farrenghast's sarcophagus, a great slab of black stone that had been brought from its resting place in the Misty Hills. Farrenghast himself sat within, bony hands clutching the sides. He was partially mummified, his face still bearing vestiges of skin, hideously shrunken, like ancient, tanned leather. A long, white beard hung from his jaw, and strands of white hair framed the twisted face beneath a crown of tarnished gold. The eyes were small slits, and only a hint of golden witch-fire glimmered within them.

The sarcophagus was dragged toward Waiqar, flanked on

either side by Farrenghast's guards, the Children of Nerek. They were equipped with bronze armor, their skeletal remains moving with the creaking jerkiness of great age. Despite their seeming antiquity, Waiqar knew better than to underestimate them. He had fought them enough times to know that they were almost the equals of his own knights.

Farrenghast's procession came to a clattering halt, and two skeletons carrying rusting carnyx sounded them, the death magics causing the relic instruments to vent forth their braying noise. Waiqar felt a pulse of disdain as he considered the ridiculous trappings Farrenghast still clung to.

Another of the old king's emissaries, a curious creature that was part skeleton, part phantom, stepped forward between the lich priests and called out in a rasping voice.

"Behold, His Majesty King Penacor, the Eternal, First of the Immortals, King of north, south, east, and west!"

The carnyx made their ugly sound again. Waiqar remained still and motionless on his mount. Ardus rode forward past him and bellowed, his voice echoing around in every skull within Kelipa.

"Behold, Waiqar the Great, the Undying, Rightful King of all Terrinoth!"

Ardus made way for Waiqar to spur his horse alongside Farrenghast's sarcophagus. The guards of both undead lords formed a semicircle around them, which only four others remained within – Ardus and Mirabelle, Farrenghast's herald, and the lupine Voldart, who slunk into sight from behind the sarcophagus's bulk.

"Why are you here, Penacor?" Waiqar demanded, fixing

Descent: Legends of the Dark

his gaze on the wizened, dead king. "You must know you cannot win. Your time has long since passed."

"One day I will teach you a lesson in respect, Betrayer," Farrenghast rasped. "Perhaps sooner than you think. The power of the Everliving Engine is wasted on you."

"That is why you have come then?" Waiqar asked. "To steal what I have built?"

"You could not have built the Engine," Farrenghast scoffed. "Perhaps you found it unfinished down there in the depths and were able to complete it, or perhaps you sold some part of your pathetic soul to a demon in exchange for the knowledge. But do not claim a genius of your own, Betrayer. You have always been in the shadow of others."

Waiqar knew Farrenghast was trying to spite him into striking a blow. That was likely why he had requested a parley in the first place. Kill Waiqar, and the battle would be over before it began. Still, he was confident the ancient fool would not dare.

"I have not sought you out, Farrenghast," he said. "It is you who comes here seeking me, seeking battle. Leave while you still may, and both our armies will remain intact. There are more important matters looming than our old rivalry."

"You speak with contrition," Farrenghast said. "A rarity for you. It only shows you for the weakling that you are. I know the truth. I have been shown it. Where are your blood-drinking slaves, hmm?"

"Closer than you think," Waiqar said. "Did the one who told you the truth also tell you that Bilehall serves Zorgas once more?"

Farrenghast vented a dry, dusty laugh.

"I do not believe you, Betrayer. You have been abandoned by your allies. You are weaker than you have been for a long time. I will not pass up that opportunity. I summoned you only to offer you a chance to surrender. Unbind your army and go, and I shall accept your exile. It is more than you deserve."

Waiqar's anger seethed. His grip tightened around Bitterbite, the sword still sheathed by his side. With a dull scrape, the guards all around began to slowly raise their own weapons, deadlights flickering dangerously.

"*Do not,*" Baelziffar murmured. "*Not yet.*"

Waiqar unclenched his grip on his sword, forcing down his ire.

"We will end this feud upon this hill, Penacor," he spat. "You have insulted me for the last time."

Ignoring Farrenghast's cackling, he turned his steed and spurred back toward the crest of the barrow.

CHAPTER EIGHTEEN

It began as it so often did. Farrenghast threw forward a loose line of reanimate archers intending to rain arrows down upon Waiqar's hilltop position. Waiqar in turn willed his own archers down the slope to intercept them before they found their range.

Against mortal foes, the shards of bone loosed by the long-dead bow warriors of Zorgas were terrifying weapons. The thrice-cursed projectiles bore spells of withering and decay that could rot a living being inside-out in seconds or age them into oblivion in just as little time. Against other reanimates, however, they possessed no particular potency.

Waiqar watched the skirmish from the back of his steed, looking over the serried ranks of the dismounted Deathborn down the slope. He remained unimpressed. Farrenghast, it seemed, was still hidebound by old, stale strategies. Perhaps he hoped to goad Waiqar down from the barrow mound, but the Undying had no intention of shifting his forces prematurely. He was in a good defensive position, blocking the Penacor from his objective. If the Misty Hills wished to claim the Everliving Engine, they would have to climb the slope.

Eventually it seemed Farrenghast also grew disillusioned with the archery duel. The bow-armed reanimates withdrew back to the main ranks of the Penacor army.

Whatever alacrity had prompted Farrenghast to march on the Everliving Engine, it now appeared to have gone. The formations of reanimates remained still and unmoving. Eventually, Waiqar discovered why.

Lady Falgor materialized in his presence. He could sense the apprehension of the ghastly spirit as it shivered before him, speech badly out of sync.

"The dead speak of another host approaching, Great Necromancer," she said, voice only a little short of a howl. "From the west, one that hungers for slaughter."

The news did not surprise Waiqar. He dismissed Falgor curtly, already able to sense the oncoming menace in the stirring of magics around him. It was a gamble, he knew, but he had weighed the odds well. He always did. Now only time would tell if his calculations were correct.

Soon the host itself became visible, passing up onto the crest of one of the lesser barrows to the west, on the right flank of Waiqar's legion and the left of Farrenghast's. Waiqar could see the black and crimson banners of Bilehall and the personal crest of Naythen Torvic, the horned dragon. More importantly, his sister's standard was flying alongside it. That was well. The sister had proven herself the more manageable of the pair. She had come to Waiqar and forced her brother to do likewise just as news of the march of Farrenghast's host had arrived. Offering them the suggestion of a pardon would serve his needs, for now.

The Bilehall host paused upon the mound. A deathly stillness settled over the ruins of Kelipa. The howls of the barghests receded, and even the shrieks and wails of the gheists haunting both sides grew muted. Waiqar could sense the attention of his advisors and lieutenants on him, but he made no move, gave no instruction. Even the elemental Mortos surrounding him remained still.

The note of a single, lonely carnyx sounded from amidst the ranks of Farrenghast's army, far below. It was taken up by more, until the braying tones resounded through Kelipa. Waiqar could feel the power transmitted by the arcane horns stirring the ranks of the Penacor host.

There was an audible clatter of armor and bones as the undead cohorts moved forward. In lockstep, the three forward sections of the Penacor host – the main battle, with the vanguard on the right and the rearguard on the left – began to advance on the barrow hill.

Waiqar sent a wordless command to the Deathborn lieutenants commanding the regular reanimates of his own force. They acted as conduits for his will, ensuring he did not have to puppet the entire army alone. They spread his command through the energies linking every walking corpse back to Waiqar. As one the hunched skeletons stood straight and tall, bringing their shields clattering together and hefting spears or drawing swords. The horn blowers sent out defiant calls, battling against the rival blaring of the carnyx.

"Begin your ride, Ardus," Waiqar instructed. The

Deathborn inclined his head and wheeled his steed away, signaling to his cavalry to close in as he did so. Waiqar could sense his lieutenant's cold will energized by a fiery desire to emulate past glories against the Penacor. Despite himself, Waiqar felt a momentary thrill of his own. He had not anticipated facing Farrenghast, and yet here he was, drawn forth from his fastness. It was an opportunity to gain true, total control over the entirety of the Mistlands, once and for all.

"*Do not pass it up,*" Baelziffar murmured.

The Penacor army began to climb the slope. The Zorgas formations opposing their central battle were mostly reanimates from the summoning fields – Waiqar had placed his Deathborn cohorts either on the barrow's flanks, or in reserve. He had no intention of wasting any more of his old legion than was necessary.

As the Penacor infantry began to mount the incline, the archers once again started to play. A blizzard of bone shards fell upon both sides, cracking off ribs and skulls or jarring against ancient shields, helms, and breastplates. Several of the Deathborn nearest to him raised their shields to protect him.

A barbed hail of death. Blood in the rain, swilling in the bottom of the valley. Uthuk roars, the howling of demons, coming for him.

He thrust the unbidden memories angrily back down to the depths where they belonged, and dismissed the shield-bearers with a thought. The Penacor missiles were falling short of him, striking the front line of his reanimates.

On Farrenghast's main battleline came, driven by the

ancient king's arrogance and defiance. As they neared the crest and the razor-crown of swords and spears that waited for them, the wind caught their standards, whipping the mold-blotched streaks of cloth, showing the Penacor device of the crowned – now skeletal – griffon as it reached its claws to lock with the antlers of the stag of Zorgas.

Seconds before Farrenghast's line dragged itself to contact, Waiqar thrust an imperative into the skulls of his own reanimates. They stepped off, thrusting themselves down the dozen paces of barrow-dirt into the oncoming foe.

The two sides collided upon the slope with a thunderous crash. Shield met shield as a furious bout of pushing, driven by the necromantic masters on either side, saw one line attempt to force the other back. Spears stabbed and swords and axes rose and fell, clanging from helmets or breastplates or splitting and shattering bones. The standards of both armies wavered, but neither gave ground.

Waiqar didn't move. He had fought and commanded in a thousand battles, some while living, many while dead. There were times for action, and times for stillness. Now was the latter.

Reanimates did not tire like living mortals, and so the slope of the barrow mound had presented less of an obstacle to the Penacor advance than it would have done to any other attacker. There were no muscles to ache, no sinews to strain, no breath to struggle in lungs or throat. Nevertheless, height still offered an advantage to Waiqar's front line. His reanimates were able to drive downward with their spears and slash at heads and shoulders, while the Penacor dead were forced to raise their shields high to guard themselves from the blows of those striking from above.

After a short while, the advantage began to tell. More of Farrenghast's host were falling, ribs shattered and skulls staved in. Yet even then, many still rose clumsily from the mud and continued the fight until they had been hacked into splintered shards. Waiqar could feel the reason for their defiance in his own bones – it was the Everliving Engine, buried deep below but still exerting its awesome power over the dead of both armies, revitalizing them and keeping them intact even when the willpower of those controlling them waned. Waiqar had anticipated its influence, and could hear the ticking of the great wheel, grinding up the living and churning out the dead. It filled him with such energy, such potency, that it made him want to ride straight down into the enemy and unleash his full might.

He restrained himself. The time for that would come.

Penacor's front line withdrew down the slope a few dozen paces, keeping their formation. There they halted, marshalling themselves, the magic that had momentarily grown weak around them redoubling.

The carnyx horns brayed once more. Again, the dead were driven up the slope, and battle was rejoined.

Ardus signaled a halt. The rest of his cavalry cohort pulled up behind him, ancient armor scraping and clicking as the knights of Zorgas reformed.

He had brought them down the eastern slope of the

barrow, riding through the ruinous streets of Kelipa until they reached one of the ancient, overgrown squares near the edge of the lost city. It gave them the space to reform, and for Ardus to assess their position.

While the wind had driven much of the mist from the barrow itself, it continued to hang about the lower reaches of the city, rendering the ruins as gaunt, jagged silhouettes surrounding the cohort. There were shapes moving there as well, accompanied by snarls and howls. Loosed by their masters, the barghests and razorwings that had flocked to both armies were battling in the ruins, fangs and talons put to use in a feral fight for supremacy that mirrored the main battle nearby. None dared approach the knights of Zorgas though.

Ardus stood in his stirrups, gazing intently forward and then right. He could sense the presence of the right flank of Penacor's army, its vanguard, somewhere ahead, but he could not yet see it. After their initial advance, Farrenghast was holding his wings back, letting the central battle drive up the barrow. That would make turning his flank difficult, meaning the advantage of having a broad front striking at the narrower enemy formation would be negated. There would be no immediate repeat of the Battle of Black Bog.

There were two solutions. Ardus knew he could ride further east, coming wide around the Penacor flank and eventually turning it. Alternatively, he could hold his position here in the square and wait. His lord's position atop the great barrow mound was a strong one. He had no doubt that at some point, Farrenghast would be forced to commit the infantry on his wings. At that point they would expose themselves, and Ardus would be able to drive into them from the side.

That was the plan. There was a third option, of course, the one that appealed to Ardus the most – ride forth immediately, and charge head-on into the center of the enemy's right. The thought caused him to tighten his grip on his axes until the bones of his hands cracked.

He had lost much since his first death. Existence was a cold, numbing experience, but if there was one thing that made him feel as though he was alive again it was the slaughter in the midst of battle. He knew that it was a peculiarity restricted to a select few of the Deathborn, that most of his undying kin now thought nothing of their unfeeling existence, but he could not throw off the need to experience that rush, even if it was only the phantom memory of a pounding heart and strong sinews. It was an addiction he craved, one that could only be sated in combat.

And yet, the time had not yet come. He had been commanded by his master to remain close upon the wings and wait for the proper moment to commit Zorgas' mounted might. He was nothing if not utterly loyal. Orders were orders. In life as in death, it was that discipline that ran as a single, unbreakable thread throughout his existence.

The killing would come soon enough, of that he was certain.

CHAPTER NINETEEN

Farrenghast shifted himself in his sarcophagus, hacking up a series of dry coughs. They were not true coughs, of course, for his throat was now bone with only a few scraps of leathery flesh bound to it by moldering tomb shrouds, but it was force of habit. He leaned forward, his ancient bones creaking, witch-fire flaring golden in his eyes.

He drove his main battle up the slope for a fourth time. The barrow mound of Kelipa loomed over him, surmounted by the bristling array of Waiqar's host, the accursed horned skull standard of the Betrayer fluttering from its pinnacle. Farrenghast craved to tear it down and rip it to shreds with his own shaking hand, before having Waiqar's remains crushed under the weight of his sarcophagus. Even more, though, he craved what lay beneath the barrow and the battling armies.

He needed Waiqar's invention, the great machine he had heard stories of down the millennia. For a long time, he had thought it a myth, an invention of propaganda designed to raise Waiqar's stature. The spirits he had captured and interrogated down the ages could not all be lying though. He could hear the Engine now, a relentless ticking, and he could feel it. It reached into his old remains and charged them as though with a bolt of lightning. It put strength and vitality into his limbs and clarity into his thoughts.

He felt something that he had long ago forgotten, something that had turned to dust in his flickering consciousness and lain disturbed for eons. He felt *alive*.

He had to have it. He had to have the Engine. Crushing Waiqar to reach it only made it all the sweeter.

The enemy were pinned to their crest, locked in a futile, grinding struggle with Farrenghast's infantry. He twisted in his sarcophagus to address the figures standing either side. They were partially mummified, bearing the brass icons of the Penacor kings – his lich priests.

"Begin the summoning," he instructed, before addressing Voldart, who had just returned from the left flank.

"What of the parasites of Bilehall?" he demanded. The arrival of the vampiric host on his left had given Farrenghast a moment's pause. The elf, Zarihell, had assured him they would not fight alongside Waiqar. In fact, almost nothing that had occurred since he had marched from the Misty Hills had followed the *Daewyl's* predictions. Waiqar was supposed to be locked in a draining war with the vampires, and the mythical engine of Kelipa was meant to be unguarded, yet he had arrived to find Waiqar's host in full and positioned to defend the entrance to the machine. Zarihell herself had simply disappeared not long after Farrenghast had marched forth. He suspected treachery, but he had come too far now. The stories of the rift between Zorgas and Bilehall seemed true enough, and while the vampires remained on the hill to the west, refusing to fight alongside the Betrayer, Farrenghast would never have a better chance at victory. Perhaps, if the tide was in his favor, the vampire nobles would even attack Waiqar as well, though the Penacor king had no desire to enter into an alliance with such disgusting, cretinous creatures.

"The red and black standards have not moved, my king," Voldart informed him. "They remain on their hill."

Farrenghast nodded in satisfaction as he heard his priests coming to the end of their summoning rites. There was a piercing scream, and death energies exploded from the Penacor icons, wreathing them in pale green ghost fire. From the conflagration came shapes, writhing and contorting. They were the spirits of those slain by Farrenghast when he had still enjoyed a demon's favor. Dark pacts had bound them to the icons, forced to serve when called upon. Now Farrenghast watched as they were unleashed. They billowed like a flailing cloud up over his sarcophagus, the two streams meeting directly overhead in a maelstrom of howling skull-faces and grasping talons.

"Go forth," Farrenghast screeched, raising his ancient, notched sword. "And wipe the barrow bare!"

With a wail that made the weathered stones of Kelipa tremble, the spirit host surged toward Waiqar's standard.

Waiqar watched the terrible swarm of unquiet spirits rising toward the crest of the barrow. It had been a long time since Farrenghast had last employed his icons in a battle with Zorgas. Waiqar had doubted that any spirits yet remained at the Penacor's behest, but it seemed as though he had been marshalling his strength for just such a clash.

"Lady Falgor," Waiqar said, the words laced with an arcane imperative. The invisible magics of the afterlife linked him to the ethereal consciousness of the dead noblewoman.

"My lord," he heard her respond.

"Take your host and free these pathetic slaves," he instructed her.

By way of answering, Falgor let out a screech that echoed out over the barrow top. It was answered by the rest of Zorgas' spirits, who had been arrayed above the infantry of Waiqar's main battle. There were many lost souls among them, barely substantial creatures that offered nothing but their rage and spite, but in among them, too, were more powerful wraiths. There were the ghost knights of Falgor's own household and other powerful warriors who had fallen down the ages, those who had sworn oaths in desperation or fear so that they did not pass over into an uncertain afterlife. There were also the creatures churned out by the Everliving Engine, a broiling mass of fangs and talons and hunger.

Beneath phantom standards of their own, the spirits that had been arrayed overhead surged forward, Lady Falgor and her ghastly knights riding at the head, the hooves of ghostly steeds galloping upon the twisting strands of the energy that darted just ahead. They met the rising tide of Penacor spirits in an explosion of death energies that rang like a thunderclap through Kelipa. Battle was joined on both the ground and in the air, spirits ripping and tearing at the essence of one another as below skeletal warriors hacked and stabbed.

This time neither side gave way. Waiqar's attention was fixed on maintaining the necromantic conduits to his host, yet a detached part of him continued to assess the battle as it unfolded, judging when the moment was right.

How many times had he done this? He did not know. Before he had practiced magic, before he had died, before he had become the greatest necromancer to have ever existed, he had been a warrior and, more importantly, a general. He remembered nothing now of his early life, of a mother and father, or where he had been born or grown up. But he remembered his first combat trial as a young warrior – blood and sweat and a relentless midday heat he could no longer feel. He remembered his first battle as well. He recalled being chosen to lead in his first campaign against the Uthuk Y'llan, and he could still see the moment Timmorran had promoted him, singling him out from among the other junior commanders and giving him leadership of the legion.

There had been pride that day, and hope. He'd proved his abilities in the years that followed, in the battles won. Timmorran had taken him not only as a general, but as his apprentice, teaching him spellcraft to further augment his natural aptitude for conflict.

All of that felt as though it had been cut away in the Black Citadel. In truth, Timmorran had never been worthy of him. He had won more battles since the Black Rain.

And of course, there had been so many clashes against Farrenghast. So many like this, two immortals venting their pain and wrath upon one another. It had become almost a tradition. But in truth it was a distraction. Waiqar had grown tired of it.

Movement from down the slope arrested his attention, banishing the reverie he had been slipping into. Part of the formations that comprised Farrenghast's reserve, still arrayed at the base of the mound, had started to climb up it. The Penacor king was beginning to commit himself, realizing that he had to break Waiqar's forces on the crest. They were tramping up the slope beneath their rotting griffon banners, leaving only the Children of Nerek with Farrenghast himself.

Even more importantly, there was motion on the flanks as well. He could see indistinct blocks of reanimates emerging from out of the mist to the left and right of where the main line was embroiled in its melee. Farrenghast was inverting his wings in on the center, hoping to turn the Zorgas main battle on both sides and overrun the hill. If he succeeded, Waiqar's host would be crushed.

Waiqar felt a moment of tangible, sweet delight, the instant that came when the decisive point was reached in any battle. This part, he never grew tired of. Victory beckoned.

"Ardus," he said aloud, projecting his voice into the head of his most loyal lieutenant. "Strike."

"We go!" Ardus bellowed, raising an axe and driving a killing imperative into the minds of every knight at his back.

Without waiting to see if they followed – he knew they would – he rode for the mist ahead. Force of habit made him rake back his spurs into the decaying flanks of his steed, his willpower driving the undead construct furiously onward. The air resounded to the clatter of hooves and armor as the mounted cohort formed a wedge, Ardus at its tip.

On they surged, along a street that had been abandoned when the world was still young. The ruinous stone on either side trembled at the passage of Zorgas' elite, and the mist itself seemed to quail and flee before them, revealing what lay ahead.

It was everything Ardus had hoped for. The right wing of the Penacor line, the vanguard, was no longer directly facing him. Instead, it had wheeled to its left, beginning to advance up toward the south-eastern face of the barrow mound. If it continued it would crash into the flank of Waiqar's main force, but in doing so it had exposed its own right side and rear to the Zorgas knights lurking in the mist.

Ardus was presented with his favored target, a packed mass of infantry facing the wrong way.

"Sound the charge," he snarled at his horn-bearer. Again, it was an affectation, but one that thrilled him. As the dolorous, magic-infused notes pealed out he once more urged his steed forward, the black and purple standard of the Undying unfurling behind him.

Impelled by some base form of necromantic sentience, the rearmost of the Penacor reanimates sensed the charge. They began to turn, and the entire phalanx of skeleton infantry came to a shuddering halt at the base of the slope.

They were too late. Ardus screamed and stood in his saddle as his steed crashed in among the back ranks. He hacked down with his axe, cleaving through helm, skull, and ribs, striking with such force that the first reanimate simply exploded in a hail of splintered bone. He swung again and again, cleaving skeletal foes like so much lumber, his wicked steed lashing out with iron-shod hooves and snapping its fangs.

So precipitous had his charge been, that he had raced ahead of the rest of the cohort. For a few seconds he fought alone, the mass of bodies barely checking his advance, carving a solo route through the soldiers of the Penacor. Their bronze swords and shields struck back at him, clattering off his plate armor or stabbing and tangling into his mount. He never once faltered. This was what made undeath bearable. This was what he loved, more than anything else.

Then the rest of the Deathborn crashed home. They did so like a thunderclap, lances splitting and splintering as they drove through the reanimates still attempting to reform and face them. Bodies went down, crushed to powder, or were slammed back with such force into those behind that bones split and shattered, the reanimated remains coming apart like toys as the necromantic energy binding them was obliterated. The wedge of knights carried deep into the Penacor host, and while they lost momentum after the first few seconds, they cast aside broken lances and drew swords, axes, maces, and hammers. They laid into the warriors of the Misty Hills, carving them apart, breaking them, the deadlights in their skulls gleaming brightly as they feasted on the death energies their savagery was stirring up.

"On," Ardus roared. "On!" There would be no stopping, no wheeling away to reform and charge again. Momentum was everything. This killing was everything. For a few precious moments he was alive again, in the midst of the fray, splattered with blood, his axe hacking its way through flesh.

There was none here, only brittle bones and bronze, dust and grave-dirt, but Ardus let himself slip into the fantasy, reveling in it. He was recreating a thousand past slaughters. He would not stop. He could not stop.

On, the knights of Zorgas charged.

"My king," Yolland began to say, but Farrenghast silenced him with a gesture that bound his soul from speaking.

"I know, you fool," he snarled, fighting down another bout of coughing. "I can sense it."

The right flank was in peril. Waiqar had committed his vaunted knights, led by the cretinous oaf that acted as his champion. It was just as before. Truly, the Betrayer was an unimaginative, predictable fool. Did he really believe Farrenghast would fall for the same trick that had first seen him undone at Black Bog?

No, there would be no such repeat. Farrenghast had predicted this exact maneuver. It was just what he had hoped for. Waiqar may have succeeded in halting his spirit host with one of his own, but now he had overcommitted.

"I was leading armies long before your sires were even spawned, Betrayer," he hissed at no one in particular. Yolland made a grunting noise.

Farrenghast ignored him, laying back down in his sarcophagus and crossing his arms over his chest. He cast the net of his consciousness wide, seeking the bestial presence that had been lurking in the mist from the start, prowling amidst Kelipa's ruinous remains.

"Voldart," he uttered, latching onto the mind of the ancient creature, forcing it to once more obey him. "Now is your time."

CHAPTER TWENTY

The vanguard of the Penacor host was almost broken. Ardus's knights had simply crushed it. Waiqar's chief captain had cut so deep from the rear that he had almost broken out through the front ranks. He sundered yet another helmeted head and clove through the pole of one of the Penacor standards, the moldy cloth falling to be crushed into the mire that had been churned up by old boots and hooves.

The battle was turning. On the barrow mound above, the center of Waiqar's line remained unmoved, the Great Necromancer's banner still flying. Spirits still clawed and shrieked at each other above, a maelstrom of death energies unleashed, but the forces of Zorgas would not yield. And now, with the Penacor right flank broken, their center was also exposed. So, for that matter, was Farrenghast himself. Only his Children of Nerek stood to oppose Ardus now.

"Reform," Ardus finally ordered, willing the other Deathborn to reorder ranks broken up by the melee. They did so as they trampled and crushed the last of the disintegrating block of Penacor infantry, their own numbers barely thinned. Bronze swords and spears were no match for the thrice-cursed armor of Zorgas' elite, while the bones of the Deathborn themselves were like iron compared to the crumbling remains of their enemies, so heavily soaked were they in necromantic energies.

Ardus was contemplating whether to storm up the slope or around its base to strike at Farrenghast himself when he heard a sound he hadn't anticipated. A drawn-out, mournful wail rose from the mist still clinging to the left flank. It was quickly joined by more, the sound of what Ardus took to be hundreds of barghests answering the call of their pack leader.

The Deathborn captain experienced a rare emotion – uncertainty. He drove the imperative to rally into his knights, forcefully drawing them back into formation and wheeling them away from the barrow and toward the mist just as the first bestial shapes came loping from between the ruins.

Too late, Ardus realized that Farrenghast had not, like Waiqar, been content to simply let the barghests run feral. They had been leashed to a powerful, cunning will, one that Ardus recognized. It was Voldart. The half-beast had brought his pack into play.

"Charge them," Ardus snarled as the barghests streamed toward them. He would not allow himself and his knights to be challenged. None faced down the elite of Zorgas, certainly not a rabble of mangy, half-rotten animals.

The barghests were quicker though, and the Deathborn cohort didn't have a chance to gain momentum before the beasts were upon them. Ardus's mount reared, and there was a hideous crack as its hooves split the skull of one lunging barghest. The movement allowed another to dart underneath however, and rake the steed's underside with its claws and fangs.

Ardus felt the necromantic energies binding the reanimated horse flicker, like a candle guttering in a gale. He twisted his steed so it could stamp down on the beast beneath it, but while his attention was on the barghest, something else approached, something inhumanly fast and deadly.

It leapt and struck him from the right, flinging him from the saddle. He slammed with a thump into the dirt, rolling with it, grappling. His senses had long been numb, but he could feel mangy fur, and the glowering intelligence of beast melded with man, even before the jaws clamped like a vice against his right shoulder.

It was Voldart himself. The half-wolf ripped away his pauldron with a twist, massive fangs scissoring through ancient, cursed metal like it was mere gossamer. He was in his wolf form, a hulking, black-furred canine that snarled and drooled.

Ardus heaved against him before Voldart could latch back down, bellowing as he cast the creature off. He had lost one of his axes when he'd been thrown from his steed, but the other was still at his hip. He ripped it free and hauled himself up with an ugly scrape of armor.

His shoulder was wounded, the bones there cracked and split, but he rebound them with a thought. Voldart twisted and turned at bay, jaws hanging open, a deep, powerful growl rising in his throat. All around, the Deathborn were engaged in a desperate melee with the snapping, snarling monsters. Ardus levelled his axe at Voldart.

"The tale of your pitiful existence ends here, animal," he shouted. "I will skin your mangy hide and present your pelt as a gift to the Undying One!"

Voldart said nothing. Instead, he howled, and lunged.

"Lord," Mirabelle said softly, looking from the ferocious combat playing out on the slope of the barrow to Waiqar. She had urged her steed forward slightly so she was alongside her master, the only one of Waiqar's entourage who had dared do so.

"Lord, should we commit the reserve?" she asked.

Waiqar didn't reply. He was angry, angry that an old fool like Farrenghast had come so close to outwitting him. Angry that he was still daring to challenge him in the first place. This should have ended centuries ago.

The Penacor had learned from previous defeats. Waiqar could sense Ardus, who should have delivered the killing blow, embroiled in a desperate fight of his own off to the left. The cavalry of Zorgas had become bogged down. Both sides had played their hand, and now only the reserves remained unengaged.

On the barrow itself the main battles of the opposing hosts were still engaged. The combat there was reaching a fever pitch, made even more so by the presence of the Everliving Engine, far below. Waiqar could hear its ticking growing louder as it fed on the feast of death that both sides had brought to bear, in turn churning out more to empower the rival armies. Even without Waiqar's bidding, reanimates who were struck down would reknit, dragging themselves back up or continuing to hack at feet and shins from where they lay. The deadlights blazing in the skulls of the skeletal warriors were piercingly bright, the vigor of the Engine adding fuel to the necromantic will binding both sets of warriors. As one fell, another would stagger back into the fray.

Waiqar turned his attention from the slope to his right flank. There, on the lesser mound to the west, the banners of Bilehall were still visible above the mist. He could sense the presence of Naythen Torvic and the rest of his foul brood. Until now they had made no move for one side or the other, seemingly content to enjoy a prime view of the brutal slaughter. Well, Waiqar would permit that no longer.

"Bring me one of the Deathborn from the reserve," he ordered Mirabelle.

"Just one, lord?" she asked, confused.

"Yes," Waiqar said. "I have a message for Naythen Torvic."

Lucrezia strode from amongst her own retinue to her brother's side, the lesser vampires hastily making way for her. She was fully armed and armored, clad in spiny, red plate mail and with her long, white hair bound up. She exuded equal parts anger and determination, the elemental Mortos like a jagged, snarling beast surrounding her.

She reached Naythen just as he was turning away from the towering Deathborn that Lucrezia had seen ride up the slope moments earlier.

To her relief, her brother hadn't struck down the warrior

of Zorgas. It seemed as though the siege of the Red Keep, and the brush with extinction it had represented, had helped refocus his mind at least a little.

"What news?" she asked him. The vampire lord looked troubled as he turned his gaze on her.

"The Betrayer demands we strike," he said. "In his favor."

"We promised to do so," Lucrezia pointed out. "Now is the last opportunity we'll have to make amends to Zorgas."

Privately, she wanted to scream at Naythen. She had risked everything to bring them back from the brink, to get them to this point. After beheading her brother's idiot thrall Pentageist, she had brought the remains before Waiqar, when he had still been invested outside the Red Keep. The timing had been fortuitous – word had just arrived that the old Penacor king in the Misty Hills was marching on Kelipa, doubtless trying to take advantage of the feud between Zorgas and Bilehall.

Choking down her pride, Lucrezia had knelt on both knees before the Undying One and pleaded for the un-life of both her brother and the rest of the coven. She had promised that Bilehall would ride to Waiqar's aide against Farrenghast. She had told him that they would submit to whatever tithes he demanded. Afterward, when he had permitted her to enter the Red Keep and talk with her brother, she had vented her fury at Naythen. They had bared their fangs, snarled, hissed, their anger potent enough to send her brother's underlings fleeing from their presence. And by the end of it, Naythen Torvic had submitted to her.

He had realized his mistake. In truth, he had known it the moment the witch Zarihell had vanished. She had misled him, for whatever reason. The host Waiqar had been able to raise in a single night to challenge Bilehall's insurrection had been beyond all expectation. Naythen had been trapped in his crypt-fortress, watching as it was demolished one stone at a time, knowing that he had been a fool. Lucrezia had been the only one powerful enough to force her brother to admit as much.

They had sworn to follow Waiqar to Kelipa. When they had reached its ruins, however, Naythen had ordered a halt. The combined forces of the vampires of Bilehall had remained in place, watching as the Penacor's reanimates had assaulted the city's great barrow mound.

Lucrezia could sense her brother's dilemma. Waiqar was before them, embattled by an enemy almost as powerful, his forces committed. One final betrayal, and Torvic's vampire knights could fall upon his flank, striking the decisive blow and finally ending the tyranny of Zorgas. It was an opportunity that would not present itself again for many centuries, if ever. She suspected some of the other Bilehall nobles, like the vicious Lord Vorun'thul, were even urging it.

Had it been any other force assailing the Great Necromancer, Lucrezia suspected Naythen would already have made his play. Farrenghast, however, was the last being any of them would have sought as an ally. The particular loathing the ancient undead king felt toward vampires was infamous. Bilehall had fought hard against him at Waiqar's side on many past occasions. Lucrezia had reminded her brother that even if Waiqar were defeated, it was certain that a battle between Bilehall and the Penacor would follow immediately after. Farrenghast would not permit Bilehall's independence, nor share his spoils, especially where the Everliving Engine was the prize.

So Naythen had hesitated, his vampiric servants uncertain of his will. Lucrezia had urged him forward, but the Lord of Bilehall would not be moved.

Until now. Waiqar had summoned them directly. The Deathborn waited on his hellish charger a little way down the slope, witch-fire flickering as he glared up at the assembled coven.

"We must ride," Lucrezia hissed under her breath, clutching her brother's vambrace in her own gauntlet. "We do not win this if we side with Penacor. We do not win this if we sit idle on this hill. If we strike now, against Farrenghast, our house will be saved."

"Saved, only to endure an eternity of servitude," Naythen said bitterly. Lucrezia bared her fangs in frustration.

"If you will not go, I will. I refuse to allow you to destroy our noble line, brother. It will endure with me, if need be."

Naythen looked at her, his expression icy.

"I am the head of this coven, sister," he said. "And that will always be the case."

He took in the sight of the battle raging before him one last time, then turned to his retainers.

"Mount your steeds," he ordered. "We have watched this pathetic display for long enough. Let us show both these moldering old fools how the red knights of Bilehall win a battle."

CHAPTER TWENTY-ONE

The sound of war horns rose over the clatter and rattle of the melee and the shrieking of the spirits still tearing at one another above it. Waiqar cast his gaze west once more and, finally, was greeted by movement.

The host of Bilehall came sweeping down from their hilltop, red and black pennants streaming, the last of the day's pallid light catching on the wicked tips of lances and barbed red armor. Waiqar watched their course carefully, ready in an instant to drive a command into the minds of his reserve. If Torvic was fool enough to betray him again, every last one of his Deathborn, along with every shambling reanimate and craven spirit, would have to be committed to the front.

For a few painful moments, it was unclear if Torvic's course would take him into Waiqar's right flank, or Farrenghast's left, both embattled against one another at the foot of the barrow's western side.

Then, the oncoming vampiric knights leading the charge veered to their right. Their lances came down in a glittering array. With a crack that reached Waiqar a second after the visible impact, the vampires crashed into the side of Farrenghast's forces.

Waiqar allowed himself the briefest moment of satisfaction. He had been right to show Torvic clemency, for now. Everything was proceeding as he had intended.

The vampires plowed through the ranks of Farrenghast's rearguard on the left, impaling, trampling and crushing. Even the power of the Everliving Engine wasn't enough to put the fallen Penacor foot soldiers back together again now.

Waiqar could feel Farrenghast's dismay. It translated through the writhing lines of magical power. All through the Penacor formation, the reanimates faltered. Waiqar snarled as he redoubled the vigor of his own warriors, driving home the advantage. Skulls shattered and ribs caved in as the front ranks of Penacor's legion were hacked down. All along the line, the legions of Zorgas gained ground.

Victory was near. Even after a millennium, Waiqar still felt the thrill of it. There were few things that could compare.

"*Complete it,*" whispered Baelziffar. "*Destroy the old usurper, once and for all.*"

Waiqar looked beyond the melee that was now rapidly driving itself down the slope before him. Past the base of the hill, he could see Farrenghast's bronze and gold armored guards, not yet engaged, arrayed around their king's sarcophagus. He realized that they had started to move backward.

The Penacor was retreating.

The fury Waiqar had felt earlier, when it seemed his own host had been checked, returned with a vengeance. Without thinking, he found himself driving his mount forward, Bitterbite sweeping from its scabbard. He heard Mirabelle calling out in confusion behind him, and sensed the sudden uncertainty of his own Deathborn guard, but he cast them aside.

He was going to destroy the Penacor, that withered, bitter old cretin who had defied him so many times. Suddenly, nothing else mattered.

The reanimates ahead of him parted, allowing his steed to crash through into the remains of Farrenghast's main battle line. The warriors of the Misty Hills did not even give him pause. He cut through them, their remains crumbling in his wake as he surged onward, down the slope.

"*Ta-ba bur erim nam-úš,*" he cried, voice booming across the battlefield, filling the twilight. Ethereal energies surged, pouring toward him from throughout Kelipa, adding to his strength. In that moment he felt unstoppable, charged with the raw powers of undeath, an avatar of annihilation unleashed.

The Children of Nerek locked ranks as he stormed toward them, blocking his path to their king's sarcophagus as it was borne hastily away. Waiqar struck like a lightning bolt, Bitterbite singing in his skeletal fist. It seared through tarnished bronze and pitted iron, cleaving bones and mummified flesh, his steed's hooves trampling the remains of Farrenghast's elite.

The Children of Nerek fought back. Spears and glaives rung against his armor, the ancient runes inscribed in the cursed metal igniting with pale balefires as they repelled each stroke. Waiqar lost momentum, his steed impaled and run through. Still it struggled on though, its body bound to

Waiqar's unshakeable will. He would not allow it to fall. It drove into a clattering wall of tall shields, spears snapping, skulls and shoulders crunching and cracking as the sheer weight of numbers pushed back against the charge of the Undying One.

None could match him, but they could slow him. Waiqar raged, raising his other hand, fingers splayed. He spat the Invocation of Unmaking, a spell normally reserved for severing the connection between a necromancer and their puppets. Instead, he turned it upon the Children of Nerek, an act only the most powerful of necromancers would have dared contemplate.

The magics Waiqar had summoned clashed with those being used by Farrenghast. There was a booming report, like a thunderclap, and roiling winds swept through Kelipa, bringing with them a chorus of disembodied howls. The coruscating essences of death twisted and writhed, crashing against one another, locked in a destructive embrace.

Waiqar hissed more words of power, drawing upon his vast reserves of strength. The energies of the Everliving Engine added even more, a furious necromantic tempest engulfing him as he wrestled with Farrenghast's hold over his warriors.

It was almost too much. Waiqar's whole body locked, rigid, the reanimates throughout his entire legion beginning to tremble and rattle as they suffered the aftershock of the power he was seeking to control. His bones ached, the wind that surged around him eroding at first his armor, and then his body, flaying the edges of his very essence, trying to drag him piece by piece into that unwelcome, numbing eternity.

His words became an incoherent roar. His consciousness

flickered, momentarily leaving him. He saw things any being, living or dead, should not see.

He saw his past, his present, his future, spliced and entwined, a deranged tableau of death and rebirth, of day and night, of a tomb sitting in the sunshine that bore his name, and a palace in the darkness that bore his soul. He saw fire, and the glittering scales of a great and terrible dragon. He saw gods, and demons, and all the things in between. He saw eternity. He saw his own obliteration.

Baelziffar was speaking to him but, for the first time, he could not hear him.

Then, with an audible crack, Farrenghast's power broke. A shockwave blasted out from Waiqar, destroying the Children of Nerek utterly. From head to toe, they were turned to dust, the Penacor king's ancient hold over them wiped from existence. The slow march of time that Farrenghast's will had held in check reasserted itself, and they crumbled to nothing.

The Corpse Wind blew itself out, whipping away the last of the Children of Nerek with a sigh. All that remained were scattered pieces of antique armor, littering Kelipa's long-abandoned streets.

A terrible stillness fell over the battlefield as Waiqar tried to recover. For a while, filled with horror, he believed he had gone too far, that some essential part of himself had been swept away by the hungry winds of death.

He could not think. He could not move. His body remained locked, and the pain in his bones pierced even the fug of numbness that usually clouded his physicality.

"*Awake*," Baelziffar hissed. That voice, deep, heavy, sweet like slow-dripping honey, finally reignited Waiqar's full consciousness. He shuddered, stirring, regaining control.

The battle of Kelipa was over. He realized that, in his wrath, he had not only unmade the Penacor's guards, but the whole of Farrenghast's host. The army that had warred against Waiqar's legion across the barrow mound were now nothing but dust and broken shards, and the jagged remains of their armor and weapons.

It was as complete a victory as he had ever won. And yet, a single failure stood out, a shortcoming that checked the brief moment of weary triumph Waiqar experienced.

Farrenghast was gone. The last of his minions had carried him into the mist that loitered with ill intent at the edge of Kelipa, far enough away from the epicenter of Waiqar's power to avoid annihilation.

Waiqar urged his mount forward, but a force not of his own checked him.

"*You must rest,*" Baelziffar warned. "*To go on now would be foolish.*"

That sparked Waiqar's anger.

"He is ours for the taking," he snarled. "I will track him through the marshes and end his defiance once and for all. No more will he seek to usurp Zorgas."

"*His pet hound yet lives, and is by his side,*" Baelziffar said, slowly, as though explaining something to a child. "*You have not had a moment's rest since the summoning fields. If you ride on now alone, even I will not be able to guarantee your survival.*"

"I have endured until now," Waiqar snapped. "The old fool and his beast will not be the end of me."

"*Your arrogance gets the better of you, Waiqar,*" barked

Baelziffar, and suddenly those slow words that trickled so easily, so sweetly into his thoughts were replaced by a voice of iron and fire, the roar of a creature that had worked its evil ways long before even Waiqar had been born.

"You will not risk the unmaking of all that I have carefully laid these many centuries! I do not permit your destruction, not yet!"

The voice was accompanied by a sudden burst of pain within Waiqar's skull. He cried out and reached up, clutching his head, the agony unbearable. He had forgotten what it felt like.

"Forgive… me…" he hissed.

The pain remained there for a moment longer then, slowly, began to recede. Baelziffar spoke once more, the words becoming less jagged, no longer scraping around inside his skull. It was a relief, and for a moment he felt shame at the reminder that he was subordinate to the creature's power. Only for now, though.

"Penacor's threat is ended forever," Baelziffar soothed. *"Never again will he have the strength to challenge you. He is defeated, and when the time comes, you will march into the Misty Hills, slight his keep, and reduce him and the last of his servants to dust, just as you did his army."*

"Yes," Waiqar agreed, feeling suddenly thankful. The pain had brought back his clarity. There was no reason to risk himself. Farrenghast's power had been broken. It would be foolish and pointless to overextend.

"You will not escape for long, old king," he said into the mist, then twisted in his saddle to look back over the battlefield. His forces stood still and silent, witch-fires glimmering faintly. None of his council were close enough to have witnessed his moment of weakness.

"*You should return to the barrow,*" Baelziffar advised. "*You have renewed oaths to receive.*"

Abruptly, Waiqar remembered the presence of Torvic and his brood. The vampiric host remained on the right flank of the Deathborn Legion. They had not dared approach the barrow itself yet.

Waiqar glared for a moment at the red and black banners of Bilehall. Then, without another word to Baelziffar, he rode back toward the crest.

Naythen Torvic and the closest members of his coven halted at the edge of the barrow's crest and dismounted from their rotting steeds.

Waiqar awaited them, suppressing his disgust. He had regained control. Now was not the time for reprisals. Now was the time to adhere to the plans he had made.

His closest retainers stood with him – Mirabelle, as well as Melkor and Karrok, who had both survived the brutal melee with Penacor's host. Ardus had returned as well from the left flank. His armor had been rent as though by great, savage claws, and many of his bones were fractured or split. He had withstood worse though. He bore in one fist a long, bloody fang, a prize he had ripped from the jaw of Voldart. According to Ardus's report, he and the beast had been locked in combat before it had suddenly broken off and loped away, around the same time that Waiqar had summoned the full weight of his powers. Ardus did not say who had been winning. Waiqar had never doubted that he would triumph.

Waiqar stood to receive the leaders of Bilehall as they advanced the last few paces. Naythen was at the fore, his sister Lucrezia close on his left. She was the one who had stayed Waiqar's hand. She seemed altogether wiser than her brother. Perhaps that was a good thing, or perhaps it made her more dangerous. Waiqar had not yet decided.

He tried to study Naythen's expression, but it was difficult for him to remember what thoughts flesh betrayed. The elemental Mortos that clung reluctantly to the vampire lord was far clearer. He was apprehensive, and ashamed and, deep down, still angry. There was fear, too. Since the start of his little rebellion, he had witnessed Waiqar's full might, first before the walls of his keep and now, in the midst of battle. He knew that he had made a mistake. All that remained was to see if his pride was still so great that it overcame his reason. A part of Waiqar hoped it would, so that he could cut the arrogant fool down where he stood and watch his marble-like flesh wither and dissolve.

There was a brief silence between the two parties, before Lucrezia Torvic knelt. Her brother followed her example, and the rest of the coven did likewise. The horned dragon standard of Bilehall was dipped in reverence before the black and purple of Zorgas.

"I come into the presence of the Great Necromancer, Waiqar the Undying," Naythen said, his voice a dry rasp as he recited the Mistlands oath, his eyes fixed on the ground.

"Louder," Waiqar said. Naythen hesitated, and Waiqar enjoyed the moment of anger and shame before he repeated the words clearly, carrying on.

"I crave your forgiveness, my lord. I have betrayed you

and, in doing so, betrayed the very cause of undeath itself. I am not worthy to be counted among the meanest of your servants. And yet, I kneel before you, craving your forgiveness. I ask that we be spared, lord, that we might renew our declarations of loyalty and prove our usefulness to you, as we have done in some small measure by joining your legion in battle this day."

Waiqar said nothing, letting the silence that followed Naythen's fawning stretch. He could feel the urge of his own warriors to once more draw their blades and strike down these parasitic wretches. He could also feel the tension among the vampires, riven with fearful expectation. Some of the thralls, unable to control their twisted, animal-like nature, hissed softly.

Eventually, growing bored, Waiqar delivered his pronouncement.

"You are forgiven," he declared. He watched Naythen's posture, still kneeling, sag slightly with relief before carrying on.

"But the tithe that you refused to pay, the one that you claim drove you to this pathetic rebellion … I will double it. That may be recompense enough for your disloyalty."

Waiqar didn't need his arcane senses to sense the anger that gripped Naythen. His armor rattled faintly as he shuddered with fury.

"My lord, Bilehall will be ruined," the vampire choked but, abruptly, Lucrezia laid a hand on her brother's pauldron, speaking before he could go on.

"My brother accepts the new tithe, my lord," she said firmly. "As do we all. Bilehall rejoices at this unprecedented act of mercy. Let none say that you are not a wise and just ruler."

The groveling almost made Waiqar reconsider, but he checked himself, looking not at Lucrezia but at Naythen. He wanted to see if the vampire could control himself.

Finally, Torvic managed to nod.

"It is as my sister says," he declared. "May you rule for eternity, Undying One!"

"For eternity," the rest of the vampire's brood chorused. Waiqar managed to hide his disappointment. It was well that Naythen had submitted. Now the rest of the plan could proceed.

"You will all join me at Zorgas on the first Moonsday of next month," he said. "To reaffirm your oaths in the proper manner. We will enjoy a banquet that will make the Night of the Red Feast seem like paltry peasant's fare and put our... disagreements behind us. What say you, Naythen Torvic?"

Naythen hesitated, understandably. Waiqar had anticipated as much.

"No harm will come to you, but if it would reassure you, I swear before you now that none of my Deathborn will enter the citadel while you and your brood are present. You will be under my protection."

"You are as generous as you are forgiving, lord," Naythen said, sounding a little more contrite now, though still hesitant.

"Then it is settled," Waiqar said. "I will be expecting you all, at Zorgas."

CHAPTER TWENTY-TWO

"Again."

The words were followed by another charge of green lightning, throwing strange, twisted shadows across the ruinous chamber.

It jolted Tomaz out of the fugue state he had slipped into. He wasn't properly aware of how long he had been watching the latest bout of experimentation being conducted by Tristayne and Kyndrithul Dalibor. They had no concept of day or night, of rest, or seemingly of time in general. For his own part, he couldn't remember when he had last eaten, yet he also didn't really feel hungry. He had caught sight of himself in a broken, grimy mirror in one of the old castle's abandoned chambers, and had found his wasted, drawn reflection unrecognizable. How long had it even been since he had been taken in Greyhaven by Viktor and Wilem and… what were the names of the others?

He was starting to forget the time before his kidnapping. At first, everything had felt like a nightmare, and he had prayed to every god that he had ever heard of that he would wake up. Now his past seemed like a dream. This was the true reality, one of old bones and the mustiness of the grave, of dust and blood and malformed monstrosities that once would have left him trembling and weeping with mind-numbing terror, but which now barely gave him pause.

Such creatures surrounded him. Not long after first being introduced to Tristayne, with the aid of his craven thralls, Kyndrithul had shifted his arcane contraptions to the wreckage of Castle Dalibor, the old citadel where the noble family had once dwelled before the building of the estate. He had apparently feared discovery, and had told Tristayne that Waiqar's Deathborn underlings were less likely to seek him at the old crypt-fortress. While the age of almost all the holdfasts in the Mistlands meant they were ruinous to some degree, Castle Dalibor had been slighted, the parapets of its walls and towers demolished, its gatehouse collapsed. Only the central keep remained intact, sitting at the end of a winding, narrow track that led up a wicked crag of rock. Even by the standards of the other places Tomaz had visited in the Mistlands, it was a crooked, melancholy place. It seemed even the spirits had abandoned it.

That was until the return of its master. Kyndrithul and Tristayne had worked tirelessly, their apparent misgivings about one another smothered for the time being by their shared obsession. The two had set to crafting hundreds of abhorrents, transfusing the dust-charged blood from one to another, penning them in the rubble-strewn shells of the old castle's chambers where the scraping of their claws on stone and the deranged screeches of their sutured throats resounded night and day.

Tomaz watched now as, at Tristayne's command, another was struck by the lightning of the cursed brass orbs. Unlike the early abhorrents, this one wasn't destroyed by the blast, but shrieked, transfixed, its malformed bone structure briefly visible through its flesh. Blood ran thick from its pores, drooling down through the grille beneath it.

He listened to the vampire and the necromancer resume their chanting, the shrieking energies of undeath once more flaring through the ghastly chamber. He had come to learn the sounds of their most common spells, if not the actual words. He dared not try and speak them though.

In the pit beneath the orbs, more bones and offal stirred, dragged back from beyond the realm of the living by the efforts of the unholy pair. Reanimates already stood around the edges of the chamber, raised from Kyndrithul's crypts by the blood of the abhorrents. They trembled slightly, the binding on them weak, but they were still standing, still obeying Tristayne's will.

Even with Tomaz's limited understanding of the necromantic arts, it was clear that his master and his newfound ally had made progress over the past few weeks. Whether that was a good thing in the long term or not, he wasn't sure. It seemed clear that what Tristayne was doing was a betrayal of Waiqar, yet Tomaz had never known the necromancer in such a good mood before. It made his own existence considerably easier when the gaunt, walking corpse wasn't snapping at him or dragging him from one cursed location to another. Tomaz simply had to stay near his master, and not interrupt him during the endless rites he was using to raise and bind more and more bodies to his will.

He scratched fitfully at his throat. It seemed to itch all the time now. He was starting to worry it wasn't just subconscious copying of Tristayne's own habit of scratching his neck, and more an arcane aftereffect of being in the baleful necromancer's presence so frequently. He knew Tristayne's first death had been a hanging, and that the memory of it seemed to haunt him still. Sometimes he would clutch his bony throat, as though there was still flesh there that ached or stung, in need of relief.

The energies of the orb cut off. The abhorrent chosen for the latest bout collapsed, writhing and rattling, but not dead. Somehow Kyndrithul was succeeding in making them more resilient, or had learned to better modulate the output of the orbs. Either way, it meant they didn't destroy as many abhorrents during each session. More fodder was constantly being brought into the castle by wagons and charnel carts, carrying remains from gods only knew where. Tomaz assumed graveyards were being pillaged from the borders of Carthridge to Strangehaven. Some of the more humanoid abhorrents had been tasked with unloading each festering delivery, hauling pale, broken flesh and bone to what had once been the castle kitchens, where gaunt thrall-things, Kyndrithul's lesser vampire servants, stitched and sutured and chanted the black rites. It had gone from a series of petty experiments to an almost industrial effort. Tristayne commanded him only to watch and wait – at times he hardly seemed to be aware of Tomaz's presence at all. He had grown completely obsessed with his experiments.

What did Tristayne hope to achieve by the end of it all? Tomaz hardly dared wonder. Was he creating an army, a legion of his own, part monsters, part reanimates? Did he hope to use it to challenge Waiqar? From what Tomaz had seen of the power of Zorgas, even the horde of horrors Tristayne had amassed so far was paltry in comparison, but as he had learned, time meant little to a creature that could not die. As long as Tristayne had unlocked the secret of re-animation, he could continue to build his strength in secret.

That was assuming Kyndrithul continued to aid him. And then there was a final, enigmatic factor, one that presented itself to Tomaz just as, exhausted, he began to drift off again, sitting against the wall in a corner of the chamber.

A figure had entered unannounced, sweeping past abhorrents that cringed away from her. It was Zarihell, a cape of deepest purple around her shoulders, her eyes gleaming. It was not the first time she had arrived unannounced since they had started their work at the castle. Her perfect features seemed set at first, but when Tristayne and Kyndrithul ceased their chanting and turned in surprise, she smiled.

"Don't stop on my behalf," she said, surveying the chamber and its nightmares before languidly hopping up onto one of the abhorrent cages, the thing within scrambling to the back in apparent fear. She sat there, swinging her legs like a child, seemingly content to watch her allies go about their work.

Neither Tristayne nor Kyndrithul seemed willing to do so in her presence. Tomaz sensed their uncertainty. It had been some time since Zarihell had last visited.

"We were not expecting you, my lady," Dalibor spoke up.

"Don't worry, Lord Kyndrithul," Zarihell said, still smiling. "I'm sure your servants will still have time to prepare a chamber for me."

It was impossible to tell if she was joking. Kyndrithul looked confused, but Tristayne spoke up, a sharp edge to his voice. Tomaz knew how furious he became when the experimentations were interrupted, even by Zarihell.

"You have come here for something," he said. "What is it you want?"

Zarihell tutted, as though disappointed by the necromancer's manners, but she answered him.

"I come bearing news. I thought it might be of interest to you both, since you've been confined to these crumbling old walls since you got here."

"Speak it then," Tristayne said testily. The smile had dropped from Zarihell's face. Tomaz shuddered.

"Zorgas and Penacor have met in battle atop the barrow mound at Kelipa," she said. "It ended just today."

"You're certain?" Tristayne demanded. It seemed impossible that news could travel so quickly, but then there were all manner of arcane arts that Zarihell used. She came and went as she pleased, literally vanishing sometimes, and her knowledge of everything that happened in the Mistlands seemed absolute. She had informed them that the old Penacor king Farrenghast had marched against Waiqar not long before. Tomaz had heard stories of the ancient undead, supposedly the first human to be afflicted with such a twisted form of immortality. Like so much else, he had discovered that they were much more than just stories. Once the knowledge that such a being was now marching abroad in the Mistlands would have filled him with fear, but now he found himself considering the power ramifications of this latest news, wondering how it would affect Tristayne's own plans.

"Do you doubt me, Tristayne?" Zarihell asked.

"Who won?" Kyndrithul asked before Tristayne could respond.

Zarihell let the question hang heavy for a moment, as though it amused her to drag out the sudden tension in the blood-stinking air.

"Penacor was crushed," she said eventually. "The king himself escaped, but his power is broken. He has fled back to the Misty Hills."

"Damnation," Tristayne barked. "And Waiqar survived unscathed, I'm sure?"

"Thanks to Bilehall," Zarihell said.

"Their rebellion is over then?" Kyndrithul asked.

"Yes. Waiqar lifted the siege at the Red Keep to face the Penacor. Torvic and his coven then rode to his aid... eventually. They have reaffirmed their oaths to Zorgas."

"Waiqar is growing soft," Tristayne said spitefully. "Even a century ago he would have slighted their keeps, staked them out at noon and banished the mists to let the sun eat them up."

Tomaz saw Kyndrithul shudder at the suggestion.

"Perhaps," Zarihell responded, smiling briefly again. "The Betrayer is hosting a banquet to celebrate the reunion between Zorgas and Bilehall."

"Has he questioned my absence yet?" Tristayne asked,

sounding abruptly alarmed. With Waiqar on campaign and Tristayne forbidden from taking part in it, the necromancer had expressed little concern to Tomaz about being away from Zorgas, or his master's side. If the conflict between Waiqar and the vampire brood had been resolved though, it would surely become more difficult for Tristayne to justify his absence from Zorgas.

"I doubt you are at the forefront of Waiqar's thoughts, dearest Tristayne," Zarihell said mockingly. "Now that he has broken one enemy and yoked another, his attentions will turn to the baronies. Final preparations for his long-awaited return are underway."

"Then we must be ready too," Kyndrithul said, his long fangs bared. "We will never have a better opportunity to strike than when he marches south."

"I see your work here is progressing well," Zarihell noted. Tomaz could never quite tell if she was making fun of them or not.

"There are still... frustrations," Tristayne admitted, with some difficulty. "Binding reanimates for a lengthy period is possible, but to do so with an army would require more energies, and more willpower, than we can currently harness."

"I'm sure you'll acquire the means eventually."

"If you would aid us, things would progress quicker," Tristayne said. "Your abilities are legendary. Why do you not add your powers to our own?"

Zarihell laughed – almost giggled – and jumped down lithely off the cage. She stalked toward Tristayne, reminding Tomaz of one of the wicked mottled southland felines he had once seen at a travelling circus.

"How very charming of you, Master Olliven," she said, reaching out and running her slender fingers lightly over the gaunt features of Tristayne's skull. The necromancer didn't react to the touch, but his scythe rattled in his grip. Tomaz held his breath.

"But trust me, I am helping you more than you already know," the elf said, breaking the contact and turning away abruptly. "I will bring you more news once it transpires. Until then, continue your work."

She strode for the door, but Tristayne's voice checked her.

"If you want to destroy him, why not lend us your full powers? Do not claim you have already done so. What holds you back?"

Zarihell looked at the necromancer.

"It's not just about destroying Waiqar," she said, eyes gleaming beneath her hood, like a predator in the dark. "It's about what happens after he's no more."

Then, without another word, she was gone.

Sometime later, Tristayne retrieved a length of thornwood, fashioned into a staff. He gave it to Tomaz, who was so tired he initially clutched the barbed lower part of the staff and yelped in pain.

"From henceforth, this is yours," Tristayne told him as he adjusted his grip. "I will teach you a minor incantation or two. You will use it as your locus, to channel whatever meager power we may find you possess."

A moment's excitement broke through Tomaz's weariness. At last, here was a sign of progress. Perhaps he was no longer to remain nothing but Tristayne's half-forgotten servant. Perhaps there was a place for him in this new existence.

"Am I to be your apprentice, master?" he asked.

"No, you fool," Tristayne snapped. "But I need someone to attend this feast Waiqar intends to throw for the Bilehall cretins, someone to excuse my absence. You were Waiqar's gift to me, and if he thinks I have elevated you he may be pleased. A channeling staff will give you more authority to speak on my behalf. Act as though you are my trusted councilor and emissary."

Tomaz felt stung at the comment, but even Tristayne's dismissiveness couldn't quite dispel the moment of unexpected pride he felt. Incantations, a staff – it was more than he had ever hoped for, more than he thought possible when he had first beheld the horror of Zorgas or the nightmarish court of the Great Necromancer. He knew it was foolishness, and yet a part of him couldn't help but suddenly imagine a future beyond his current drudgery, one where he acquired at least a fraction of the power he had seen displayed by his master.

"Of course," he said to Tristayne, gripping the staff tightly.

"You must give nothing away," Tristayne stressed, physically clutching Tomaz's shoulder in his bony grasp. "Let it be known that I am studying at the ruins of Morrowheim to any and all who ask. Fail me, and I will rip your soul to pieces and consign it to the Black Realm."

"Of course, master," Tomaz repeated, bowing his head.

Tristayne let him go, seeming to regard him for a moment more before speaking again.

"Go and find somewhere to sleep," he said, apparently remembering that mortals required such petty diversions. "Look for me when you awake, and I may teach you a spell or two."

The silver stars cascaded loudly across the stained table, the coins shining in the candlelight.

Hektor, the self-proclaimed finest mercenary captain north of the Flametail River, stood admiring the hoard, before taking his seat with a groan. He still ached from head to foot, a sad reality he was only slowly coming to accept. In his youth he had fought knights and demi-dragons and had sprung up the next day, ready to do so again. Now, a long march and a melee at the end of it left him seized-up and stiff.

Time to pack it all in, perhaps. The pile of coins before him said otherwise. His body might no longer be willing, but his mind still loved the sight of all that ill-gotten wealth. All his now, or almost all.

He began to dutifully count out the pennies, running through the sums under his breath. Below him, the sounds of carousing rose and fell like the sea lapping on the shore at night. His warband were in fine spirits. Old Sir Elias had offered less resistance than anticipated, and now his devious son had inherited his land and titles, and Hektor and his mercenaries had inherited a good wedge of his wealth, via said son. Only Jericha and Moldern had been killed and, truth be told, neither of them were great losses.

Now the band of sell-swords had retired to the Crossed

Arms in Archaut, their favorite watering hole and the place to go to celebrate another job well done. Hektor had left the party early to go upstairs and count the loot. A lifetime as a freelancer had taught him to assess the weight of a payment down to almost the last coin, but it still had to be checked and divided out at some point, piece by piece.

He was about halfway through the pile when his candle guttered. He felt an unexpected draft, and cursed softly when he realized the room's shutters were still partially open. He rose, grunting with the effort, timber floorboards creaking underfoot as he crossed the room to close and latch them.

Only when they were shut did the candle on the table actually go out.

He froze. A lifetime of both front- and backstabbing had honed his senses to a wicked edge, one that age hadn't quite yet dulled. The hairs on his forearms and the nape of his neck prickled.

He whirled around, the knife at his belt in his hand in an instant. There was nothing though, or at least nothing he could see, for the room was almost pitch black. The only illumination came from the faintest outline around the door, the light of the torch in the corridor outside.

He felt his way back to the table and managed to find the matches and striker next to the candle. Fumbling and awkward because he refused to put down his knife, he succeeded in sparking a light to the wick, cupping the flame, trying to nurture it until it gave off proper light.

At first, it seemed that nothing was untoward, that it

really had been just a strong draft. As he moved to retake his seat though, he realized that something was wrong, horribly wrong.

The first inkling was the stillness. There was no more noise coming from below, or from the rest of the tavern. It was as if the rowdy celebrations had instantaneously stopped. More than that, he thought. It was like the building had been wholly abandoned.

Only then did the state of the room he was in become apparent. It was the best the Crossed Arms had to offer, but no longer. The corners were cobwebbed, and the bedsheets blotched with mildew. The floorboards and the table before him had rotted, and fat wood lice and maggots could be seen writhing in the flickering light of the candle. It was as though the tavern had stood deserted and decaying for years.

Worst of all was the money. The silver lay where it had fallen, but now it was tarnished, its luster gone.

"Gods no," Hektor stammered, dropping the knife and clutching desperately at the worn coins, his heart pounding so hard against his ribs that it ached. This was a nightmare. It had to be.

"The stars will do you no good, Hektor," said a quiet voice.

He started up, knocking over his chair, the soreness in his muscles and joints superseded by his horror.

There was a woman standing where no one had been a moment before, tall, pale, carrying a simple staff and clad in a white kirtle. She looked to be perhaps fifty or sixty years of age, but Hektor knew that to be an illusion.

"You," he hissed, as the candle guttered once more. He fumbled for the burning hand token he wore around his neck, holding it up. The woman smiled coldly.

"You will need that, and more, where you are going," she said.

"I'm going nowhere," Hektor said loudly. "I've paid my debt to the Great Necromancer. We're finished."

"If only you knew how wrong you are, Hektor," said the woman. She snapped her fingers and the burning hand sigil – the mark of Kellos – and the chain it was on began to glow red-hot. He yelped, yanking the chain off and dropping it on the sagging table before it scorched him.

"You and your merry band shall serve Zorgas once more," the woman said. "It is a very specific task my master has in mind for you this time. A very… bloody one. As ever, the compensation shall be great."

"What use is coin if I'm not alive to spend it, Mirabelle?" Hektor demanded.

He had considered such a conundrum before. This was the fourth time the servant of the Great Necromancer had sought out the abilities of his mercenary band. He had hoped the last contract, a successful hunt for a forbidden tome almost a decade before, would be the end of his dealings with the denizens of the Mistlands. It had been years before the nightmares had dissipated, and sometimes he still woke in a cold sweat, uncertain if the phantoms that haunted him were real or not. He had dared hope Mirabelle and her master had forgotten him.

"If I were you, I would be trying to acquire as much lucre in your remaining years as possible," Mirabelle replied darkly. "Spend it lavishly. Live a wild and thrilling life, because you shall know nothing but pain once you pass over. I can personally vouch for the horror that awaits your particular soul."

"You can't make me," Hektor said, trying desperately to bargain the specter away. Surely there were other desperate souls she could call on? "Nor my followers. They won't go back to the Mistlands, not after last time!"

"I will visit them in turn," Mirabelle said. "Have no fear of that. You can all remain here and rot, if you so desire."

He looked down and realized with a jolt that there was a figure sitting in the chair he had occupied before he'd risen to close the shutters. It was skeletal, slumped over, but the remnants of its clothing left him in no doubt about its identity. It was him.

Feeling numb, he reached out and lightly grasped the corpse's shoulder. The skull fell from the neck with a crack, bouncing from the table amidst the silver, and the rest of the remains collapsed with a rattle of old, dry bones.

"Please," he gasped, looking back up at Mirabelle. "Just tell me what you would have me do."

"You will know when next you awake, mortal," the woman said. "You and your band are expected at Zorgas before the first Moonsday of next month. Do not be late, or a worse fate than this awaits you."

Abruptly, the candle went out again. Behind it was left an afterglow, a luminous phantasma imprinted onto the darkness. It was Mirabelle, but horribly changed, her face now a pale, glowing skull, her dress the shrouds of the grave. By the time Hektor had succeeded, on his fourth attempt, at relighting the candle, both the physical woman and the incorporeal, nightmare shade, had vanished.

The room was as he remembered, brushed and clean. He could hear the bawdy celebrations of his fellow mercenaries once again, rising up from below.

Most importantly, there was no corpse sat before him. The chair was empty.

His sigil of Kellos, the little burning hand, was still where he had cast it on the table. He reached out tentatively and discovered that the icon was quite cool.

Shaking, he snatched it up, hung it around his neck once more, and began to pray.

CHAPTER TWENTY-THREE

Waiqar was not accustomed to swearing oaths to anyone, let alone those he considered beneath him, but his oath to Naythen Torvic that no Deathborn would enter the Black Citadel while he was present had been necessary to reassure the vampire. He went even further when the Bilehall nobility arrived, on the night of the first Moonsday of the new month, showing how he would bear a null stone, a form of runestone that deadened magical potential. Privately, he considered it utterly demeaning, but if all was to progress as it should, he knew he would have to make these last concessions.

Because of this, his only other companion in the throne room, besides the cattle herded in earlier, was Mirabelle.

To her own credit, Waiqar could sense little of the tension he was certain his chief advisor felt. She masked it well. There was danger here, he knew. If Naythen decided to renege on his promises after all, if the coven turned on him in full, there was no guarantee of survival, let alone victory, not with Ardus and the other Deathborn banished to the rest of the citadel and the null stone draining Waiqar's power. Even now he could feel the detestable presence of the little shard of rune-inscribed rock, sitting on the arm of his throne, dulling his senses and turning his thoughts sluggish. For one as steeped in magic as Waiqar now was, such an item was anathema.

But Waiqar had never shied away from doing what had to be done, and the reassurance provided by the stone was necessary. This was one last test for Naythen Torvic.

Waiqar didn't much care if he passed or not.

The vampires prowled in, led by their sire. Naythen looked even more unwell than usual, gaunt and draped in his musty, baggy garments. He needed to feed, clearly, and was anticipating a fine feast. In that regard, Waiqar would not disappoint. Over two dozen living mortals had been packed into the pit before the throne, all of them desperate not to be on the outside, closest to the vampires as they arrayed themselves around its edges. They stank of fear, and other flavors that Waiqar wondered if Naythen would notice.

After the vampires came other invitees not of Bilehall. Lond limped in, and several of his Arch Mortificers, leaders of the various Death Cults throughout Terrinoth. Taralin, the serpent witch of the Lakes of the Lost, was also making a rare appearance at the court of the Great Necromancer. Each stopped before Waiqar's throne and knelt, announcing themselves and their fealty before taking their own places for the feast.

Last came a mortal bearing a thornwood staff. Waiqar might have struggled to recall who he was, had he not seen him so frequently of late.

"Undying One," the man, Tomaz, said faintly, kneeling and averting his eyes.

"Speak," Waiqar demanded, unmoving upon his throne.

"My master craves your forgiveness," Tomaz said. "He is engaged deep in study at Morrowheim and would not wish to disappoint you by curtailing his progress to travel here. He sends me to act in his stead."

Waiqar regarded the cowering being for a while. He was not surprised by the news.

"Very well," he rasped. "Take your place then."

He gestured toward the lesser throne to his right, sitting empty. He almost enjoyed the fear and confusion that emanated from Tomaz.

"You are acting in my apprentice's stead, are you not?" Waiqar asked. Tomaz nodded hastily.

"Then sit," Waiqar said.

The mortal did so, looking out on the collection of undead creatures that had gathered around the feasting pit.

All were now assembled. Waiqar permitted himself a brief feeling of quiet satisfaction, as well as anticipation.

After tonight, he could finally progress to the final stage.

"You should speak now," Lucrezia urged her brother.

It had taken all her powers of persuasion to get him to agree to attend the feast. He had claimed repeatedly that it was some sort of trap, but she was sure he simply wished to avoid the humiliation of once more swearing himself to Waiqar before the rest of the coven. The lord of Zorgas had gone out of his way to reassure Bilehall that there were no further retributions planned. Lucrezia had certainly never seen Waiqar use a null stone before. Without his legion as well, he was practically defenseless before those who barely a month before had wished to see him destroyed. It was, in its own way, a potent display of power and confidence.

Naythen grimaced at his sister's demands, but stepped forward. Looking over the heads of the feast crammed into the shallow pit below, he addressed Waiqar, who sat stiffly on his throne overlooking the hall.

"On behalf of my coven, and all of Bilehall, I wish to offer my thanks to you, O Undying One," he declared, just about managing to sound sincere. "Now, more than ever, I regret the foolishness that led me into my craven and unworthy defiance. Your rule is benevolent and just, and I am... overjoyed that we may be counted among your humble servants once again."

There were dutiful murmurs of agreement from Naythen's underlings. Every last vampire from Bilehall, right down to the lowliest, freshest thrall, had been summoned to attend. Gone were the arms and armor that they had girded themselves with in preparation to battle Zorgas, replaced with finery and opulence. For a short while Lucrezia dared to hope that she had managed what had seemed impossible. She had brought her brother to heel, and in doing so quite probably saved them all from extinction.

"Your words are well met, Lord Torvic," Waiqar said in answer to Naythen's short speech. "It seems the troubles between Zorgas and Bilehall truly are at an end. I do wonder, though, where House Dalibor is to be found tonight? They, too, were invited to this feast."

Lucrezia had been wondering as much, but it hardly seemed like Bilehall's problem. Naythen said as much, spotting an opportunity.

"As you well know, my lord, Dalibor, regretfully, does not answer to Bilehall. I cannot account for Kyndrithul's absence. Were he sworn to me, I can assure you he would not offer such an insult. I fear the Kyndrithul coven have long taken your favor for granted."

"Is that so?" Waiqar said, his dry, deep voice reverberating through every being, living and undead, in the hall. "It sounds to me, Lord Torvic, as though you already seek to expand your power before even fully renewing your oaths to me."

Lucrezia stayed still and quiet, hoping desperately that her brother would turn from the path his words were leading him down.

"All fealty is to you, lord," he said clumsily. "I meant only that Lord Kyndrithul should be more appreciative of your summons, and the hospitality you show here tonight."

Silence reigned over the hall. Not one of the Bilehall coven so much as twitched. Waiqar remained utterly impassive, and were it not for the powerful deadlights that continued to play deep within his sockets, he might well have looked like some great, long-deceased king of old, left to molder upon his throne.

Almost imperceptibly, Lucrezia saw her brother's hand twitch, his claws beginning to fractionally extend.

Then, abruptly, the vampires of Bilehall heard a sound few had ever experienced before. Waiqar began to laugh.

It was a cold, scraping sound, and it echoed around the

cobwebbed hall without restraint. The noise did nothing to dispel the unease every creature present felt.

Eventually it began to fade, and Waiqar spoke again, a sort of dark mirth still lingering in his voice.

"Let none deny your boldness, Lord Torvic," he said, raising one skeletal hand and gesturing. "Come, enough idle chatter. Let the feast begin!"

The tension seemed to flush from the hall. Lucrezia relaxed once more as around her a shriek went up from her fellow vampires. Released from their fetters, they flung themselves upon the mortal cattle penned in below them.

Lucrezia was about to do the same, finally allowing the blood-hunger that gnawed at her to be sated, when some unutterable foreboding gripped her. It was so strong that she lashed out and snatched her brother's wrist just as he, too, was about to pitch in.

"What?" he barked, rounding on her, fangs bared and eyes as red as the blood that was about to be spilt.

"Something's wrong," Lucrezia began to say.

Naythen's retort never came. The pitch of the shrieking around them changed. No longer was it the sound of vampires feeding. A note of shock, and of fear, had entered it.

Lucrezia realized why. The cattle weren't cattle at all. As the vampires had lunged in among them, the prisoners had responded not with screams and desperate, vain struggles, as they always did. Instead, shouting defiance, they brandished concealed blades, and worse. Each had a burning hand icon, the symbol of Kellos, the god of light and the anathema of all undead, especially those who bore the vampire's curse.

It was a trap after all.

The effect was instant. Those nobles of Bilehall who had not yet thrown themselves into the pit recoiled, stung by the concentration of Kellos relics. Those unfortunate enough to have already leapt upon their "prey" suffered an even worse fate. Their shrieks were pitiable as they found themselves surrounded and hacked apart by the savage blades of those around them. The weaker thralls, unable to withstand the burning hand relics, found their flesh igniting, their claws and fangs raking those around them as they were consumed by agony.

"This cannot be," Naythen cried out, frozen in dismay. There had always been a chance that Waiqar would renege on his clemency, but to bring mortals bearing accursed icons like those of Kellos into his very hall, to use them against fellow denizens of the Mistlands, it seemed unthinkable.

The cattle – mercenaries, Lucrezia now realized – scrambled up from the pit and threw themselves into the remains of the coven with the desperate fury of mortals who know that a terrible fate awaited them should they not triumph. Lucrezia turned desperately, looking for a way out, but the cursed icons were so potent she doubted even she had either the time or strength to shift and throw herself from one of the hall's high, arching windows.

"What do we do?" Naythen stammered, his usual anger and arrogance rendered mute by the scale of the treachery he was suffering. Lucrezia looked at him, and drew her dagger free from her waist.

"Forgive me, brother," she said, knowing he would not.

She plunged the wicked blade up through his palate and into his skull. The red in his eyes turned instantly black and his jaw went slack, dark, stale blood trickling past his fangs. Releasing the knife, Lucrezia clutched her brother's head in both hands, claws digging in. She looked into his eyes one more time before, with a roar, she twisted and ripped Naythen Torvic's head from his shoulders.

It was horrific and glorious, and Tomaz found himself unable to look away.

He had felt fear since leaving Dalibor – which mortal sent into the presence of the Great Necromancer would not have? – but also a sense of pride. This was his opportunity. Tristayne had placed himself in his hands. All he had to do was make certain that Waiqar did not discover the true reason for Tristayne's absence. He did his best not to think about the fate that would await him were that the case, and focused instead on the position of authority he had been granted.

Being in close proximity to Waiqar still made Tomaz's flesh crawl, but he forced himself to sit quiet and still, doing his best to watch what was actually playing out before him. He had anticipated another massacre of the prisoners herded into the hall, but found himself watching something altogether more impressive.

The ghastly wailing that filled the hall was even more terrible than the screams Tomaz had anticipated. He realized that the mortals were fighting back. At first, he thought it was sheer, desperate defiance, but he soon understood that there was far more to it. While some of them did seem defenseless, others were armed with short swords or daggers which they had kept concealed. Even more importantly, they carried icons of the burning hand, the infamous sigil of the fire god, Kellos.

Tomaz stared in abject shock as he witnessed those vampires who had first leapt upon their supposed prey hacked apart and burned by the sacred icons. The hall soon stank of ancient, scorched flesh. Those undead not caught in the initial trap began to scramble toward the rear of the hall, but the mortals pursued, charging after them with a resounding roar.

Throughout it all, Waiqar remained impassive. Tomaz dared a brief glance at him, seeing the great king of necromancy sitting unmoving and still. It seemed inconceivable that he would permit those bearing the searing sign of Kellos into the literal heart of his crypt-fortress, all the while leaving his own guards absent and muzzling his magical capabilities with a null stone. Yet that was surely what was happening. There was no chance such assassins could have infiltrated the Black Citadel en masse without being discovered.

That meant that Waiqar had orchestrated the massacre not only to punish Bilehall, but to display his own supreme power. Both the living and the dead were his to command.

Tomaz thought that every last vampire would be cut down, but the ones who had initially seemed to restrain themselves were more powerful. With claws and fangs, they tore at the desperate mortals, blood splattering across the hall's flagstones, their flesh branded by the Kellos sigils but not ignited. Nevertheless, they were being herded back, and their destruction seemed inevitable. That was until one particular vampire let out a terrible shriek and held something aloft.

It was a head. Even as Tomaz watched, it began to shrivel and crumble, the weight of centuries of evil catching up with it now that the blood-born necromantic energies that had been preserving it were cut loose. Tomaz still recognized it though. It was Naythen Torvic, beheaded, destroyed, his remains held aloft by his killer – Lucrezia Torvic.

"Stop!" the vampire roared, her words punctuated by a blast of energy that even overwhelmed the null stone and sent a skein of ice darting across the floor, walls and ceiling of the hall, making the fresh, warm blood steam.

To Tomaz's shock, Waiqar raised one hand, fractionally, from the arm rest of his throne. Even unattuned to the elemental Mortos, the living beings attacking the vampires paused their assault, panting and wild-eyed.

"Bilehall has suffered enough," Lucrezia hissed, her eyes blood-red and fangs bared, still holding the half-crumbled skull of her brother aloft. "Naythen has paid for his treachery. What more do you wish from us, Great Necromancer? Would you slay us all, your loyal servants?"

Waiqar did not answer immediately, but when he did the words seemed to scratch and scrape around inside Tomaz's skull, making him gasp in pain and clutch his head.

"You deserve nothing but obliteration for the defiance you have dared show me. That you believed I would simply welcome Bilehall's return after your treachery shows the level of your foolishness. That you now try to claim you are valuable to me shows your arrogance. You and your kind are nothing, Lucrezia Torvic, nothing but parasites that leach upon my glory. I could have every one of you reduced to ash right now and be no worse off."

Lucrezia fell to her knees, and the remaining vampire nobles hastily did likewise, naturally following the lead of the most powerful survivor of the coven. The mercenaries gathered round them warily, ready at the slightest hint of resistance to cut them down.

"I make no more claims, lord," Lucrezia said. "We are at your mercy. Do as you will."

"I shall, as I always do," Waiqar's terrible voice intoned. "You alone show promise, Lucrezia. Your brother was a fool, though you realized it too late. I will spare this pathetic rump not because I am merciful, for I am not. I will spare you out of kinship. A time is coming when the living may yet unite against us. This fate, burned and butchered by the spawn of Kellos, is a lesson in what awaits you if my plans do not bear fruit. You will do everything in your power to serve me, and to ensure the triumph of undeath. If I ask anything from you, be it your castles, your retainers, your fangs, your very blighted souls, you will give them to me immediately and unquestioningly."

"Yes, lord," Lucrezia said, still kneeling. "Bilehall is nothing without Zorgas."

"And this time I will make sure you remember it," Waiqar said. "Take the shrunken skulls of your kindred back to your crypt-fortresses. Impale them on spikes above your keeps and gatehouses. Whenever you feel aggrieved, whenever devious thoughts enter your shriveled, unbeating hearts, look upon them, and remember what I will do to every last creature, living or undead, who even considers defying me."

"Yes, lord," Lucrezia repeated, adding nothing more.

"Go," Waiqar commanded. "And do not forget this night. It will be played out in full if you ever give me reason to doubt you again."

The vampires fled from the hall, taking the remains of their murdered kin with them.

Waiqar let them go. A part of him still simmered with anger, but he ignored the emotion. The plan had been carried through to completion. It was time to move on to the next steps.

"You may approach the throne," he said to the mortal mercenaries who had smuggled themselves into the hall. The raggedy band still carried the accursed Kellos icons they had brought with them, but they wisely concealed them as they came toward the dais. Waiqar could feel the damnable power of the fire-worshiping priests who had imbued the tokens, an unwelcome heat on his cold bones, but he resisted it in a way the vampires were unable to.

He was tempted to slaughter them all, just for the offence of being alive in his presence, but he quashed the impulse. The work of mortals from beyond the borders of the Mistlands was still vital to his designs, and would continue to be for some time even after he reigned over Terrinoth. It would be short-sighted to slay them on a whim.

"Leave, while you still may," he told them. "Mirabelle will go with you to the outer gate, where you will be granted what you were promised. Silver and gold, and precious trinkets, enough to keep you in fine living until I call your souls to a ... more eternal form of service."

They did not need further encouragement. They left with Mirabelle in the wake of the vampires they had been slaying moments before, doubtless desperate to be as far from Zorgas as possible. The way that greed could overcome even the most dreadful of terrors never failed to impress Waiqar.

He dismissed the other unliving guests, ending the impromptu feast and clearing the hall. At the very last moment he ordered Tristayne's servant, Tomaz, to stop and return to the dais.

He could feel the mortal's abrupt fear, bleeding into the death energies that filled the dark, echoing space. He stood before the throne, clutching his thornwood staff.

Waiqar considered him for a moment. The mortal had started to make progress, it seemed. Then, Waiqar gripped onto the armrests of the throne and rose. He did so stiffly, bones cracking, forced to obey his indomitable will. It had been days since he had last moved, he realized.

"Look at me," he ordered Tomaz. The man dragged his gaze up until he was looking into the burning sockets of the towering skeleton.

Waiqar stared down at him for a while, trying to remember the features of his sallow, pallid face, the details of flesh and the meaning of the expressions they held. It was so difficult to do that now. He wondered what the mortal saw in turn. Nothing less than death incarnate, he suspected.

"Do you remember when last we spoke, Tomaz?" he asked.

"No, lord," the mortal whispered, fear warring with confusion.

Waiqar said nothing. Clutching Tomaz's head with one hand, he twisted, and broke his neck.

CHAPTER TWENTY-FOUR

The next evening, Waiqar reconvened the Deathless Council. A gray gloom lay about the hall, the blood of the vampires now dark markings across the floor, left to dry.

The feasting pit was once more occupied by its table, surrounded by Waiqar's inner circle.

"We had a chance to exterminate them," Ardus was saying, a note of bitterness in his voice. "Bilehall deserves nothing less."

"We can do so whenever we please," Lond pointed out, his pallid hands splayed flat on the table. "They are no longer a threat, and nor is Farrenghast."

"Still, they linger," Ardus said. "They have patience, like all our kind. Either may rise again to challenge us."

"My dear Ardus," Waiqar intoned, feeling the slightest flicker of amusement. "If you had your way every being beyond these walls, living or dead, would be slaughtered."

"I only wish them to receive what their actions merited, lord," Ardus responded, his bloodlust undimmed.

"You are my hunting hound," Waiqar mused. "But for

now, the hunt is over. Do not chafe too harshly against your bonds. There will be more killing to occupy you soon enough."

The Great Necromancer turned his attention to the other two Deathborn present, the ever-faithful Melkor and Karrok.

"Does the Legion still stand?" he demanded.

"It does, lord," Melkor said.

"And for how long can you maintain it?"

"Indefinitely, lord, if we are permitted to return the greater part of the other reanimates to the summoning fields."

"Make it so," Waiqar said. Now that the campaign against Bilehall had been successfully concluded, the great host that Waiqar had personally drawn from Zorgas' crypts and charnel pits could be laid to rest once more. It would leave behind only the Deathborn Legion itself, rather than the fodder which supported them, thus granting rest to the lesser necromancers who helped keep those without a consciousness of their own standing.

"If the Legion is to remain intact, lord, let me take some to the Misty Hills and finish the Penacor cretin," Ardus said. "I could manage it with a single cohort."

"Perhaps," Waiqar allowed, willing to indulge Ardus's bloodthirstiness. Sometimes it grew vexing, but normally he appreciated a subordinate with Ardus's single-minded intensity. "I will consider it. Lond, what of the cult in Archaut?"

"Their work is being completed as we speak," the necromancer said, his spirit orbs whispering to him as they drifted about his seat. "If the barons will not meet your demands, they will not live beyond the next Stormtide."

"We shall see," Waiqar said. "What of news from Molten Heath?"

"The drakes are present in ever-increasing numbers," Lond answered. "Hybrids flock to their nests. It will not be long now. Another month, maybe two."

"Then all is almost set," Waiqar mused. "At long last."

"What of Olliven?"

The question came from Mirabelle, and almost caught him by surprise.

"What of him?" he replied.

"He has been seen around Zorgas only sparingly since the beginning of the conflict with Bilehall. I wondered if you were… aware."

Once more, the necromancer was bringing to light news that Waiqar doubted any of the others would have dared share. As much as he valued that, he had little time for it at the moment. His absence was entirely expected.

"My apprentice's work is of no concern to this council," Waiqar said. "He progresses. That is all that is important."

"Of course," Mirabelle said, lowering her gaze briefly.

"All is then ready," Waiqar declared. "You may depart."

He had Mirabelle return later, after the others had dispersed.

"What made you question me about Tristayne?" he asked, for once more curious than displeased.

Mirabelle hesitated before answering. She knew she had more leeway than even Ardus, but she also knew not to overindulge her privileges.

"You know more about Tristayne's absence than you are admitting to your council, lord," she said. "There is something untoward at work. Since you charged me with investigating the absence of bone dust from the crypts, I thought it my duty to mention it."

"Your perception does you some credit, Mirabelle," Waiqar responded. "Unlike Lond's. I expected more from my chief of spies. And likewise from Lady Falgor. Has no wandering soul reported back to her about the comings and goings of my apprentice? Or are my most trusted advisors keeping their knowledge from me?"

"None would be so foolish," Mirabelle said firmly. "These have been busy, taxing times for the council."

"They will become busier yet," Waiqar said sharply. "But no matter. I long ago resolved to deal with this myself. I have been… taking steps."

"Surely this is a matter in which we can assist you, lord?" Mirabelle asked. "In which *I* can assist you? The traitors in our midst could prove dangerous, once they are exposed."

Waiqar decided against checking his closest advisor's ardor. She alone had some inkling as to what had been unfolding. While the rest of the council had dedicated itself to quashing the unrest in Bilehall, a far more perfidious threat had grown, like rot working its way through a great oak. Permitting its existence had disgusted Waiqar, had gone against his very instincts, but it had been necessary. Now that Bilehall had been humbled, it was time to cut it out.

"If I have need of you, I will send for you," Waiqar allowed. "In the meantime, ensure that preparations here continue. The time to march upon Terrinoth is almost upon us. I can feel it."

"You will remake the whole of Mennara anew, my lord, of that I have no doubt," Mirabelle said. She bowed, and withdrew.

Darkness fell. Ghost lights winked in the windows and behind the arrow slits of Zorgas. The crypts and corridors were unusually quiet, even the most desperate and deranged spirits sensing the cold will that animated through the air that night. Out beyond the walls the Deathborn shuddered, while even those lesser reanimates already consigned back into the muck of the summoning fields stirred and twisted in their graves, their rest uneasy. Their master was abroad.

Waiqar stalked the walls of the Black Citadel's pinnacle alone, the wind that perpetually buffeted the uppermost parapets snatching and clawing at his purple cape. The mist was hanging low tonight, leaving Zorgas on its crag, making it seem like the dark citadel had pierced the very clouds themselves. Overhead the black vault was decorated by a glittering array of stars, ruled over by the moon's great, silver disk.

It had been a long time since he had last gazed upon the firmament. He stood atop the highest tower of the keep, taking in each star in turn, recalling how Timmorran had once taught him the names of the constellations. There had been a time when it felt like all he knew was down to the efforts of that great wizard. How long ago that now seemed, yet still those particular memories lingered, brought to the fore on rare nights like these.

The stars reminded him of his failures. They reminded him of a very different time, riven by a furious storm, laden with dark destiny. They made him recall the shattering of the Orb of the Sky, its priceless fragments now scattered across the ends of the earth by Timmorran's treachery. Once, he had sworn to collect them all, to reconstruct the work of his former master and finally prove himself, once and for always, the greatest sorcerer to have ever existed. That ambition still lingered on, fed by the collection of pieces – the Stars of Timmorran – that he had managed to amass down the millennia, most of them sealed deep below Zorgas. But he was still nowhere near to completing his oath. Time had run out.

That was not something he was accustomed to admitting. He drew his eyes away from the sky, raising his hand and looking at it in the silvery light of the moon. There was flesh there. He clenched it, felt the rush of blood, the tension of muscle and tendon around his bones.

"*Do not let yourself slip,*" whispered Baelziffar, voice low, as though even the demon was afraid of disturbing the night. "*You have come too far now.*"

"Why do you always stop me?" Waiqar whispered, grimacing slightly. "Just when I'm about to escape. When I remember."

"*Too much has been sacrificed for that, my friend.*"

"You are not my friend," said Waiqar.

"*Would you rather call me 'master'?*"

"No."

"*Then accept my lie.*"

He looked up once more at the stars, seeing how they

glimmered. They taunted him. They were beyond his reach and would always remain so. No power in creation could bring them all together in his grasp. That realization left him feeling icier than he ever had before. Bitterness seemed to suffuse his every thought.

Again, he looked at his hand. Now it was skeletal, gleaming cold and hard. He unclenched his fist. No warmth, no vitality, only a numbing ache and the dull tugging of the elemental Mortos.

That was his existence now. That was the price he had paid on the day he had shattered the Orb of the Sky and drenched the Tower of Meringyr in the blood of his master.

Whether it was worth it or not had yet to be determined.

He reached into a pouch at his waist and drew out the two objects he had brought with him to the castle's pinnacle. One was a small, crystalline shard. As soon as his fist closed around it, he felt its power, its potential. It was choked with the energies of the Verto Magica, a more potent tool than any mere channeling object like a staff or tome. It was a Star of Timmorran, the first he had recovered, the only one he had been left with on that fateful day at Meringyr.

The second object was a single, skeletal digit, the finger of one of the Deathborn Legion, Sir Yarvek. Waiqar clenched it in his own iron grasp and squeezed, hearing a small, dull crunch. He maintained the pressure until it had been reduced to dust. A precious, priceless handful, the most that would ever be used for the summoning of a single entity.

Looking out into the night, he cast it into the air, letting the Corpse Wind whip it away. Then, he began to chant.

It was a murmur at first, but it built steadily, ancient words describing an ancient horror, calling upon it. Bolts of death energy arced down from the battlements like pale green lightning, lashing against the base of Zorgas' jagged crag. Waiqar used them like a weapon, striking with them again and again against the stone, calling into the night as the wind rose to a howl around him.

At the height of his chant, he raised the Star of Timmorran. It blazed, its magical properties twisted to do Waiqar's will.

He felt the consciousness that he sought begin to stir. It was sluggish and reluctant at first, then angry as it realized it had been awoken. The Star and the finger of Sir Yarvek combined had done their jobs.

Waiqar drove invisible fetters formed by arcane words into the mind now communing with his own, lashing it and goading it until it was fully awake. It protested and resisted. The Great Necromancer gripped the parapet with his free hand, ancient stone cracking and crumbling beneath the force of his hold as he focused every ounce of his power to bending the creature to his will. This was the most difficult, the most vital moment. The Star of Timmorran blazed in his fist, lit by arcane fires.

Like all dragons, the spirit of the great beast before Waiqar had not fled to the afterlife upon its death. It had remained redolent in its ancient bones, lingering but dormant. When Waiqar had first called upon it, centuries before, a furious battle of wills had raged, but this particular terror had long since been tamed. Now, as the death magics awoke it, Waiqar called upon it as an old friend, roaring the final words of the wakening rites into the howling gale.

"Še-ga ur-mah Garathule! Ki lá lugal kaš!"

The creature obeyed. There was a crash of shattering stone as it tore itself free from the death-lair that lay deep within the caves of Zorgas' crag.

It surged upward, arching over even the tower where Waiqar stood. He watched as it soared above him and spread its great wings, and the elemental Mortos lightning struck it, transfixing it and illuminating every last one of its bones with pale energy.

It was a barrow wyrm, a great drake, long dead. Only a handful of necromancers had the willpower and ability necessary to tame the ancient bones of one. Waiqar permitted himself to marvel at the sight of it, to take in the great bones and huge, raggedy wings, the elongated skull and huge fangs. It remained there, transfixed for a moment, blazing like an undead comet above Zorgas, lighting up the turrets, battlements and parapets below with the raw energies of death.

Behind it, the stars had disappeared.

"Ku nu," Waiqar ordered it sternly, feeling a part of its reanimated consciousness still chafing against his control. After a moment's silent struggle it obeyed, sweeping down with just a single beat of its great wings. It alighted with a crunch upon the parapet beside him, its form perching, hunched over, on the edge of Zorgas' pinnacle, before it lowered its wicked skull, finally submitting in full to the one who had called it from its grave beneath the fortress.

"You will feed on flesh and blood once more, my friend," he told it, reaching out and planting one hand upon its skull. Its name in life had been Garathule, and in death its consciousness still lingered, the drake's memories and understanding more acute than even many of Waiqar's Deathborn.

He could sense its question. It wished to know why it had been awoken.

"We have work that must be done," Waiqar told it. "One final task before I claim my destiny. You must take me south-west, tonight. To Dalibor."

PART THREE

DALIBOR

CHAPTER TWENTY-FIVE

Tomaz woke up in his dorm in Greyhaven.

That was what his addled, exhausted mind managed to convince him of for all of one second. Then the base of the Black Scythe dug into his gut, making him cry out.

"Get up, you cretinous oaf," Tristayne snapped, towering over him. The half-dream about Greyhaven he had been drifting through dissolved, and grim reality reasserted itself.

He was on the floor in one of Castle Dalibor's ruinous chambers. He tried sitting up, and groaned. His neck ached from where he had been lying awkwardly.

"Where have you been?" Tristayne demanded. "I've been looking for you."

"I... I don't know," Tomaz admitted, clutching his head. Everything was a haze. He vaguely remembered returning to the castle after the massacre at Zorgas and reporting it to Tristayne. Both the necromancer and Kyndrithul had displayed genuine fear at the news. Waiqar had not been growing lenient after all, and his slaughter of Naythen

Torvic and so much of his brood apparently pointed to either dangerous unpredictability or a terrifyingly high degree of cold calculation. Either way, it had taken the reappearance of Zarihell to calm the two conspirators.

After that, however, Tomaz had no idea what had happened.

"This is happening more and more regularly," Tristayne complained. "Perhaps you are starting to lose your mortal bonds."

"You mean perhaps I'm dying?" Tomaz asked, having no memory of disappearing before. The thought no longer seemed to hold quite the same meaning it once had.

"We'll find out eventually," Tristayne said. "In the meantime, you are not to leave my sight unless I give you permission. I would confine you to this miserable chamber as punishment, but I need to reorder my thoughts, and for some reason that is easiest when I teach you."

That much seemed true. Over the past month Tristayne had occasionally taken time to try to discover whether Tomaz possessed more than a mere scrap of magical potential. The answer, apparently, was yes. Tristayne had been able to coax and bully him into tapping into the barest sliver of death energy, an act that had left him feeling frigid and shivering with a cold that now never seemed to leave him. In doing so, Tristayne appeared able to acquire a degree of focus that allowed him to gather himself after long days spent with Kyndrithul's experiments. In some ways the gaunt skeleton reminded Tomaz of his tutors back in Greyhaven.

For his own part, Tomaz was glad to be making more

progress. He had feared Tristayne would demand he return the thornwood staff he had gifted to him after making it back from Zorgas, but he had allowed him to keep it and employ it in channeling the spectral power. He was finally learning something of the art of necromancy.

"Up then," Tristayne repeated, tapping the Black Scythe's base on the stone floor threateningly as Tomaz finally managed to find his feet. He grunted with the effort. Everything ached, though nothing more than his neck. He bent slowly to retrieve the staff.

He expected Tristayne to usher him out into the courtyard, where he usually taught him incantations, but instead the necromancer just stood motionless. Tomaz stared at him tiredly, wondering if he was about to be reprimanded, or if this was some new, strange test.

"Something's wrong," Tristayne said abruptly. "Dalibor has ceased his work."

Quite how Tristayne could tell when the vampire was conducting his experiments and when he wasn't, Tomaz didn't know, but there was no uncertainty in his rasping voice.

"Follow me," Tristayne said, turning sharply and striding from the ruinous chamber. Tomaz set off after him, struggling to match his long stride as he emerged out into the inner courtyard of the castle.

Dalibor was already there. He looked wide-eyed and almost as skeletal as Tristayne, his white features stretched with anxiety.

"You can feel it too," the vampire said. Tristayne stared for a moment before answering.

"He's coming."

"What do we do?" Kyndrithul stuttered. "Where is Zarihell? She promised this wouldn't happen!"

Tristayne turned, and Tomaz found the Black Scythe poised before him, shuddering with the desire to cleave him in two.

"It was you, wasn't it?" Tristayne snarled. "Verminous traitor! You told him!"

"Who?" Tomaz said, feeling increasingly panicked as he tried to keep up with what was happening.

"Waiqar," Tristayne said. "He's coming! We can all feel him. Did you tell him what we've been doing here?"

"No," Tomaz exclaimed, suddenly feeling as worried as Tristayne and Kyndrithul appeared to be. "I would never... I would never dare!"

He tried desperately to recall if he had ever let anything slip, had ever mentioned anything when Tristayne had sent him to speak for him while he was with Dalibor, but he had hardly said anything at all to Waiqar.

Tristayne seemed to believe him. He lowered the scythe.

"If we flee, it will cement our guilt," he said to Dalibor. "Get your experiments into the dungeons and crypts, and keep them silent. We will meet him in the lower bailey."

"But what if he knows?" Kyndrithul whined.

"Then we strike now, and destroy him," Tristayne snarled. "He comes alone. This will be as good an opportunity as ever!"

Tomaz began to edge back to the chamber where he'd been woken up, but Tristayne snapped at him to stay close.

"I told you, you will not leave my side," he said. "If it

was you who has led him here, an eternity of torture in the Black Realm will seem like a mercy!"

Tomaz obeyed, rejoining the necromancer as he strode from the inner courtyard downhill through the second gatehouse, into the lower bailey. It was an open space that sat just within the remains of the castle's curtain wall. The outer defenses were even more damaged than the inner, the walls tumbled down, the gateway itself broken open, and the cobbled courtyard littered with rubble. Gaps that had once been doorways leading down into the dungeons yawned around the edge of the desolate space, while at their backs the keep loomed on its crag, crooked and derelict.

It was not a place prepared for defense, but if Waiqar really had come alone, he would be hideously outnumbered by Kyndrithul and Tristayne's spawn. He would only stand a chance if he truly was as powerful as the stories claimed.

The vampire joined Tomaz and Tristayne in the courtyard. Dawn was not far off, a dull, grey radiance seeping the merest hint of color into the wrecked walls and struggling to drive the long shadows back into the dungeon doorways. It only made Kyndrithul look even more haggard. The vampire was muttering to himself, clutching his long fingers together as he fretted. Tomaz simply stood shivering, fighting back rising fear. If what Tristayne had been doing was discovered, he had no doubt he would share whatever terrible fate Waiqar devised for his treacherous apprentice.

"Say nothing, both of you," Tristayne hissed. Tomaz fixed his eyes on the ruined arch of the gateway, feeling his heart hammering as he stared into the dawn that was trying to break through the perpetual mist.

When the darkness came, it wasn't through the gate.

It surged suddenly from above, eclipsing the light. Tomaz looked up, instinctively stumbling backward and almost falling as a massive object hurtled from the mist and slammed down into the courtyard, just in front of the trio. Stone cracked and dust surged, kicked up by the flapping of immense, musty wings.

Tomaz regained his balance, only to find himself rooted to the spot, staring up at a nightmare given form. Before him was a great drake, long dead and now reanimated in all its dreadful glory. It was almost wholly skeletal, bar the strips of leathery, decaying flesh and tarnished scales that still hung from its bones, like the outer layer of a fish that had been abandoned in the midst of its gutting. The wings themselves, ragged as the sails of an old barque and just as large, remained splayed as it towered over them, challenging them. Its skull was wholly fleshless, its fang-riddled jaw agape, great balefires of deepest purple blazing in its sockets.

Sat atop its back, between two of the great barbs that ridged its spine, was Waiqar. The Great Necromancer was garbed in his finery, bearing his skull-engraved heavy armor and mantle of purple. His skull was horned by great antlers, and his broadsword was in his fist, his axe at his waist. He resembled nothing less than undeath itself given form, eternity channeled into a singular will and purpose. He was too terrible in aspect for Tomaz to gaze at for more than a moment.

The mortal was vaguely aware of Tristayne and Kyndrithul falling on their knees beside him. He did the same, his staff clattering to the cracked cobbles.

The drake – Tomaz knew it could only be one of the legendary barrow wyrms – finally furled its wings and lowered its withered body toward the ground. Waiqar dropped down with a crack of steel on stone. He stood, observing the trio.

"Rise."

The word made Tomaz's skull ache and sprang blood from his nose. He found himself back on his feet, not by his own will, but compelled to obey. He stared at the ground, quivering.

"What brings you to Dalibor, my apprentice?" Waiqar asked Tristayne.

"My research," Tristayne started to answer, but trailed off. Tomaz had never heard him so cowed before.

"A strange place for research," Waiqar mused. "A broken, empty castle. Or perhaps it is not so empty any longer?"

Waiqar was silent. None of the trio dared speak, so he continued.

"You were missed at the last feast, Lord Dalibor. Your kindred from Bilehall learned much that night, even more than I suspect you're teaching to my apprentice."

"My apologies, lord," Kyndrithul managed to whisper, voice a dry croak. "I-I found myself detained…"

"Is that so?" Waiqar replied. "You have not encountered Garathule for some centuries, have you? But you must know that the legends about the barrow wyrms are true. Garathule's breath will have your secrets from you."

Tomaz glanced sideways at Tristayne, who had dared to look directly at Waiqar, the Black Scythe rattling in his skeletal grasp.

"I have been trying to further your work, lord," he said. "I believe I am close to a breakthrough. Soon you shall have no need of even the bone dust of the Legion in order to reanimate the dead."

"Yet to achieve this, you have been stealing that very bone dust from the crypts of Zorgas," Waiqar said, his voice like a knife now, scarring Tomaz's brain. "My own apprentice, complicit in a plot against me, betraying me, just like everyone else. And now you have the arrogance to stand before me and claim it has all been done to further my own work."

Dalibor had started edging back, and now as Waiqar finished he turned and ran, heading up the steps toward the keep. Tomaz felt an overwhelming urge to go with him, but Tristayne stood his ground.

"You are one to speak of arrogance, my lord. Perhaps if you weren't so blinded by your own self-belief, you would have solved these problems long ago. Instead, you obsess about plots and manipulate all around you, rather than actually taking action. In just a few short months, I have done what you have failed to do in ten centuries or more."

"I doubt that, Tristayne," Waiqar said. "But if you really have been so successful, then perhaps you would like to show me the products of your labors?"

Tristayne didn't hesitate, snapping a string of arcane words that Tomaz didn't recognize. A dreadful wailing filled the bailey, ringing up from the dungeons. With it came the scraping of claws on stone, before a tide of abhorrents sprang from the arches and doorways all around the courtyard, a flood of misshapen flesh, shrieking faces and bared talons that poured into the confined space.

Waiqar, sword already in one hand, drew his axe with the other.

Tristayne turned to Tomaz and uttered a single word.

"Run."

Waiqar had expected nothing less.

The first abhorrent to lunge at him was almost as big as an ogre, and it died without Waiqar even raising a hand. He simply looked at it, and it was unmade, the pathetic life-force that gave it sentience snuffing out like a doused candle. It collapsed, its momentum carrying it to Waiqar's feet.

"Destroy them," he told Garathule. The great barrow wyrm let out an arcane roar, a sorcerous gale channeled through its ribs and jaw, before whipping around. Its spine-ridged tail swept in an arc that disemboweled the leading edge of the monstrosities charging from the left side of the courtyard, their tainted blood drenching the cobblestones. The wyrm then twisted right, lunging with its forearms and ripping apart another clutch of the creatures with its talons.

Waiqar took a few paces forward to give Garathule more room to slaughter, ignoring the rest of the oncoming abhorrents as he gazed after Dalibor, Tristayne, and Tomaz. They were scrambling up toward the central courtyard, the vampire already passing in through the ruined gateway.

He had experienced a rare moment of uncertainty as he

had flown to Castle Dalibor. What if, against all evidence, he was mistaken? What if there was some deeper scheme he was unaware of? But now, there was no doubt. Now it was writ large all around him, a betrayal more pernicious than any of the arrogance displayed by the likes of Bilehall.

Waiqar roared and swung Bitterbite. The first screeching abhorrent to reach him was bisected, its deformed muscle and bone offering not even the slightest resistance to the ancient broadsword. He followed up with Doom's Edge, bringing the axe cracking down on the next monstrosity, hewing it clean in two. Stinking black blood drenched him, glistening across his armor and bones. It felt unclean. It only heightened his disgust.

He began to kill, methodically at first, but with a rising fury. Abhorrents, any one of which would have proven a fearsome foe for even an experienced mortal warrior, were cut down almost as an afterthought, more of them pulverized and torn apart at Waiqar's back by Garathule. The wyrm grasped two of the creatures in its foretalons and flung them like discarded toys over Waiqar's head, slamming them into the castle's inner wall and leaving them as bloody smears that dripped slowly down the ancient stonework.

Waiqar could feel the essence of the Deathborn Legion in the blood splattering him. That even a fraction of the noble warriors who had followed him in both life and death had been stolen and used toward this perverted end disgusted him. It was desecration, blasphemy, a treachery of the highest order. He would permit it no longer.

The thieves had underestimated him. They believed they had evaded every trap in Zorgas' depths, warded away every wandering spirit, but they had failed to realize that not all the bodies they were stealing from were inanimate or asleep. Waiqar had breathed consciousness into some, just enough for them to be able to remember who had stolen from them. They had confirmed his suspicions.

With a thought, he summoned the razor wind. It came howling around him like a tornado while leaving him untouched in its eye. The closest abhorrents were voided of flesh in a blink by the invisible hail of a million blades, blood forming a fine, crimson mist in the air. The crimson skeletons left behind collapsed as Waiqar advanced between them, no longer even deigning to look at the unnatural creatures as he reached the inner gatehouse.

He had barely passed through when the dead came for him. Screaming spirits surged from the open crypts and passageways that lined the interior of the courtyard directly below the central keep, unphased by the razor wind. They were the Dalibors of yore, Kyndrithul's cursed ancestors who lingered on, viewing the ruination of their home and the corruption of their lineage with anguish. They struck at Waiqar with ethereal blades and talons, their ghastly, insubstantial features contorted with hatred.

Waiqar's armor glowed as it repelled the ghostly assault, each skull engraved upon it pulsing with power. He struck back, and the dead shrieked as Bitterbite cut them, its notched edge as fatal to phantoms as it was to beings of flesh and blood. Those shorn through dissipated, their consciousness finally evaporating as the slender thread they maintained with the mortal realm was severed.

Onward Waiqar advanced, slicing and hacking, like

a man trying to chop his way through a mist. It worked though – the souls of the dead had not held any fear for him for what seemed like eons.

He mounted the final steps leading into the crooked keep and paused, glancing back. There was a crash as Garathule slammed itself through the gatehouse and into the inner courtyard, sending stone tumbling down onto the abhorrents still trying to swarm it, crushing the shrieking horrors.

"Annihilate them," Waiqar commanded, driving the imperative into the savage consciousness of the barrow wyrm. Then, turning his back on the carnage, he stepped into the darkness that still held sway within Kyndrithul's final fastness.

"We should flee," Kyndrithul hissed, his eyes wide with panic. Tristayne cursed him for a coward.

"To what purpose?" he demanded. "To etch out a miserable existence in the bogs, like all the other fools he has defeated down the centuries? To flee south, and spend an eternity trying to hide what you are? You are in no fit state for either such venture, Kyndrithul. We have a chance to beat him, here and now. Show some courage."

They were bold words. Tristayne tried to convince himself they were true. His worst fears were being realized. They had been discovered, far sooner than he had hoped. They weren't ready. Just what had brought Waiqar here now seemed obvious enough. It had been a trap from the very beginning.

Zarihell. It had to have been her. The idiot Tomaz was too

cowardly by half to tell Waiqar what had been happening in the Dalibor holdings. He doubted the mortal even properly understood any of it. That left only the *Daewyl*. He suspected it had been a plot all along. She was still in league with Waiqar. Perhaps she had never stopped being as such.

"Turn your device on him," Tristayne told Dalibor, trying to focus his mind. With Tomaz panting along behind them, they had retreated to the hall of the keep, where the two great brass orbs had been set up.

"Surely it has the power to destroy him, if he has been weakened by the abhorrents," Tristayne pushed on as Kyndrithul hesitated, clutching on to a desperate, almost manic hope. "Between that, and our own abilities, we can defeat him. Then we shall reign supreme."

Not that Tristayne had any intention of sharing power with the withered vampire, but now didn't seem like the right time to admit as much. Kyndrithul nodded, hurrying to throw the lever that activated the orbs.

"Can you direct it, when he arrives?" Tristayne demanded as green lightning filled the chamber.

"Yes," Kyndrithul said, drawing down a long, copper lance from the wall. "I have been planning to experiment in its use as a weapon."

The vampire connected a tube from the base of one of the orbs to the lance's bottom, holding it like a spear. The green lightning surged up its length, fizzing and sparking at its tip.

Tristayne struck the base of his scythe against the ground and began to chant. The reanimates, momentarily abandoned around the chamber, started to stir, called to life by the necromancer's will. Despite the danger, Tristayne felt a thrill. This was his power to command now, not Waiqar's. He would never relinquish it.

There were more abhorrents crammed within the keep, squirming, thrashing, sightless things that reached for Waiqar with dirt-encrusted talons.

He slew them with Bitterbite and Doom's Edge, adding their blood to that of their kin. There was a heaviness to his limbs now, the eternal, dull ache rising to become something almost akin to pain. The past months had taken a great toll, and summoning up Garathule had almost been too much. The creatures ranged against him by his wayward apprentice were pathetic, but they were numerous, and every one slain sapped another fraction of his strength.

Perhaps Mirabelle had been right. Perhaps he should not have come to this place alone.

"*It is too late now for doubt,*" Baelziffar snarled. "*Kill! Kill!*"

Waiqar obeyed. He cut down the beasts relentlessly, unflinchingly, chopping his weapons again and again through every last nightmare creature that barred his path, ignoring when their claws and fangs scraped against his armor or chewed into his bones. He found the stairs that led up to the keep's higher levels and began to ascend them, slaying at every step, digging deeper and deeper into his anger and determination. He was Waiqar the Undying, the Great Necromancer, master of death itself.

He would not stop.

He could not stop.

Blood ran thickly down the cracked spiral stairs of the

keep, slicking Waiqar's feet. The narrowness of the ascent made it all the harder. Blows became short and brutal, cutting through skulls and shoulders and ribs, grinding horrors underfoot when they refused to die.

Finally, he mounted the head of the staircase, shouldering his way into the space beyond.

The energy struck him immediately, a bolt of raw, green lightning. It blasted the skulls on his breastplate and darted across his body. Sudden, searing agony, the likes of which he had not known since the day of his ascension to undeath, transfused him. He roared, trying to take a step forward, but his bones had stopped responding. Instead, he found himself falling, clattering forward onto his knees.

The lightning cut out, though it continued to spark across him. He managed to take in its source. Kyndrithul Dalibor was standing in the center of the keep's hall, clutching a long, copper lance connected to two great brass orbs. The green energies crackled around the spheres and darted up the lance's length, seemingly recharging after their first blast. Kyndrithul's ghoulish face was contorted with equal parts shock and glee, taking in the fact that he had just struck the Great Necromancer down onto his knees.

Tristayne was present too, Tomaz cowering as ever behind him. As Waiqar looked toward them both the necromancer raised his hand and chanted. Death energy, fashioned into a spear, darted toward Waiqar, but he dropped Bitterbite and reached up, grasping the ethereal haft and crushing it from existence.

"You will need to try harder than that, my apprentice."

He rose, forcing his remains to obey his will, now more

than ever. With a shriek, Kyndrithul triggered the lance again. Another actinic blast slammed into him, making him roar with pain.

He tried to keep going. He had to. It could not end like this. In betrayal and death.

"But it did before," Baelziffar whispered.

"Do not... abandon me..." he begged, managing to take one shuddering step forward, close to collapsing again.

"Then find your strength, Waiqar," the demon barked, its wrath momentarily eclipsing even the searing power of the orbs. *"Find it, and prove to me once and for all that you are worthy of all that I have given you!"*

Amidst the agony, Waiqar remembered.

CHAPTER TWENTY-SIX
Long Before

The Wizard's Vale was burning.

Waiqar stood at the heart of it, in the shadow of the great gateway that led into the Tower of Meringyr. All about him his legion fought, storming the lesser towers that clustered along the valley's sides, battling with the guards and apprentices that sought to protect their master, Timmorran.

Timmorran the fool, Timmorran the traitor. Timmorran, who had left him in the clutches of Llovar. Who had come too late, who could only carry him from that place of nightmares after his body had already been broken and his mind claimed.

Waiqar had tried to forgive. He had allowed time to pass, hoping the slow march of the seasons would blunt the wicked edge of the betrayal he felt. But it had not. Instead, the opposite was true. While scars had healed, his thoughts had festered, made worse by the changes he was seeing around him. Timmorran assuming more responsibility throughout the realm. Claiming power, and prestige, after the enemies they had battled together were defeated, while Waiqar was left in his shadow.

He was no longer Timmorran's apprentice. Their friendship had turned stale. Baelziffar had predicted that worse was to come. As much as Waiqar had not believed the demon, every prediction had turned into reality. Timmorran had grown addicted to power, and recent events had only confirmed it. He was creating something he shouldn't be. Only Waiqar, with Baelziffar's guidance, could see it. Only Waiqar could stop him, now, before it was too late.

The great iron ram fashioned by Waiqar's engineers crashed once more into the gateway, the ancient lengths of oak barring their path creaking in pain. Arrows were raining down upon the warriors crowding the base of the tower, but Waiqar ignored the deadly, barbed hail. The air was thick with ash and screaming, and stank of blood and burning.

One of the towers to the right, further up the valley's side, collapsed, crushing friend and foe alike and kicking up a surging cloud of dust. There was a hiss as a sheet of boiling oil was cast down from the machicolations over the gateway just ahead of Waiqar, more agonized screams ringing out as some of it found its way through the battering ram's protective covering and seared those beneath. Those who fell were immediately replaced as more of Waiqar's soldiers pushed forward. The ram's next shuddering blow fell, but still the gate stood.

"My lord, it will not break," Ardus said. Waiqar's

lieutenant was splattered with blood, his strong, bluff features flushed with the fury of combat. "The wizards have surely enchanted it."

A dark rage gripped Waiqar. He had cut his way along the length of the Vale, leaving none alive. He would not be defeated now, so close to his final objective. Timmorran had to be stopped, before it was too late.

He reached up with one hand and began to spit words of power. His consciousness delved into the blood-drenched earth beneath his feet, finding the languid, dense spirits of rock and stone, demanding their allegiance. Using incantations Timmorran had taught him, he began to tear great boulders from the ground just before the gate, not caring how the sudden seismic activity flung his own soldiers to the side.

He held the mass of boulders in the air before him for a moment, soil cascading down, before roaring and flinging them over the top of the ram and directly into the gate.

Golden magical power flared across the ancient oak as the enchantments strengthening the entranceway sought to stymie the power of Waiqar's assault, but it was too much. With a crash, rock shattered and stone split, a hail of stone shards and splinters raining onto those below.

"Again!" Waiqar roared at the warriors crewing the ram. With a bellow of effort, they swung the great siege engine one last time.

With a crack like thunder, the gate to the Tower of Meringyr burst inward.

"Forward, you dogs," Waiqar shouted. "Kill them all! Bring me the Orb!"

With a howl, his legionaries charged the open gate. The response was immediate. A line of Timmorran's warriors and apprentices waited in the wide hallway beyond, bows drawn. They loosed, and the first three ranks of the charging mass were punched off their feet, the deadly missiles ensorcelled with charms of force and sharpness so potent they sliced through two or three legionaries at a time.

The shock of the volley momentarily checked those behind, but Ardus was pushing forward now, the black and purple banner bearing Waiqar's white stag held aloft.

"Into them," Waiqar howled, throwing himself through the gateway. "Kill them all, before they reload!"

Shrieking like demons, the legion charged once more, trampling over their own dead and dying packing the gateway's arch.

Waiqar followed them, looking up. He got a final glimpse of the great, arcane tower soaring above him before the archway hid it. There, near Meringyr's pinnacle, a single figure stood alone upon a balcony, clad in blue robes that flowed in the ash-choked wind. He was too far away for Waiqar to discern his features, but he knew immediately that he was looking up at Timmorran.

Hatred suffused him. He shoved his way forward into the tower's front hall, the high, vaulted space ringing with the clash of arms and the screams of the wounded. Ardus's charge had stormed into the first line of defenders, and now they were being ruthlessly hacked down by the rush of Waiqar's legionaries, their pleas for mercy ignored.

"On me," Waiqar demanded as he forged a path to the

grand stairs that led up through the tower's core. Ardus fell in alongside him, chopping down a screaming acolyte that fell in their path, the man's blue robes turning dark with blood.

More of the Wizard's Vale guards protected the bottom of the stairs, locking shields. Howling, Waiqar threw himself into them. There was no generalship here, no clever tactics or grand strategy. There was only killing. The simplicity of it was thrilling, but it was still only a distraction. Waiqar saw none of the faces of those he slew, was barely even aware of their strikes or parries. He fought furiously, Bitterbite a blur of death that stabbed through breastplates or clove open helmets. Beside him Ardus's progress was just as relentless, even as he fought with one hand still clutching the great standard.

Waiqar began to ascend the stairs. All who tried to stop him fell. Their blood began to run down it, staining the white marble a bright crimson.

Not long after the first spiral had taken him out of sight of the entrance hall, he felt a sudden impact against his right shoulder, and a sharp stab of pain. He stumbled, the mistake saving his life as another missile whipped through the space his head had occupied a moment before.

"Lord," Ardus cried out, catching him before he could fall backward. A clutch of legionaries who had been following their master up the stairs pushed past to protect them both from a sudden charge of Timmorran's acolytes coming down the stairs.

Waiqar looked at the arrow protruding from his shoulder. A volley of the missiles had come slicing out of small ports in the stone of the central spiral's wall, a deadly trap that had almost succeeded where all else had so far failed. Waiqar snarled, letting the pain stoke his anger, and reached up to snap the shaft of the arrow, leaving the tip still buried in his flesh.

"The treacheries of Timmorran's lair will not stop me," he said, setting off once more.

Further up, there was a cracking sound, and a section of the stairs gave way beneath the legionaries who had pushed ahead of Waiqar. They fell, screaming, into the darkness beneath, leaving Waiqar teetering on the edge. Another trap, he realized. Meringyr was riddled with them, Timmorran's cunning given shape and form.

He vaulted the gap and beat aside the weapon of the guard trying to hold him back, throwing the man screaming into the pit after his own warriors.

He could not stop. Timmorran had created something terrible, a device he was calling the Orb of the Sky. It was a concentration of pure magic, given crystalline form. Anyone could utilize it, even the unattuned and the uninitiated. With it, the lowliest practitioner could rival even the likes of Timmorran himself. No one should have such power at their command. Even worse, if the great wizard was to lose his artefact, or if it were to fall into the wrong hands, the consequences could be catastrophic. He had to be stopped. The Orb had to be destroyed.

"*You are Terrinoth's only hope, Waiqar,*" said Baelziffar, rallying him as Ardus joined him on the other side of the gap. "*You must retrieve the Orb before something terrible happens.*"

"Press on," Waiqar panted to Ardus, once more beginning to climb.

A part of him wished it had not come to this. He had tried to warn Timmorran. Even after all his former master had done to him, leaving him to suffer in Llovar's Black Citadel, Waiqar had still attempted reconciliation. The Orb was too powerful. But Timmorran was obsessed. He had claimed that by creating an alternative to the Verto Magica, he was cutting out the dangers of the Ynfernael, ensuring its corruption would no longer taint those who sought to utilize the arcane arts. Waiqar didn't believe such a thing was possible. In fact, he feared the opposite was true. When he had last seen Timmorran, the once proud and noble magician had looked a shadow of his former self, drained and stooped, almost broken by whatever was compelling him to craft the Orb.

There was still time to stop it. It had to be now, or never.

"There is foul play at work here," he said, pausing as Ardus dispatched another guard. There were few left to oppose them now, and similarly the rest of Waiqar's legionaries had fallen behind. Sounds of desperate, slaughterous fighting echoed up from below, but here they were almost alone.

"How much longer can these stairs endure?" Ardus panted. Waiqar's limbs ached, and his lungs struggled for breath – in his prime the climb alone would have been punishing, but after the brutalities of the Black Citadel and the hard fighting that had raged throughout the Vale, it was almost more than he could endure. The pain from the arrow head still lodged in his shoulder made him wince, sharpening his thoughts, giving him fresh determination.

"Some sorcery is being employed against us," Waiqar said, looking further up the stairs. It was only natural that Timmorran would seed his lair with magic traps, as well as the mundane ones they had already encountered.

"*You are right*," Baelziffar whispered. "*Still the wizard seeks to trick you. Strike the wall to your right.*"

Waiqar did so without questioning, expecting the enchanted steel of Bitterbite to ring from stone. Instead, to his surprise, he found it lodged in a wooden door. The tall, arching entrance hadn't been there a moment before.

The illusion of the endless stairs disintegrated before them. They stood in an antechamber, leading to the rune-inscribed doorway that Waiqar had just hit.

Fierce triumph filled him. He dragged Bitterbite free and prepared to strike again.

Before the blow could land, a shockwave of tremendous energy slammed through the tower. The antechamber's stained-glass windows blew out in a blizzard of multi-hued shards, and the great door itself shuddered, the runes glowing white-hot and molten as they absorbed the worst of the blast. Both Waiqar and Ardus stumbled, feeling the very heart of the tower quaking all around them.

The shock subsided, and horror gripped Waiqar. What had Timmorran done? Was he already too late? Had all of this been in vain?

"Timmorran!" he roared, and threw himself at the door. Dropping Bitterbite, he drew out Doom's Edge and hewed at the enchanted timber and metal like a deranged woodsman, splitting and cleaving. Finally, something gave way, and the doors swung open before him.

He stormed inside, wrathful, ready to cut down all who opposed him. But instead of a host of acolytes, he found only Timmorran himself, kneeling upon the steel floor of his workshop. Arcane devices, books and scrolls lay broken and scattered all around, tossed aside by the destructive force the wizard had just unleashed.

"What have you done?" Waiqar breathed, halting, shaking, before his old master.

"What had to be done," Timmorran replied. He was a shadow of his former self, gaunt and exhausted, his flowing azure and purple robes hanging heavy from his withered frame. But as he looked up, Waiqar experienced a spark of that same fearsome willpower that had first drawn him into the wizard's service.

"The Orb of the Sky is no more," Timmorran said.

"Liar," Waiqar snarled. "Where have you hidden it?"

"I have broken it," Timmorran corrected, his voice weak. "I cast it down and shattered it into a thousand pieces."

In one trembling hand, he held up a single crystalline shard, its edges gleaming with magical resonance, like a diamond refracting the light.

"No," Waiqar hissed, realizing that the shards still held the power of the whole, their dangerous potential remaining. "You cannot have. Where is the rest? Where?"

"Gone," Timmorran said. "Born away by an apprentice far more loyal and pure than you, Waiqar. He will scatter them across Terrinoth and beyond, and ensure that only those with good intentions receive them."

Waiqar quaked with rage, knuckles white where he gripped the haft of Doom's Edge.

"How could you do this?" he choked, tears of frustration in his eyes. "Now anyone could claim the Orb's power. It should have been me! Only I can stop it from being misused!"

"If that is so, Waiqar, then here is the first shard," Timmorran said, pressing the fragment into Waiqar's hand. "Take it, and prove me wrong. Prove that you still have some good in you."

Waiqar felt the power of the shard – that even a piece so small contained such potency made him realize just how much arcane energy the full Orb must have held. It only frustrated him further.

"I am sorry, Waiqar," Timmorran murmured, barely audible anymore. "I failed you. At the Black Citadel, and every day since. I believed you were dead, but I should have still tried. I should have come for you sooner. I fear something rancid has taken root in your soul, something too deep for me to now extract. I only pray that you can free yourself, in life, or by death."

For a moment, regret and sorrow gripped Waiqar. It was too much, too overwhelming. The bitterness, the horror, it threatened to paralyze him. Abrupt rage, black and fiery, replaced it all, an altogether easier emotion to process.

Waiqar screamed, and swung Doom's Edge. Timmorran made no move to block the blow. The wicked axe caught him in the neck, and severed his head with a single, almighty slice.

Although Waiqar had expected blood – there had been so much of it already – instead the wizard's robes simply collapsed. There was no sign of his body. Even the head had vanished. It was as though he had never existed.

Waiqar clutched the single shard of the Orb so tightly it

cut his hand, blood running over the crystalline fragment and dripping down onto the floor. Rage broiled and seethed within him, unquenched by Timmorran's demise. Even at the very last, the damned wizard had tricked him.

He was dimly aware of Ardus standing next to him, asking what was to be done now. Ignoring him, Waiqar strode over Timmorran's empty robes, across the workshop toward the open archway and the balcony that lay beyond.

When the legion had started their assault up the Vale it had been a bright spring morning, but now a premature twilight had gripped the once-pleasant valley. Great plumes of black smoke and eddying swirls of ash broiled between the burning towers, and the sky itself had turned dark, low, gray clouds blocking out the light. Waiqar could feel the way the shattering of the Orb had momentarily broken the very spirit of Mennara itself, an act of desecration that had drawn forth its wrath.

Vainly he searched from the balcony for any sight of Timmorran's apprentice and the stolen shards, but there was nothing. Whatever means had been used to spirit the thief away, they were now long gone. Waiqar seethed, gazing down upon the great mass of his warriors as they filled the valley below.

Ardus joined him, the ash-choked wind catching his standard and making it ripple. Meringyr taken, Timmorran slain, and all in vain. All for nothing.

He screamed, and the scream became words, the sole remaining shard of the Orb raised in his fist, blood running down to fall in crimson droplets over the balcony's edge.

"I will find the rest of the Orb! I will rebuild it, piece by piece, until it is whole again. No one else will claim even a fraction of its power! I will not rest for a moment until it is done, and all who seek to stop me will know my wrath! This I swear!"

A sound pierced the haze of his fury, the last noise he expected to hear. Laughter. It was Baelziffar, but for once the voice didn't seem to be in his head. It resonated through the whole valley, deep and mirthful at first, but rising in a maniacal crescendo, a sick, depraved cackle that made Waiqar's blood run suddenly cold.

It was eclipsed by a crash of thunder. Lightning flared within the torpid clouds, illuminating their underbelly. Waiqar, his elemental magics attuned to nature, felt a terrible change occurring all around. Now it was not just the wrath of the skies that hung heavy over the valley. Something else was present, something his words, and the bloody shard in his fist, had inadvertently summoned.

It began to rain.

The first drop struck the edge of the balcony, just in front of him. He felt another plink from his pauldron, and a third against his outstretched arm. Within seconds, the air was full of droplets as the skies vented forth their rage, a seething, hissing deluge.

One of the drops fell upon Waiqar's face. He recoiled, clutching at where it had struck, hissing in pain. It was like being stung, and it left behind a burning sensation even after he cuffed it off.

The downpour, he realized, was not just water. It was black, and bore something more than rain, something much, much worse.

Below, the warriors of the legion began to scream.

More droplets found Waiqar's flesh. He cried out, trying to shield himself, but the rising pain made it difficult to move. He attempted to twist away from the balcony, to get back into the shelter of Meringyr, but something gripped his shoulders, something with claws that dug in, making the arrow head embedded in him dig deeper.

"*Fleeing already, Waiqar?*" Baelziffar whispered in his ear, voice rich and mocking.

Waiqar could see nothing, his eyes screwed shut. He tried to fight the grip, but could not. He heard Ardus beginning to scream beside him.

The agony became unbearable. Waiqar howled, clawing at himself, every inch of his body feeling as though it was on fire.

Beneath him, his warriors suffered the same fate. The black rain drenched them, and as it fell it began to liquify them. Skin ran molten, a foul, stinking steam rising into the air. Legionaries writhed in agony, incoherent with pain, driven feral by their suffering. Swords and shields were abandoned, and warriors ripped at their helmets and breastplates, desperate to salve the source of their pain. Wizard's Vale echoed with the tumultuous screaming of thousands, its peace forever shattered, its sanctity blighted by an intensity of suffering that would forever haunt it.

And Waiqar suffered with the rest. He fell upon his knees, unable to scream anymore. He could taste only blood and bile. It was worse even than the Black Citadel, worse than any suffering he had known. He was blind, and for a moment became deaf as well, his senses destroyed, his mind cutting out, unable to process the horror.

He saw burning eyes in the darkness, and heard the voice, that damnable voice, the last he would ever know.

"You are damned, Waiqar. Damned for eternity."

He lost consciousness. Everything simply ceased to be. His last thoughts were a prayer, to every god he had ever known, that the void would swallow him whole, and his very existence would be snuffed out.

For a long time, it seemed as though that was what had happened.

The first thing he knew was an ache. It suffused his entire body, from toes to fingertips. It made him moan, though no sound came out.

He was lying down, he realized, on the balcony. It was raining, but more gently now. The droplets were no longer black.

He tried to move, but could not. He lay still, battling the agony that still suffused him. It was not as terrible as what had come before, though.

Finally, through sheer force of will, he made an arm obey. He planted his hands under him and, with a dull scrape of armor, forced himself up onto his knees.

Ardus lay beside him, the standard next to him, drenched through. Waiqar managed to crawl the few paces and reached over to grasp his lieutenant's pauldron, rolling him onto his back.

A nightmare presented itself, making Waiqar cry out, though again his throat failed him. Ardus Ix'Erebus was no more. The black rain had destroyed everything but his bones. Now only his skeleton remained, still clad in his armor, a grinning skull staring sightlessly up at Waiqar, glistening in the rain.

As he clutched at his old friend, Waiqar noticed his own hands for the first time. They too were now fleshless, mere bones that seemed to be bound tight and articulated by invisible sinews. He raised one before his face, shaking, staring, unable to comprehend what he was seeing.

Slowly, he touched his own face. He could feel almost nothing with the nerveless fingers, but he found himself probing the outline of a fleshless jaw and teeth, high cheek bones and the ridges of a nose and eye sockets.

Perhaps Waiqar screamed. He did not know. Eventually, and without warning, the horror paralyzing him ceased. An unnatural sense of calm, icy, bitter and firm, settled over his thoughts. What had come before was finished. Something new had now begun, and nothing could change that.

"*Now, you start to see,*" whispered Baelziffar's voice in his head, tiny and barely perceptible.

Waiqar reached out and gripped the edge of the balcony then, slowly, used it to haul himself up. The ache was in his bones, deep and throbbing, but it seemed less insistent now than it had been before, as though it was receding.

As he gained his feet, he found himself looking out across Wizard's Vale.

The valley was a scene of utter devastation. Between the broken towers, their fires now quenched, a great mass of bodies lay, stretching away as far as Waiqar could see. They were his legion, he realized, or their remains. The black rain had annihilated them, melting each and every one down to the bone. They lay now in heaps and piles, bodies hideously twisted in the throes of their final death-agonies, a vast field of bones, blades and armor that gleamed wetly as the natural rain continued to fall.

Some distant, rapidly receding part of Waiqar's mind expected to feel horror at the realization of what had become of his loyal warriors, a plunging nausea, a derangement the likes of which he had not experienced since the Black Citadel. But there was nothing. He felt cold. That was the only enduring thought.

Something moved out among the bodies. Waiqar looked, and saw a substance drifting across the valley, winding its way through, between and around the great piles of remains. He took it to be mist at first, but realized that it bore within it a strange, pallid luminescence. It wasn't just down among the corpses, he recognized, but in the air all around him, coiling and twisting.

It was magical, certainly, but not of a sort he had ever seen before.

"*It is the elemental Mortos,*" Baelziffar told him. "*The essence of the Sphere of Death, transmuted into the mortal realm.*"

There was a strand just before Waiqar's face, twisting languidly back on itself, glowing a sickly, pale green.

"*Reach out,*" Baelziffar instructed. "*Grasp it.*"

Waiqar did so. As soon as his bony fist clenched around the strand, he felt a shock run through him. Abruptly, the ache was gone, though the bitter cold seemed to redouble. He could hear faint whispers as well, and far-off cries, not the familiar tones of Baelziffar, but echoes from a plane of reality beyond the one in which he stood. This energy, the very essence of death, was a conduit between the two.

Gripping the strand, he pulled it taut.

Across the Vale, bodies stirred. Like puppets drawn slowly up by their strings, the corpses of Waiqar's legion began to shift and rise, bones clacking, armor scraping, their remains shuddering as a new, unnatural un-life took hold of them.

Waiqar held tightly onto the elemental Mortos, feeling its power, feeling too how his own mind transmuted through it, running out via every last strand to connect with the warriors who had given their lives for him. He could feel them, their consciousness, their individual minds as they began to stir. There was little horror there, little dismay. They were cold, like him. More importantly, they were loyal, loyal still to the general who had led them from here to the Ru Steppes. That brought Waiqar a sense of relief he had not anticipated, coupled with a fresh surge of determination.

He heard the sound of armor on stone next to him, and looked over to find Ardus rising as well. The skeletal remains looked to Waiqar, and as they did deadlights ignited in their sockets, a witch-fire that blazed a deep purple.

"Master," Ardus croaked, the words issuing not from his fleshless jaw, but seemingly within Waiqar's own skull.

He felt the acknowledgment not just of his lieutenant, but of all his warriors, the weight of his entire legion re-swearing their oaths to him. It wasn't just for life anymore, but for eternity. Briefly, he knew a moment of humility, of thankfulness.

"Unfurl the standard," he ordered Ardus. He retrieved Waiqar's fallen emblem and raised it in the rain, the wind cutting about the high tower making it billow. The terrible deluge had not harmed it, but it had changed it, just as it had changed everything. Now the white stag's head was gone, replaced by a leering, antlered skull. The sight of it only further hardened the cold resolve that had gripped Waiqar.

He had changed. He had survived. He would endure. That was what mattered. Baelziffar had given him a chance, the ability to fulfil the oath he had sworn.

He let go of the strand of magical energy, tentatively at first, fearing it would cause his warriors to collapse again, but the magics flowed to him, binding themselves around him. He felt their power, their vitality, banishing the aching weariness that gripped his new form and sharpening what remained of his senses.

A glimmer at his feet caught his eye. He looked down, and discovered the sole shard of the Orb that he had been able to retrieve. He had dropped it when the rain had struck, and it teetered now on the edge of the balcony, the downpour having cleaned it of his blood.

He regarded it for a while, then stooped to pick it up in fleshless fingers, bone scraping. The magic properties within seemed to surge to meet him, and the death energies redoubled, glowing brilliantly, a constellation of death magic whose pale light refracted through the crystalline shard.

"I need… more," Waiqar whispered, holding it before his face, gazing into its lustrous depths.

"And you shall have them all, if you prove yourself worthy of what has happened here this day," Baelziffar told him.

Waiqar lowered the shard, looking down once more upon his legion – his deathless, reborn legion – and seeing how, like Ardus, their skulls had ignited with purple flame, the essence of their renewed consciousness.

"What now?" Waiqar asked.

"I have given you eternity," the demon said. *"Now, you need only awake."*

CHAPTER TWENTY-SEVEN
The Present

In a split second, Waiqar saw it all.

He saw it, and remembered, and in doing so he forgot the pain.

It would never compare to the agony he had felt at Meringyr. He had forgotten it for a while, just as he had forgotten his oath. That changed today. He would endure no further distraction.

He rose, and advanced. The power being unleashed by Kyndrithul was terrible. It filled the chamber with crackling and sparking energy, the green bolts lashing furiously at the Great Necromancer. Waiqar's armor was beginning to run molten, and his bones were disintegrating, tiny fragments eroding away under the intensity of the onslaught. But on he came. There was no more agony, only that coldness he had known the moment he had accepted his true fate, so long ago.

He was inevitable, and there was nothing either the living or the dead could do to stop him.

Tristayne's chanting faltered, the elemental Mortos momentarily abandoning him as Kyndrithul attempted to retreat. He tripped over the tubing that connected his copper lance to the brass orbs, and fell with a cry. The lance's energy lost direction, striking upward instead, blasting stonework from the hall's vaulted ceiling and causing the entire keep to shudder.

Waiqar stood over Dalibor, verdant charge still dancing across his armor and bones and playing like a halo around his antlers. He raised Doom's Edge, like an executioner's axe. Kyndrithul whimpered.

The wicked weapon fell. With an ear-splitting crack it cleaved the lance in half, severing it in Kyndrithul's grip. There was a surge of light as the green energies arched back through the device and its cabling, earthing themselves into the brass orbs. With a crash, they exploded, sending shards of ruptured, twisted metal hurtling through the chamber, cutting down stumbling reanimates and clattering off Waiqar and Tristayne's bones.

In the aftermath, a dreadful silence began to settle. It was broken when Waiqar lunged forward with his other hand and gripped Kyndrithul by the throat.

The vampire tried to plead for his un-life, but Waiqar's grip was too strong.

"Would you have me spare you, Kyndrithul Dalibor?" he demanded, eyes ablaze with purple fire.

The vampire managed to wheeze an affirmative, claws scraping against Waiqar's vambrace, legs windmilling in the air.

"Very well," Waiqar said. He momentarily slipped

Doom's Edge back into his belt, then snatched Kyndrithul's jaw with his free hand. He lodged the vampire's two elongated front teeth between his fingers and, with a grunt, ripped the fangs free. Black, rancid blood squirted forth, spattering up Waiqar's arm as the vampire found the ability to shriek, squirming wildly in the unrelenting grasp.

"Save your strength," he told Kyndrithul dispassionately. "I will have you impaled above Zorgas' gatehouse. I will feed you the blood of beasts and crows, enough to maintain your existence, enough to keep you conscious. You will serve as an ever-living, forever-tortured example of what happens to those who steal even a fraction of the remains of my legion."

He dropped the vampire and turned, stepping over him to confront Tristayne. Tomaz, who was cowering in the far corner of the chamber, simply stared wide-eyed as his master met with Waiqar.

Tristayne did not back down. Instead, he raised the Black Scythe.

"This isn't over," the necromancer hissed.

"I know," Waiqar agreed. "But it will be soon."

"*She is here,*" Baelziffar whispered.

Waiqar paused and turned. He discovered that another figure had entered the chamber, materializing seemingly from nowhere beneath the smoking wreckage of one of Kyndrithul's orbs.

"What a mess," Zarihell said. She was sitting cross-legged on the floor, her hood drawn back, smiling. "I leave you boys alone for a few weeks and look what happens!"

"At last," Waiqar murmured. "The hidden hand shows itself."

"Hardly hidden, Waiqar," Zarihell said, pouting. "You only needed to call upon me, and I'm sure I could have explained everything."

"Treachery," Tristayne hissed, looking from the elf to Waiqar. "Just as I suspected! You led him here, didn't you? You've been working for him all this time. Working to expose all those who would defy him!"

Zarihell rolled her eyes.

"Sometimes I doubt the wisdom of turning you against your master, Tristayne, I really do. I had no part in Waiqar discovering our little scheme, though it hardly surprises me that he has. I honestly thought it would be sooner."

Waiqar felt a stab of anger at her arrogance, but also justification. He had been right, as always. Her scheming would come to nothing.

"If you aren't with him, then help us," Tristayne pleaded.

"Perhaps," Zarihell responded. Pushing up only with her legs, she leapt to her feet. Waiqar slipped Doom's Edge free once again, but the elf made no further move toward him.

"Though I must admit, I'm intrigued to find out exactly how you came here with such certainty that Tristayne and Kyndrithul were conspiring together," she said, cocking her head to one side, like a curious avian.

"I was told," Waiqar said. "A confidante gave me ample evidence."

"Who?" Tristayne demanded, seemingly desperate to know. "Name them!"

Waiqar gestured dismissively with his ax, past Tristayne, at where Tomaz was cowering.

"You," Tristayne hissed. "I should have known!"

"B-But I never," Tomaz wailed, looking wide-eyed up at his master. "I swear it! I swear!"

"The truth never left his mortal lips," Waiqar admitted. "But if you had only paid attention when I taught you, Tristayne, you would know that there are other ways of exposing a secret."

Tristayne still seemed uncertain, so Waiqar drew forth a small piece of stone from a pouch on his belt. It was a runestone, carved with an arcane marking.

"The Soulbinder," Waiqar said. "It took a long time before those I dispatched were able to find it. Almost too long. Alone, it is highly useful, but combined with the high art of necromancy, it becomes invaluable. Do you know what it does, my apprentice?"

"A runestone… it's capable of forcing a spirit to remain with its body," Tristayne said, still struggling to comprehend.

"A rare and powerful ability indeed," Waiqar said. "Though not of much use if the body is incapable of bearing the soul any longer. Still, I am a master of more than just the necromantic arts."

"Surely you could not," Tristayne breathed.

"I could, and did," Waiqar replied. "Healing magics, bent to my will, repaired the damage dealt to your servant."

"You interrogated his spirit," Tristayne said disbelievingly. "Just as you taught me."

"Again and again," Waiqar said, looking past his

apprentice at Tomaz. "Taking him from his cell where you left him, or whenever you sent him to me to act in your stead."

It had been a simple thing. A slit throat, or a broken neck. As the body of the former Greyhaven student had slumped, Waiqar had snatched and bound the terrified, screaming soul as it broiled up from the fresh corpse remains. He had torn the truth from Tomaz in between screams and pleas – where Tristayne had gone with him, who he had met, what he had spoken of.

Tomaz had divulged all, every time, from the first encounter with Zarihell to the journey to Dalibor, and the foul pact that had been made with the treacherous vampire. Waiqar had watched the plot unfold from afar, allowing it to ripen, and only striking when all other distractions had been dealt with. It had been difficult, to play at obliviousness, to let his arrogant apprentice think him a fool. But it had worked. Tristayne had led him to the one who had been stealing the dust of his Deathborn. A final enemy among his own ranks, exposed.

"The mortal was my loyal spy and servant, without ever even realizing it," Waiqar said. "When he had imparted his news, I wiped the memory of the encounter from his spirit and then forced it back into his body using the Soulbinder. I healed him with hardly a blemish left behind, then returned him to you."

Tristayne was shaking, his bones clacking. He had not only been defeated, he had been humiliated. While he had been plotting and scheming, Waiqar had been observing him all along, like a parent who was entirely aware of their child's antics, but who chose to turn a blind eye until it became impossible to feign ignorance.

He gripped his scythe all the tighter then, abruptly, he screamed and threw himself at Waiqar. The great, curving blade swept down, the air itself shrieking as it was cleaved asunder.

With a crack, the steel plowed down through Waiqar's shoulder, cleaving ribs, hacking halfway through the Great Necromancer's torso.

Such a blow had been enough to eviscerate kings and demons, their bodies destroyed and their souls dragged howling into the scythe's depths, to suffer an eternity of torment in the Black Realm. But when the dread weapon came to a shuddering stop within Waiqar, he merely looked at Tristayne, unbowed, seemingly unharmed.

"The demons of that infernal plane you call yourself a prince of know better than to try and claim me, my apprentice," Waiqar said. "My soul is promised to one far more powerful."

The Great Necromancer grasped the Black Scythe by the haft and ripped it from Tristayne's hold, tearing it from his own body with a dull crunch and spinning it, reversing the grip.

"Let us see if they would prefer your soul instead, Tristayne Olliven," he went on.

"No, no," Tristayne screamed, but Waiqar wasn't listening. The scythe fell again, splitting Tristayne's skeleton body from crown to pelvis. The bisected halves began to collapse, but before they had even hit the ground there was a nightmarish howl, and a thick black substance surged from the scythe's head and shaft, dragging the cleaved remains into it. In the same time it had taken Waiqar to strike, Tristayne had disappeared, body and soul, returned to that same hellish prison that Waiqar had once rescued him from, consigned there until he was freed.

The stillness that followed was disturbed only by the soft whimpering of both Tomaz and Dalibor, followed by a harsh clapping sound. Zarihell was applauding.

"You know, I wondered if you would actually go through with it," she said, approaching Waiqar and stopping before him. "To kill your own apprentice, just as you once killed your own master. Delicious irony, almost poetic. I love it!"

"Tristayne is imprisoned," Waiqar corrected her, still gripping the Black Scythe in one hand. "I have yet to find a way to kill him permanently. Was that what all this was about? A game, to see if I had come full circle?"

"Something like that," Zarihell replied, shrugging. "I thought I might be able to overthrow you. Gather your enemies together, destroy Zorgas, cut you apart, and cast your dust to the wind. But no matter. It was always unlikely. I just wanted to see if you were still the Waiqar I once knew."

"And am I?"

"Not really," she said, reaching up with one hand. With exquisite lightness, she brushed the tips of her fingers down Waiqar's skull, tracing the sharp definition of cheek bones and jaw.

"I could destroy you," Waiqar warned without moving.

"I was about to say the same of you," Zarihell said.

Waiqar snatched her wrist, her fingers still poised, and

for just a second his body was as it had been a millennium before. Waiqar stood tall and whole again, his face pale, noble, hair swept back from his brow, his eyes a deep gray.

"You've had your fun," Waiqar said. "But I cannot risk you striking again when I march south to claim my destiny."

He saw something in her gaze he was unaccustomed to – pain. He released her arm, realizing he'd been gripping her wrist where her own manacles had once bound her. The scars were still there, markings of subservience, of damnation.

They reminded Waiqar of their shared past. Of why, despite the fact that she had striven to overthrow him, he could not raise a hand to harm her. Not unless there was no other choice. That was a reality he would not admit even to himself, at least not until that moment.

Zarihell lowered her hand and turned away, composing herself in an instant. There was no hint of the weakness she had shown.

"I'm flattered that you think I still have cards left to play," she said, stepping away from Waiqar. She patted the prone Kyndrithul's bald head as she passed him, making him whimper louder.

"It wasn't such a strong hand I held in the first place," she added, smirking back at Waiqar as she stood above the prone vampire.

"Nevertheless, you will return with me to Zorgas, and be confined while I am absent," he said firmly.

"Sounds boring," Zarihell said. "Are you sure you wouldn't rather put my abilities to good use? The baronies won't look kindly on your return. Carthridge, for starters…"

"I have only just purged my ranks of those I cannot trust," Waiqar pointed out. "It would be unwise to add the least trustworthy of them all back in."

Zarihell held her hands up, as though accepting the accusation. Waiqar heard the sounds of footsteps, ringing up the stairs behind him. He began to turn around, sensing a familiar presence approaching.

"My lord," exclaimed Mirabelle, stepping into the wrecked hall. She was followed by Ardus and a clutch of Deathborn, their blades drawn and dripping with abhorrent blood.

"I did not send for you," Waiqar said harshly, as Mirabelle took in the sight before her. "What are you doing here?"

"Forgive me, lord," the necromancer said, bowing hastily. "But news has reached Zorgas. I sought you out to inform you, but could not find you. I followed the lines of death energy here. Ardus insisted on coming as well."

"I feared I was missing out on vengeful slaughter," Ardus said with a rare hint of humor. "It seems I was correct! Let me behead this craven vampire, lord!"

"I have a better fate in mind for him," Waiqar said, ignoring Kyndrithul's moan of terror. "What news is so vital that you dare disturb me once again?"

"Word has come from the north-east," Mirabelle said, even the stoic councilor displaying a flash of excitement. "Levirax has been sighted beyond the Molten Heath. The dragons are on the move once more."

"Then it is time," Waiqar declared. "We shall return to Zorgas immediately, summon the council, and set the final plan in motion. The Legion will march south, tonight."

"At last, Terrinoth will once again know the name of Waiqar the Undying," Ardus said triumphantly.

"Take Dalibor," Waiqar instructed the Deathborn. "And Zarihell."

For once, his servants hesitated to follow his command.

"Zarihell, lord?" Mirabelle dared ask.

Waiqar looked back at where the elf had been standing, and was unsurprised to see that she had vanished.

"She was behind all this, as we suspected," Waiqar said, gesturing at the hall's ruination. "She lured Kyndrithul and my apprentice into stealing the bone dust, and I have no doubt she helped set both Bilehall and the Penacor against me. She thought that by uniting the Mistlands against their true master, she could finally overthrow me."

"Then she was a fool," Ardus said. "Allow me to hunt her down for you, lord."

"There will be no need," Waiqar said. "Her power is broken, for now. Besides, her nature is capricious. I suspect she has grown bored of attempting to undermine me. She will do us no harm, for the time being. And I will need all my warriors with me when we enter the mortal lands. These distractions are now at an end. The true quest lies before us."

"As you wish," Ardus said dutifully. The Deathborn marched forward and snatched Dalibor, who was still drooling blood from his fangless jaw. He began to babble as he was hauled past Waiqar, but the Great Necromancer ignored him.

"What of the mortal?" Mirabelle asked quietly. Waiqar took a moment to realize who she meant. He had almost forgotten Tomaz, curled up in a corner, half hidden behind the remains of one of Kyndrithul's orbs.

"I will deal with him," Waiqar told his advisor. "Wait for me in the upper bailey. Send Ardus back immediately to prepare the Deathless Council at Zorgas."

As the others left, Waiqar hefted the Black Scythe, and paced across the room to Tomaz.

Amidst the lightning, and the screaming, and the words that made his skull ache, it had all come back to Tomaz. Every death. Every moment of existential horror, as he endured the bitter chill of existence beyond his own flesh, coupled with the agonies inflicted by Waiqar. He had seen into the afterlife, again and again.

In many ways it terrified him. But in others, it gave him a strange sense of icy calm. He looked up from where he was hunched on his haunches, finding Waiqar towering over him. Waiqar, that king of undeath, a myth whispered of by Tomaz's old, forgotten friends, a demi-god that haunted the nightmares and stalked the legends of every corner of Terrinoth. Waiqar, now stood before him, fleshless, scarred by his latest battle, covered in the slowly drying blood of his enemies.

For the first time, Tomaz's sense of awe eclipsed his fear.

"Rise," Waiqar commanded, and Tomaz obeyed. He forced himself to his feet, clutching his thornwood staff, feeling small and child-like before the greatest avatar of necromancy to have ever existed.

"You betrayed me," Waiqar said.

"Yes," Tomaz croaked, looking down.

"But I knew you would. I intended you to. I plucked you from your meaningless existence and gave you to Tristayne, knowing that you would serve him faithfully, and in doing so betray him to me. It is the natural cycle of things."

Tomaz had now realized as much. The question of why – why him, why had he been taken from Greyhaven, why had he been kept alive by these undying monsters – finally made a degree of sense. He had been a pawn to the greatest of them, and he had played his part.

"Tristayne had begun to teach you the necromantic arts, had he not?" Waiqar asked. Tomaz nodded.

"Did you display any aptitude?"

"I ... do not know."

"Then let us see."

Waiqar held out the Black Scythe. Its haft was dripping with a thick, foul black substance, oozing from the unnatural plane it was connected to. Tomaz hesitated, heart racing.

"Take it," Waiqar ordered.

Tomaz obeyed. He let the staff Tristayne had given him clatter to the floor and, with shaking fingers, grasped the scythe.

Screaming filled his head. He screwed his eyes shut, and found himself surrounded by the souls of the damned, the wailing imprints of those claimed by the scythe down the centuries. Their agony was overwhelming, and the hunger of the scythe itself twisted in his gut, the haft vibrating against his grip.

And yet, he kept hold of it.

"Be... silent..." he snarled through clenched teeth, his determination taking over. He had endured enough. He was not going to fail now, not when he had been given a chance. Now he was the one with the power. Now he could cast down those without it.

One by one, he directed his will at each of the specters in turn, banishing them to the scythe's depths, to the Black Realm where demons toyed with their ravaged souls. Eventually, he was left with only one, clutching at him with spectral hands. Tristayne Olliven.

"Please," the necromancer begged. "You have to release me!"

He was whole again, clad in flesh, but white and ethereal. There was a noose tied around his neck.

"I cannot endure this place again," he babbled. "Beg Waiqar for me, or do it yourself! Just let me out!"

"I said be silent," Tomaz snapped, feeling a surge of power the likes of which he had never known before. "You will not speak again unless I summon you!"

With a snap, the noose was drawn abruptly tight, and Tristayne was dragged, choking, after all the others, cast back down into the same dark prison that he had known before.

Tomaz opened his eyes. The spirits were gone. He could still feel them, railing against their entrapment, but their voices were faint now, an afterthought. The black slurry clinging to the scythe had enveloped his hand.

"Impressive," Waiqar allowed. "Tristayne was wrong about many things, but you do not appear to be one of them. You will replace him."

"Replace him?" Tomaz repeated, wondering just how he could be expected to replace a centuries-old necromancer.

"As my apprentice," Waiqar said. "You already know what awaits you should you fail me, or betray me."

Tomaz fell to his knees, his momentary calm evaporating in a rush of both fear and hope.

"I... I will strive to prove myself worthy, lord," he stammered.

"If you do so, then eternity awaits you," Waiqar said. "Arise, Tomaz. Soon, you shall cast the shackles of mortality aside."

He did so, and found himself speaking again.

"My lord, I have a request. A single boon to ask of you, as I pledge myself forever to your cause."

Waiqar regarded him, and Tomaz found himself wondering if he dared go on. The Great Necromancer bade him speak anyway.

"Continue."

Tomaz did so. He made his request. When he had finished, Waiqar offered a short, hard laugh, a cold sound devoid of mirth.

"An indulgence indeed," he said. "I will permit this, but only once. Afterward, you will serve me and me alone, and not your own whims and desires. Is that understood?"

"Yes, lord," Tomaz said. For the first time in what felt like an age, he experienced a rush of exhilaration, of hope. With it came a fierce desire for more. He had survived. Now, he would do more than that. He would become powerful, truly powerful, more so than Tristayne. Waiqar himself would see his potential and acknowledge his abilities.

There would be a reckoning.

•••

Waiqar marched down the blood-slick steps of the keep, over the bodies of the hundreds of abhorrents he had slaughtered. He resolved to have them burned, so that none of their tainted blood could be used against him again.

Castle Dalibor lay silent once more, as devoid of life as it had been before Kyndrithul had reinhabited it. Garathule remained in the upper courtyard, covered in the blood of the abhorrents. The great barrow wyrm was barely responsive, the embers of its reawakened consciousness fading back into oblivion. Waiqar fed a fragment of his power into it, and it raised its great skull in greeting, the flames in its eye sockets rekindling.

"You have done well, friend," Waiqar murmured to it before grasping onto one of its great ribs, using the length of bone to clamber up between the ridges on its spine.

He surveyed the wrecked courtyard, and the other further down, littered with the carcasses of the monsters that had dared challenge him. They wouldn't be the last, he had no doubt. The Mistlands were full of terrible creatures and dark powers, and few accepted a master willingly. But master them he had. Now, at last, he could turn his attention beyond the blighted borders of the marshes.

"*Are you forgetting your oath once more, Waiqar?*" asked Baelziffar. The demon sounded curious this time, rather than accusatory.

"No," Waiqar said firmly as he settled atop his drake, slipping Doom's Edge back into his belt. "I have never forgotten it. But you said it yourself. You have given me eternity. I will find the fragments of the Orb, eventually. Right now, they are not my foremost concern."

"*You have grown ambitious.*"

"Thanks to you. The time has come to make our play. All Terrinoth will submit."

"*You believe yourself ready? It is not only the baronies you will face.*"

"Mortals or dragons, they will bow or perish," Waiqar said, knowing Baelziffar was referring to the reemerging threat of Levirax.

"*Some among them will seek to use the Stars of Timmorran against you,*" Baelziffar pointed out. "*Timmorran's acolyte spread them well. Do not underestimate those so-called heroes who wield them.*"

"Let them try to stop me," Waiqar said. "They will find only death."

EPILOGUE

It was cold in the hall that night.

Wilem turned over, drawing his covers tighter and cursing under his breath. Not long to go now. A few more months and he'd have graduated, and he could leave these hard beds, thin blankets and drafty stone chambers behind. This windy, gray city on its hill could be consigned to memory, and he could return south and take up his inheritance in the hills overlooking Riverwatch.

He heard movement down the aisle at the end of his bed, the soft shuffling of feet on the bare flagstones. He assumed it was one of the younger students, traipsing into the dorm after a night in the taverns. Damn the youths. Ordinarily Wilem would have been given a room of his own in his final year of study, but the university was oversubscribed at the moment, and they had all been taken. He'd drawn the short straw, so had to see out his last months with the greater majority of the student body, in the shared accommodation. It was typical of Greyhaven. He was glad to be leaving.

His thoughts were so sullen it took him a while to realize that the footsteps had stopped. That in itself wasn't unexpected, except for the fact that they had come to a halt at the foot of his bed, and the other two students who slept to his left and right, Alisa and Molvo, were both already in their own beds and asleep.

Wilem sat up sharply, or tried to. A hand met his chest and thrust him back down. A figure was stooped over him, almost indiscernible in the dark.

He was about to snarl something at what he assumed was a drunken youth attempting to get into the wrong bed, but the hand that had pushed him went up to his face, calloused fingers lightly brushing his lips.

"Quietly now, Wilem. Quietly. You'll have plenty of time to scream later."

The words were chilling, but they paled next to the horror of realization. He knew the voice. It had been a long time since he had last heard it.

"No," he whispered back, sitting up again. This time the figure allowed it. "Tomaz?"

"Yes Wilem, Tomaz," the darkness replied humorously. The figure stood up properly, so the pallid moonlight streaming in through the dorm's high windows could pick out his face.

The emaciated, pallid being standing over Wilem was a far cry from the young student that he had once studied alongside, the same one he had abandoned on the borders of the Mistlands a year before. And yet, there was no denying it was him. The Greyhaven Death Cult's most pathetic member had returned unannounced, in the dead of night.

"It cannot be," Wilem said.

"Sometimes it can," Tomaz replied in an almost conspiratorial whisper, giving him a sickly smile. He stooped down so he was speaking directly into Wilem's ear. "You know I forgot you for a while. You and the others. Lillian. Fergas. Viktor."

Wilem realized Tomaz was clutching something in one hand, a staff it seemed, though he held it down against the bed. His heart was racing, and he was considering crying out, but dared not while Tomaz was so close, the former student's rancid breath on his face.

"I forgot all this, until the Undying One reminded me of how he had killed me. That brought some memories back. This place included. I asked if I could visit, and he said yes!"

Alisa moaned in her sleep in the next bed over and turned onto her other side. Wilem held his breath, trying to gauge whether he could subdue Tomaz physically, a part of him also wondering what he was rambling about. How had he escaped? Worse, what if he went to the authorities? Maybe he already had? After all this time, was his place in the cult about to be exposed?

He suspected a worse fate awaited him.

"I came back, to show you the Black Realm," Tomaz whispered, smiling in the moonlight.

"I don't know what you're talking about," Wilem hissed. "I don't want you to show me anything, Tomaz. Get away from me."

"Too bad," Tomaz said. "Lillian, Fergas and Viktor are whispering to me, right now. They want you to see it. They want you to join them. And so do I."

"Wait," Wilem began to say, but Tomaz didn't seem to be listening anymore. Stifling his laughter, the former student of Greyhaven brought up what Wilem had taken to be a staff.

Much too late, he realized it wasn't a staff at all. It was a scythe.

The last thing Wilem saw in the mortal realm was the moonlight, gleaming from its blade as it swept down toward him.

The two border watchmen remained upon their knees in the mud at the side of the road. It had been raining fitfully since the previous morning, and the track itself was mostly cloying dirt, winding between the hard and fallow fields that lay upon the borders of the former thirteenth barony.

The dead did not care. They marched past, through the muck, rank after rank, bones and armor glistening, black and purple standards clinging limply to their poles. Their eye sockets smoldered with the flames of their sentience, dire deadlights on a gray day.

The watchmen were father and son. They both shook where they knelt, their befouled, green capes drenched through. They had been surprised in the middle of the night, taken from the tower they were manning by skeletal horrors that now stood over them with drawn swords.

The father at least attempted to master his fear. He looked up, expression set, as a group of figures approached them and their captors, pausing at the side of the road while the risen corpses continued to tramp implacably past. The

Mistlands were on the march, and who now would warn of their coming?

Waiqar sensed rather than saw the man's defiance melt away as he laid eyes upon him. He halted before the pair, towering over them.

"Shall I behead them, lord?" Ardus asked. He, Mirabelle, and Waiqar's other councilors stood close behind, looking at the pathetic excuses for cold, wet life.

"No," Waiqar said, sending an impulse that froze Ardus in place. He stood watching the mortals for a while, trying to match their expressions to the emotions he could feel emanating from them, trying to understand, to remember.

"*Do not waste time,*" Baelziffar urged. Waiqar grunted.

"Go on then," the father stammered, finding the courage to speak. "Just… get on with it. Kill us."

Waiqar felt a stab of annoyance. Kill them? As though that would change anything.

"I'm not going to kill you," he told them both, sensing their disbelief flare as they looked at one another.

"Return to your watchtower," he went on. "And resume your duties. The dead do not march abroad to conquer the living. We come to bring salvation. We come to offer hope, and a new beginning, a time when Terrinoth will no longer squabble over petty differences and cower whenever the darkness beyond its borders rises. Where there is division, I will bring unity; where there is despair, I will bring hope. I have defeated death itself, and given time, I will show you all how to do likewise."

The mortals stared up at him. Now it was the son who found his voice.

"Are the legends true? Are you ..." He trailed off.

"Yes," Waiqar said. "They are all true. I have returned. I, the Undying One, Immortality Incarnate. Waiqar."

ACKNOWLEDGMENTS

A huge thanks goes out to the Aconyte publishing team, from editors to proofreaders, from marketing to logistics, and all the other myriad jobs that make creating books possible. A special thanks also to the talented Joshua Cairós for the amazing cover art. Lastly, to my mum, who probably won't read this book as it's too spooky.

ABOUT THE AUTHOR

ROBBIE MacNIVEN is a Highlands-native History graduate from the University of Edinburgh. He is the author of several novels and many short stories for the *New York Times*-bestselling *Warhammer 40,000 Age of Sigmar* universe, Marvel's *Xavier's Institute* and the narrative for HiRez Studio's *Smite Blitz RPG*. Outside of writing his hobbies include historical re-enacting and making eight-hour round trips every second weekend to watch Rangers FC.

robbiemacniven.wordpress.com
twitter.com/robbiemacniven

DESCENT
LEGENDS OF THE DARK™

Epic fantasy of heroes and monsters in the perilous realms of Terrinoth.

Explore the dark pasts of Terrinoth's most notorious villains.

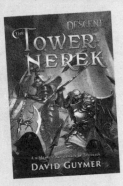

Legends unite to uncover treachery and dark sorcery, defeat the darkness, and save the realm, yet adventure comes at a high price in this astonishing world.